PROMISE OF
SPRING

PROMISE OF SPRING

a novel

KRISTEN McKENDRY

Covenant Communications, Inc.

Cover image by Tetra Images © 2008 Jupiter Images

Cover design copyrighted 2008 by Covenant Communications, Inc.

Published by Covenant Communications, Inc.
American Fork, Utah

Printed in Canada
First Printing: April 2008

15 14 13 12 11 10 09 08   10 9 8 7 6 5 4 3 2 1

ISBN-13: 978-1-59811-549-9
ISBN-10: 1-59811-549-9

To my husband, and in memory of
Grandma and Grandpa Waite

ACKNOWLEDGMENTS

First and foremost, I would like to thank my patient husband and children for their encouragement. Thanks to my parents for the priceless gift of my first typewriter when I was thirteen, and to Michael Crawley for his concise instruction. Thank you to Anna Wiggins for opening the door, and to David and Sally Lougheed for pushing me through it. I greatly appreciate Alison Clarke's kindness and helpful suggestions. Special thanks also to the expertise of Kathy Jenkins, Noelle Perner, and all the others at Covenant who have been so helpful.

While the general location of this story is real, the town and its inhabitants are fictitious. Any errors of fact in this book are entirely my own, with apologies to the wonderful people of the Panhandle.

CHAPTER 1

It was what her grandfather had called a "mother-in-law storm"—quick to move in and slow to move out. Melinda watched the boiling gray clouds spill ink spots across the brown-patched lawn. Large drops began to spatter the screen and darken the cement patio below the kitchen window.

It was a good thing she'd picked the peas that morning. It was going to be muddy. She reached down absently to stroke the large orange cat entwined around her ankles. There was still so much to do, but she was secretly relieved that the rain had given her an excuse to put it off. Dismissing the waiting vegetables, she scooped the cat into her arms and flopped on the living room couch to wait out the storm with a murder mystery.

The phone rang just as the body of Edward Rutherford washed ashore with a knife in its back.

Melinda tried to ignore it. Abigail, the cat, had gone to sleep in a warm furry ball on Melinda's stomach, and Melinda hated to disturb her. The caller was persistent. Melinda sighed and pushed the cat off onto the couch. Abigail's mashed Persian face wrinkled indignantly as her owner went for the phone.

"He's here," said the caller without preamble.

"Hi, Jack."

Melinda leaned around the kitchen wall and waved out her living room window. The tall figure standing in the window of the house opposite hers waved back. She could see that his other arm was raised, holding the phone, but she couldn't make out his expression from across the street.

"Does he have a truck or anything?" she asked.

"A U-Haul."

"Do you think he needs help unloading?"

"He won't unload in this rain. Wait 'til it's over."

"You know, he might not be so bad, Jack. Give him a chance."

She could feel the force of the scowl on the other end of the line. It sounded like Jack was speaking through clenched teeth.

"He's a wimp. You didn't know him when he was young, but I remember him all too well. It was his job to collect the eggs every morning, and he paid me to do it because he was scared of the chickens!"

"I'm sure he's changed since he was six, Jack." She couldn't help chuckling. "Jenny told me he was the manager of a cattle operation in Wyoming."

"I can't imagine it," Jack said flatly. He gave a disgusted sniff. "He was scared of cows too."

"He wasn't!"

"He was."

"Well, when the rain stops, we can help him unload his trailer, and you can ask him if he's gotten over those fears," Melinda said. Waving to the figure across the street again, she hung up. She waited until he had left the window, then went to peer out into the pouring rain.

Over the top of the lilac hedge lining the west side of the drive, she could see that a blue car had pulled up in front of Paul Delaney's ranch house. A red and gray trailer was hitched behind the car. A light came on in one window inside the house. She pictured Paul's son walking through his childhood home, now empty. She imagined him short and scrawny, in a "city kid's" suit and tie, maybe with dark-rimmed glasses and slicked-down hair. The sort who would use a nutcracker on peanuts. Of course she knew he wouldn't look like that—a cattle rancher wouldn't, surely. But Jack had painted a picture for her, and the image persisted. She imagined Paul's son walking into the old, familiar rooms, turning on lights, touching the furniture, looking at the framed photos on the walls . . .

How did she know there were framed photos on the walls? She'd never been inside. Her imagination was running away with her.

Melinda stayed at the window, lightly fogging the glass with her breath. Just looking at Paul's house with its wraparound porch and sheltering burr oaks made her sad. She hadn't known Paul very long. She'd moved in two years ago, but she'd immersed herself in work and hadn't gotten to know her neighbors very well. There had been the occasional chance meeting in town or a wave as they passed each other in their pickups on the road. Paul had seemed like a nice sort, with a pleasantly lined face and a thatch of slate-colored hair.

He'd had a heart attack just at spring planting time. Melinda had been so busy scrambling to keep the farm functional that she hadn't learned of Paul Delaney's death until a week later. The day of his funeral, she'd been at a meeting with the bank, presenting her business plan and hoping to scrounge enough money to install the windmill that now supplied half her electricity. By the time she'd emerged from the flurry, it was too late to make a gesture of sympathy—and there was no one, really, to make the gesture to.

Gazing over the hedge at the ranch house down the road, she wondered what sort of person Ryan Delaney was and whether he felt overwhelmed, having suddenly become responsible for the property another person had spent his life caring for.

The rain didn't let up until late that evening, too late for her to go meet her new neighbor. She decided to make cinnamon rolls and deliver them the next morning as a house-warming gift.

* * *

When she set out the next morning carrying the foil-wrapped plate, the gravel road was pitted with puddles. The air smelled fresh and damp, and the sun was already growing hot. Birds were chattering in the tulip poplars as she marched up the porch steps and knocked on the Delaneys' door. Melinda made a mental note to bring in the rest of the spinach before the sun wilted it.

After a pause, the door opened and a head poked around it. For a moment the two stared at each other. If this was Ryan Delaney, her imagination had been off by a mile.

He looked older than she was, perhaps in his thirties. His reddish-brown hair, rumpled and spiky, nearly brushed the top of the doorframe. His face, which was probably usually smooth-planed, was unshaven. As the door opened wider, she saw he was dressed in a gray track suit that showed a lean, athletic build.

"Can I help you?" he croaked.

Melinda's mouth hung open. It was still very early in the morning. Ryan Delaney had likely driven all day yesterday from Wyoming.

"Did I wake you up?" she asked, horrified.

Ryan extended a hand and flapped it at her. "It's all right; I have to get moving anyway. I'm Ryan Delaney." His voice was rough with sleep, but she guessed he was a baritone.

Feeling idiotic, Melinda swallowed and tried to recover her smile.

"I'm Melinda Keith, from next door." She pointed imprecisely over her shoulder. "I brought you cinnamon rolls to welcome you in."

"I thought you were a little old to be selling Girl Scout cookies."

"I didn't mean to come so early—I mean, I can come back later."

"No, no. Come in." He ushered her inside and closed the door. "Are those homemade? Great!"

"Everything around here is homemade," she answered.

"This is really nice of you. Come in the kitchen, and I'll see if I can find the milk to go with them."

"Oh, I won't stay. I really do feel terrible about waking you up."

"But you've got to share the cinnamon rolls with me. It's a rule." He set off down the hall toward the kitchen. She had no choice but to follow. Melinda caught a glimpse of the living room with its dark wooden floor, oriental carpets, and pastel furniture. She was surprised, realizing she had pictured it furnished with chunky country furniture and a pair of horns mounted over the fireplace. Smiling, she stepped into the kitchen and stopped short in delight.

The room was a dream—huge and airy. Sun flooded through broad windows that looked out toward the barn, making the white cabinetry glow. The floor was like an ice rink. Copper pots gleamed tantalizingly overhead. The table was long enough to seat ten, its wooden surface polished smooth and golden with years of use.

"What's wrong?"

Ryan was looking at her with a puzzled expression. His eyes, though red-rimmed with fatigue, were an astonishing aquamarine.

"I'm trying to figure out how to convince you to trade houses with me," she replied. "This is gorgeous."

"Haven't you ever been in here before?" he asked, pulling out a chair at the table for her.

"Never. If I had, I would have married your father just to get at this kitchen." She'd spoken without thinking and gulped, remembering that he had lost his father only three months ago. Ryan just smiled. It transformed his face, erasing his weary expression.

"It *is* nice, isn't it? It's too bad I'm not a better cook so I could do it justice," he said cheerfully. "My mother tried to teach me, but when you're ten, the only use you can see for a frying pan is hitting someone over the head with it." He pulled a jug of milk from the fridge and looked around thoughtfully. "Now, if I were a glass, where would I be? Probably above the dishwasher." He opened a cupboard.

Melinda unwrapped the rolls and held the plate out. "How long has it been since you were home?"

He sat down beside her and took one. "Before the funeral? Six or seven years."

"So long?"

"I had ten thousand acres in Wyoming. You can't just walk away from that for a holiday. And my father and I didn't get along all that well, truth be told."

"Then why did you give up ten thousand acres to run this place? You could have sold it and stayed where you were. If that's too personal of a question, just tell me," she said hastily. "I'm known for sticking my foot in my mouth."

Ryan gave a low chuckle that warmed her spirit. "It's a fair question, and one I've asked myself more than a few times. I guess when it all comes down to it, blood ties are strong. Dad spent his whole life raising cattle. He built that barn himself, and strung fence, and cleared the ditches, and—well, I guess I can't walk away from it any more than he could have."

Melinda nodded. "I understand."

"And there's something peaceful about a small spread after the operation I've been running. I mean, not that there isn't plenty to be done here. It's still a ton of work. But it's just the right kind of work, you know? It fits me."

"There, you've said it perfectly. I've been trying to say that to my mother for the past two years, and she just doesn't get it."

Ryan lifted one eyebrow. "Oh?"

"I bought the place next door about two years ago. I studied ecology and environmental restoration, and I wanted to put what I learned to the test—see if I could live off the grid and get everything I needed directly from the land, but in a sustainable way. A way that benefited the environment instead of plundering it." Melinda looked down at the roll she was absently breaking into sticky bits. She popped a piece into her mouth. "My mother thinks I've lost my mind. We aren't farm people. I grew up in Albuquerque with electric lights and gas heating and two cars in the driveway. She thinks I should sell and move back. But I can't do that. I'm determined to make a go of this. I wasn't sure when I first started out, I admit, but since then I've decided I need this. Like you said, it fits."

There was a pause as they both considered this. Ryan nodded and took another roll from the plate. "These are really good, by the way. Just like from a bakery, only fresher."

"Thanks. I wasn't sure how many to bring, because I didn't know how many of you there were," Melinda said casually.

She wasn't casual enough. His eyes slid sideways at her.

"Just two. Me and Tanner."

"You and who?" She blinked at him.

"Tanner. My son. What about you? Married? Kids?"

"No, and no. Just me."

"You're out here alone in the middle of nowhere?"

She laughed. "You sound like my mother. It's not the middle of nowhere. We're only an hour from Amarillo. It's not like this is the Sahara. There are quite a few families closer to the river."

"Still, it's a pretty isolated place. I understand why you bought land—and I think your environmental experiment is great—but why way out in Texas if you have a mother in Albuquerque?"

Melinda smiled. "Because I have a mother in Albuquerque."

"Aha. I get the picture. Live your child's life for her and call it parenting?"

"If you hit someone over the head with a frying pan, can you call it cooking?" Melinda mused. She shrugged. "I just needed the change. Texas was it."

Deep laugh lines appeared around his incredible eyes. "Speaking of changing, I think I hear Tanner. Can you stay to meet him?"

She smiled at the eagerness on his face, which was now alert and bright like a little boy's. He even looked younger. She nodded at his question. He brushed off his hands and went into a back room. There was the sound of his warm voice murmuring low behind the door, followed by a high shout from a young child. She heard something slide across the floor—a suitcase, most likely. Melinda nibbled another cinnamon roll—they *were* good—and listened. After a few minutes, Ryan reappeared, carrying a blond-headed little boy in his arms.

Melinda had never been overly fond of children, and as a teenager, she had avoided babysitting as a rule. She played with her nieces and nephews with the patient resolution of one who knew her duty. Though she sometimes contemplated—late at night and usually after reading romance novels—what it would be like to have a child of her own, she didn't really see herself as a mother, at least not at this point in her life. So she wasn't prepared to fall madly in love with Tanner Delaney.

He wasn't just cute; he was beautiful. His hair was spun honey, and his eyes were a clear blue with dark blond lashes a girl would kill for. He was about two years old, she guessed, and built like a miniature linebacker. Dressed in blue shorts and a white T-shirt, he was a small Christopher Robin, a cherub—comparisons failed her. She just sat and blinked at him. Tanner, after a blunt, assessing look, smiled at her. It lit up his whole body. She was hopelessly smitten.

"Look what the nice lady brought us, Tanner." Ryan settled the small boy on a third chair and handed him a cinnamon roll. Tanner's eyes grew round. He tried to mash the entire roll into his mouth at once.

"They're a hit," Ryan declared.

Melinda watched a moment longer, then stood up and brushed the sides of her jeans. "I guess I'd better go. I've got spinach to pick before it bolts. I probably ought to do the beans, too. Do you have much stuff in your trailer to unload?"

"Not a lot; it's just the two of us," Ryan said with a smile. He stood to see her to the door.

"I can swing by later to help if you'd like," she offered.

"Oh, you don't need to . . ."

She smiled at him, having to tip her head back to meet his eyes. "I'll be here around one, and I'll bring a picnic lunch. Nobody likes to cook when they've just moved." She went down the hall and out the door before he could protest.

* * *

August in Texas was suffocating. The temperature stayed at ninety, and the grass turned a dismal brown. Melinda could feel the sun drawing moisture right out of her skin. Sweat trickled irritatingly down her temples and back. She crouched beside the waist-high row of yellowing vines, trying to keep within their feeble shadow. She worked quickly, pulling off the skinny green beans and dropping them into her basket. A hornet zipped past her ear. She froze a moment until its buzzing faded. She didn't mind the occasional slugs that turned up in the strawberry patch or even the rare garden snake under the lilacs, but she hated hornets and other stinging things. She straightened and put her hands to her lower back, feeling the bones creak, and looked out over the bean rows.

The ground was dry between the rows of fading plants, in spite of yesterday's heavy rain. She used a system called the deep-bed method to grow her produce. In the deep-bed method, the earth was dug and loosened to a depth of three feet, with plenty of compost mixed in. The theory was that this loose ground, which was never to be stepped on (to avoid compaction), allowed the plants' roots to grow downward instead of to the side, permitting them to grow more closely together. And keeping plants closer together conserved water. This method yielded four times the amount of food that normal gardening produced. The heavy composting eliminated the need for chemical fertilizers, and Melinda used the natural repellents of certain types of plants interspersed with her vegetables to keep insects at bay. It was her first attempt with this method, but already the harvest looked promising.

The vegetable garden lay to the rear and east side of the house. Behind the house, the lawn stretched to the back porch. Melinda had plans to churn the grass up next year and plant mixed prairie grasses instead of keeping a traditional lawn. It would be wiser in this semi-arid area. Before her, the neat rows and hills of vegetables spread in a gray-green sea to the distant orchard, where the apple trees bowed under their ripening fruit. She had fenced in the orchard and was running pigs underneath the trees. The pigs loved the fruit that fell, and the trees loved the manure the pigs contributed. The animals' churning hooves also loosened the soil, allowing it to accept the infrequent rains and keeping the weeds down. In every aspect of the farm that she could think of, Melinda tried to foster a symbiotic relationship. She would even go so far as to call it an ecosystem, the parts working harmoniously. Except that her back didn't feel particularly harmonious at the moment.

Far beyond the orchard, Paul Delaney's pasture—Ryan's pasture now, she reminded herself—sloped away. His cows had trampled out all but the hardiest grasses and stripped any bushes that had been foolhardy enough to show their heads. Melinda caught the flash of reflected light from I-27 half a mile away. The silver smudge down by the highway was Dale Purdy's steel shed, where he sold fruit and vegetables, including her own.

When Melinda finished the beans, she carried them into the house and packed a quick lunch of ham sandwiches, tossed salad, dill pickles, cherry tomatoes, and leftover strawberry crumble. Then she showered and rebraided her dark hair, which never behaved itself no matter what the shampoo bottle claimed. She put on a fresh blouse and her dress-up jeans and gave herself a final glance. She supposed she looked all right, though she wished she would tan instead of sprout freckles. She considered herself no great sight to behold, but then, out in the back of beyond, you had to take what you could get.

There was no sign of life from Jack's house when she set out toward the Delaneys'. Jack's battered, black pickup was gone from the gravel drive. So much for him helping Ryan unload the trailer.

Ryan was outside, maneuvering a computer table toward the porch steps. Watching him as she came up the drive, Melinda decided she could have fared worse as neighbors went. Ryan was dressed in a short-sleeved, blue shirt that hugged his impressive biceps. Sweat was beginning to roll, plastering his sideburns darkly against his skin. He moved with a muscular grace that he surely hadn't developed sitting behind that computer table.

"Hi!" Melinda called. She set the picnic basket on the porch and went to help him.

"Hello again," he responded, and he let her take the other end of the table. "Good timing. But you should have been here for the box springs."

"How did you get them inside?" Melinda started walking backward toward the house. He followed, carrying the other end of the table.

"Lots of sweat and a couple of damaged doorframes," he replied, laughing. He had a pleasant laugh, hearty but not too loud.

They carried the table in through the front door. He directed her into the living room, where they set the table against the far wall, away from the front window because, he explained, direct sunlight would harm the computer.

"I don't know what Dad would have thought of a computer in his living room," he mused as they headed back to the trailer for another load. "He never would update his method of keeping records."

"A computer," Melinda mumbled, a finger on her chin. "That's one of those white plastic boxes with the blinking lights, right?"

He laughed. "Too space-age for you too?"

"Actually, I've been meaning to look into getting one myself," she said. "But because of one thing or another, I've never been able to afford it." Not to mention the amount of electricity a computer gobbled. When your only power supply came from what you could harvest yourself from wind and sun, every bit of it had to be thoughtfully rationed.

"I don't think I could get along without mine." Ryan paused with one foot in the bed of the trailer and looked down at her. "I'm sorry," he said. "I've forgotten your name. I wasn't very awake this morning."

"Melinda Keith."

"That's right." He waded to the back of the trailer and started pushing small items toward her.

She looked around the empty yard. "Where's Tanner?"

"I've barricaded him in his new room with a trunk full of toys," Ryan answered, lifting a box labeled *Books*. "I didn't want him wandering around. He likes to explore new places, but he doesn't know enough yet to stay out of culverts or off the road."

They worked steadily for half an hour longer, and then Ryan announced it was time for a break. Melinda retrieved the picnic basket from the porch, and Ryan retrieved Tanner from his room. They spread a blanket under the burr oaks.

"You've been a tremendous help," Ryan said. He broke a sandwich into smaller pieces for Tanner. He looked over at Melinda, where she was dishing out the salad onto paper plates. "I remembered too late that the nearest grocery store is ten miles away, and Pizza Palace doesn't deliver."

She laughed. "You'll get used to it after a while."

He lounged on one elbow, stretching his long legs and looking around the yard contentedly. "I feel like I've never been away. It's peaceful, isn't it? It's too bad it took this to make me come back."

She chewed her sandwich and thoughtfully watched him. The sun filtering through the trees caught the red in his hair and made it glow. His skin was tanned bronze. The collar of his shirt was open, and she saw a thin gold chain around his neck.

"What's this?" She pointed to the chain.

His face brightened, and he pulled the chain out to show her a minute gold pendant.

"A piano," she said. "Do you play?"

"Yes, when I get the chance."

She looked in horror at the U-Haul. "Don't tell me I have to lift a grand piano out of there."

He threw his head back and laughed. Tanner, not knowing why, joined in delightedly. "No, no. I have an electric keyboard. Very light-weight."

"Whew! I was going to say, the neighborly spirit only goes so far."

Ryan, who had finished with his meal, lay back on the blanket with his hands under his head and looked up at the sky, squinting against the blue brilliance.

"There aren't any clouds," he said, sounding surprised.

"No, the rain yesterday washed them out. But give this heat a few days and we'll have another cloudburst. They say if you don't like the weather, wait a few hours; it'll change. But you know that better than I do. You're from here."

Ryan rubbed a hand over his jaw and sat up.

"I've been away more than I've been here, though. Thanks a lot for the picnic. I'd better get back to work. Dad's men are doing well on their own, but the sooner I can join them, the better. I was lucky—they've already finished the branding, polling, and vaccinating this year."

Melinda was glad she didn't raise cattle and could miss out on those particular activities. The idea of it—the sounds and smells of dehorning, the bawling calves, the general mayhem—did not appeal to her. She found it ironic that the ranch hands both hurt the calves and vaccinated them against harm at the same time.

"Your dad had some good hired hands," Melinda assured him. "The only time I've ever heard Dayton Bridger say a full sentence was when my chicken coop caught fire, and Mark Garcia doesn't know much English at all, but they're hard workers. And Peter Clegg is the best roper in Swisher County."

"That's what I've heard." Ryan nodded. "Good. I'm glad to know the ranch was in capable hands after . . . until I got here." A half grin slid across his face. "Coop caught fire, huh? Trying to roast your chickens all at the same time, were you?"

"Ha-ha. No, I suspect it was teenagers from the new subdivision, goofing around and getting into trouble. I don't think they meant much harm by it, because they set the hens loose first. Once in a while I have a run-in with some of them, just little things. They trespass. They cut in line at the grocery store. Sometimes they sneak into my orchard and steal my apples."

"They're probably just bored. As I recall growing up here, there wasn't much to keep a teenager entertained."

"Well, they probably found it pretty entertaining watching me run around for an hour trying to catch the chickens again."

Melinda got to her feet and carried the basket back to the porch. Ryan, picking up the four corners of the blanket with Tanner inside, slung him over his back and carried the giggling bundle into the house.

CHAPTER 2

By midafternoon, the trailer was empty. Melinda left Ryan to his unpacking and went home. She sat in her large, airy kitchen, snapping pole beans into a bowl. The quiet of the house settled around her. The soft snapping of the beans, the ticking of the German clock on the mantel, and the distant squeaking of the turning windmill all combined to lull her into a pleasant stupor as her hands moved automatically at their task. Even Abigail seemed drugged by the stillness, lying motionless on the back of the couch like a discarded dust mop. There were times the quiet of the house weighed on Melinda, serving as a reminder of how alone she was. But other times, like now, it was as comforting as a blanket.

Melinda was a third of the way through the bushel when the phone rang, making her jump. She set the bowl aside and went to answer it.

"Are you still alive? I haven't heard from you all week," said the familiar voice on the other end of the line.

Melinda rolled her eyes and perched on the edge of the counter, swinging her feet. This was going to be a long call.

"Hi, Mom."

"Oh, you still remember me?"

"Ha-ha, Mom. What's up?"

"Do I have to have a reason to speak to my own daughter? I was just concerned when I didn't hear from you."

"I'm sorry. It's coming on harvest time, Mom. I'm swamped. You should see the place—bushel baskets from here to the ceiling."

"If you lived closer, I could help you."

Melinda had a brief image of her mother's plump, manicured hands snapping juicy beans. She smiled. "Thanks. But if I lived closer, I wouldn't have the farm, and I wouldn't be swamped," she reasoned.

"Well, I tried to warn you that it would be too much for you to handle alone." Melinda could picture her mother's face puckering.

"It isn't too much to handle. It's going fine. It's just time-consuming; I haven't had a chance to call you."

"I still think you're making a mistake. You shouldn't be out there all by yourself. I think you should sell the place and come back home. You could use the money for school."

"We've hashed this out already," Melinda reminded her. "I want to do it, Mom. It's not just for the research or to see if it can be done. I *enjoy* this way of living."

"But *farming*? If you're looking for something to do, you could get your old job back."

"I have a job: running this farm. You know I'll never move back to Albuquerque as long as I live, so why do you always bring it up?"

"Now, dear, just because of one bad experience with one man, you don't have to eliminate the state's entire male population."

It was an old song. Melinda was too tired to sing it again. She ran a hand through her bangs.

"Mom, I'm really busy right now." If that wasn't a universal hint, what was? Her mother happily ignored it.

"I didn't tell you—I've been farming myself lately. I have a beautiful zucchini in my backyard."

Melinda barely stopped herself from saying, "Zucchini would grow in solid concrete." She cleared her throat. "That's good. I really have to go, Mom."

"Fine, fine. But you are coming back here for Thanksgiving, aren't you?"

"That's almost four months away."

"Everybody's coming home for Thanksgiving. Did I tell you Chris got his promotion? They're going to redo their kitchen with the money. It's high time, too. And Scott got his license; he's taking Jessica on a date tonight, and I just know he's going to get in a wreck."

"I remember you said the same thing when the rest of us started driving, Mom, and we never crashed, did we?"

"No, but there was the time you knocked down the mailbox."

They were off and running. The clock read 6:00 P.M. when at last her mother began to wind down.

"Well, this is costing a fortune. You should live closer."

"I like it here, Mom. I think it's good for me."

"You didn't have to move out. Did I ever say you had to move out?"

"Mom, it was time. It's been two years; why bring it up now?"

"I'm just saying is all."

"Can we please not do this tonight?"

"You should have stayed after the divorce and finished your doctorate."

"Okay, Mom."

"It's not too late to go back. You could end up a professor, even. Some women do that, you know."

"No, Mom."

There was an audible sigh from the other end of the line. "That Davis boy asked after you. You know, his mother's in my book club."

"I'm not interested, Mom."

"It doesn't hurt to look. I need grandchildren."

"You have grandchildren. Joan has given you four."

"But Anne Gilbraith has nine, and she's younger than I am."

"Good-bye, Mom."

"You're twenty-seven, Melinda. *Do* something about it."

"I will. I'll turn twenty-eight. Gotta go. Good night."

She hung up with a sigh and rubbed her ear. The conversation never changed in content; it only grew longer each time. Forget about Derek. Finish your PhD. Be successful like your brothers and sister. Marry again—and this time give me grandchildren. Stand on your head and bark like a seal . . .

Melinda blew the bangs out of her eyes and went back to her beans. The doorbell interrupted her. Muttering, she stomped to answer it.

Ryan waved a bulging, white paper bag. "Since you provided lunch, I'm providing supper."

Melinda gaped at him, then broke into a laugh. "I should say, 'You didn't need to do that,' but I'm too glad to see a sane face. Come in."

She stepped aside to let Ryan in; he was followed by a widely smiling Tanner. Melinda watched Ryan put the bag on the kitchen table and lift paper-wrapped items from it.

"Sane face, huh?" Ryan asked. "I'm not sure I'd qualify."

"I just had a conversation with my mother. *Any* face will do at this point." Melinda sighed.

"I hope you like Subway. It was the closest restaurant I could find—and I had to drive clear to Redcreek at that." He glanced at her apologetically. "They're not half as good as your homemade lunch, but we're in a pinch until I can get to a grocery store. Dad's place is practically bare. I think he lived on cheese sandwiches."

Melinda pulled plates and glasses from the cupboard and pushed the bowls of beans and bean ends out of the way.

"Excuse the mess. It's canning season."

"You should have told me you had all this work to do. I wouldn't have let you slave all day at my house."

"I enjoyed it," she replied, surprised to find it was true. "I've never spent much time with my neighbors. Well, except for Jack Peyton. He comes over once in a while. Do you remember him?"

"Jack." Ryan's face took on a thoughtful look. "How could I forget him? If ever there was someone to hit with a frying pan . . ."

"Why do you say that?"

"He made my childhood a nightmare. Once he pushed me in the river that runs across the back of his property when he knew I couldn't swim. If it hadn't been for Dale Purdy, who saw the whole thing and fished me out, I'd be dead."

"Not really."

"Really."

"He told me you used to be afraid of cows." She watched him from under her lashes, waiting for his reaction.

"Did he also tell you he once locked me in a stall with a very temperamental bull? I defied gravity getting over that wall," he said grimly. Then he gave a wry grin. "If Jack's your only social life, you might be better off lonely."

Melinda brought out the for-company tablecloth, which she'd only used twice. On an impulse, she stepped out the back door and snipped some pink roses to stuff in an earthenware jug for a centerpiece. Then she arranged everyone around the table, setting Tanner on a couple of heavy books to raise him. Ryan glanced at the titles.

"*Basic Horticulture* and *The Wives of Henry the Eighth*. Interesting selections."

"They're the thickest ones I could find on short notice. The horticulture book has come in very handy. *Henry the Eighth* is just for fun. Talk about temperamental!"

As they ate, Ryan took in his surroundings with open interest. Melinda watched his eyes slide over the spacious, well-organized kitchen with its big, stainless-steel double sinks and high-efficiency stove. Bunches of drying herbs were suspended from the ceiling beam, rows of cookbooks and how-to books lined the shelf where the microwave would ordinarily have been, and the steam canner squatted on the counter like an aluminum gargoyle. She wondered if Ryan could tell the wall opposite the windows was extra thick, made of cement, to capture the sun's heat and store it for later use. It was one of the improvements Melinda had made to the old farmhouse when she'd begun this project.

"I can see you're an industrious person," he said.

"I have to be," Melinda replied with a touch of pride. "I rarely buy anything if I can make it instead. I've learned how to make just about everything I need, except maybe shoes. I have to go to Amarillo for those."

"That's incredible. How did you learn all this?"

"Some of it I learned from courses I took in school. Some I got from library books or my textbooks. Some from trial and error. A few things I learned from my grandpa. He wasn't a farmer, but he loved to garden, and he was pretty innovative, always willing to try new things. He taught me to think about things from more than one perspective. And he had a profound respect for the earth. He was recycling and going organic long before it was popular."

"He sounds like an interesting character."

"He was. He died a few years ago." Melinda reached for her glass and hid behind it a moment as she drank. Thoughts of her grandfather still brought sadness with them.

"I imagine this way of life is pretty demanding. It must be a lot of work."

"Yes, but it's kind of fun, actually. There's a lot of opportunity for creativity. It's satisfying. I don't make much money, but I don't need much, either. I consider it a challenge, figuring out how to make something myself instead of buying it, or finding ways to get what I need from the land without harming it in return. I even had a windmill and solar collector panels installed so I wouldn't have to buy much electricity. When I can afford it, I'm putting in more panels so I'll be able to live completely off the grid. I'm determined to be completely self-reliant. And I should be mortgage-free in just a few years." She paused. "That's what my mother and I fight about. She doesn't think it's a good idea to be independent—or, at least, her children shouldn't be independent from *her*. She doesn't understand why I don't want to go back home. She doesn't think it's proper for me to be out here on my own. She has her own agenda in mind for me, and she can't understand why I don't want to live it."

"Sounds like Dad and me," Ryan mused with a crooked smile on his lips. "He didn't approve of anything I did."

"What did you do?" she asked with a smile.

His expression turned thoughtful. "Three things, really. Before I tell you, though . . . you're a member of the LDS Church, aren't you? I thought I saw a BYU sticker on the back of your truck."

"Yes, I am. I did my undergrad at BYU. Why?"

"I'm a Mormon, too. That's the first thing that bothered my dad. I don't know how well you knew him. As you might know, my mom was LDS, but my father never was. He never could understand why I wanted to go on a mission. He seemed to think it was just an excuse to get out of working on the ranch with him. He thought it was a waste of money and time. But I wanted to go."

"I didn't know that about your parents," Melinda said, sad for his experience but delighted he shared her beliefs. "I never met your mother, and I didn't know your dad all that well. Where did you serve?"

"Toronto, Canada."

"That would have been interesting. And what were the other two things you did that he didn't approve of?"

"I married Caroline." Ryan's voice grew soft. "It wasn't that he objected to her personally so much as the fact that since the marriage was in the temple, he couldn't attend. It caused some tension between us. Even though he'd always known about the temple, and Mom had told him years before that it was likely I'd marry there, he never thought it would actually happen. He saw it as me choosing Caroline and her family over him. And then, as the final blow, we decided to live in Wyoming, where her family was. To Dad, that was the ultimate betrayal—that I'd abandon him and the ranch. But as it turned out, it was a good thing we were near her family for what time we had." He gave a painful smile that tugged at Melinda's heart.

"What happened?" Melinda asked and wondered if she were treading on forbidden ground.

"She died when Tanner was four months old," Ryan said, and though his face didn't change, his voice became even softer. "We'd been married almost five years."

"I'm sorry. I didn't know." The words felt flat and insufficient. Melinda couldn't imagine what it would feel like to be left a widower so soon, having to be both father and mother to a baby. It seemed too intimate, too unfathomable a thing for him to have told her. Melinda didn't know how to react to pain like that. She was afraid, suddenly, to look at Ryan's face. As an excuse to move away, she went to the fridge and took out the peach betty she'd made for one of the women she visit taught. She'd planned to drop it by tonight, but she would wait and make another one tomorrow. Melinda rattled around in the cupboard, getting bowls, covering the awkwardness with noise.

Ryan folded the sandwich wrappers and smoothed his large hand across them. When Melinda finally stole a look at him, she was relieved to see that his face was concentratedly impassive.

"We tried for several years to have a child," Ryan said. "We were so excited when we found out Caroline was pregnant. She was diagnosed with cancer when she was three months along."

Melinda turned to stare at him fully, her hands growing still. "Oh, no."

"They wanted to operate right away and start aggressive chemotherapy, but she would have had to terminate the pregnancy." He glanced at Tanner, then away. "She wouldn't do it," he went on. "She said she was going to have him, even if it cost her her life. And in the end, it did. By the time Tanner was born, it was too late for treatment."

"Oh, Ryan." She fished for something to say, but everything that came to mind seemed trite and inadequate. She looked at Tanner, who was chewing happily on a bun. She wished intensely that she hadn't asked.

Ryan smiled at her as he pushed the wrappers back into the paper bag. "Dad came to her funeral, and he actually bent enough to tell me afterward that he thought he could understand why I'd wanted to marry her. She was a special person." He reached over and roughed Tanner's hair affectionately.

"I'm so sorry."

He gave a one-shouldered shrug. "*I'm* sorry; I didn't mean to tell you all that. We're all right now. But I'll tell you, for the first while, all I wanted to do was escape."

At these words, Melinda's mind jumped to the day she had fled from her parents' house just after her twenty-fifth birthday. They had had a party for her, a child's party, with streamers, balloons, and cake. But it was too soon after her divorce for gaiety, and all she had wanted was quiet, to be left alone. She had come to Texas, had bought this land on an impulse, and had found the tranquility she so desperately needed after the nightmarish year her marriage had lasted. Oh yes, she understood the desire to escape.

She looked up to see Ryan's blue-eyed gaze upon her.

He spoke quietly. "I think you know what I mean."

"Yes, I think so." She pushed a bowl of peaches and crumbly oat topping toward him.

"I thought there might be a reason a lovely young woman would be living on her own, miles from anywhere."

Melinda ignored his comment. "Do you want ice cream with that?" she asked.

"Ice cream!" Tanner shouted, and Ryan and Melinda both jumped, startled.

"I guess that's a yes," Ryan said and laughed. He seemed to laugh a lot, Melinda noted as she went to the chest freezer. It was an infectious sound. When you lived alone, you didn't hear laughter often.

"Would you like to come out on the porch?" she asked when they had finished eating. "It's cooler out there with the breeze."

She carried the bean bowls out through the back kitchen door. He followed with the bushel basket onto the porch. Melinda dropped onto the step and promptly began snapping beans, but Ryan Delaney stretched himself out on the padded porch swing and sighed, seeming content to enjoy the slight breeze coming down off the quiet fields.

"I've got aches and pains in muscles I never knew I had," he remarked wryly. "I can see I'm going to have to get in shape."

Melinda glanced at his lean, broad-chested frame lounging on the swing and smiled. His shape looked just fine from where she sat. She caught herself and concentrated on the beans. Such thoughts were dangerous. If anyone should know that, she should.

Tanner had discovered the rabbit hutches in the open shed and was delightedly poking his finger through the wire. Melinda saw Ryan's face soften and lose the tired lines around the eyes as he watched his son.

"You have a very nice place," Ryan said, turning to her and catching her staring. She dropped her gaze. "How much land are you working?"

"There are twenty-five acres. Half of it's workable, and the other half I'm converting to mixed forest. I have a little pasture as well. I had a steer I was raising for beef, but it got into some tansy ragwort a couple of months ago and died. I haven't replaced it."

"Tansy ragwort? Don't you spray for the stuff?"

She leveled an eye at him. "I'm trying to keep it all organic, remember? Besides, I'd never seen any growing in the pasture before, so I didn't see a need to spray even if that had been an option. I'm not sure how the steer got it, because I never did find any growing around, but that's what the vet said happened." Melinda nodded toward the hutches. From where they sat, they could just see the compact balls of white fur behind the wire. "I'm still getting up my nerve to try rabbit."

Ryan chuckled. He gestured toward the chicken coop—now rebuilt—and raised his eyebrows in amusement. "And how about the chickens? Or are they just for eggs?"

Melinda grinned and tossed a handful of beans into the bowl. "Once, I chased one in circles around the yard until it died of a heart attack. I think I've decided I'll just be vegetarian until they drop quietly from old age. Until then, they can lay their eggs in peace."

He chuckled, a deep, resonant sound in the growing dusk. Tanner heard him and waved, babbling something incoherent and pointing to the rabbits. The windmill chugged slowly in circles, sending power humming along the lines to the batteries in the shed. In the lowering light, the dark shapes of the pigs moved under the apple trees.

"You really do have everything you need here," Ryan remarked, gazing about with an approving look.

Melinda gazed around too, trying to see it all through his eyes. "Yes, I guess I do," she agreed. "Except for the solar panels, but those will come."

Ryan stood and came to sit beside her on the step. "I'll help."

"No need."

He snorted. "This after you spent hours hauling my garbage in from the trailer? Give me the bowl."

They sat quietly for a while, snapping beans side by side. Their hands worked steadily until the beans were finished and it was dark. The stars reminded Melinda of Christmas lights caught in the tree branches.

"It's been a good day," Ryan murmured. "I don't know what made me talk so much about Caroline and my dad, but thanks for listening."

When Ryan left, Tanner astride his shoulders, Melinda stood on the front porch and listened to the crunching of his feet on the gravel long after he'd disappeared into the dark. She thought about going inside to blanch and bag the beans for the freezer, but she continued to stand a while longer. Crickets vibrated in the window well. The windmill creaked. After a while, lights came on in the ranch house windows down the road. She pictured Ryan tucking Tanner in bed, maybe sitting for a while with a book before going to sleep himself. The night smelled sweetly of summer. She told herself that the calm contentment spreading through her stemmed from the peaceful night sounds, the stars, the taste of peaches. She told herself it had nothing whatsoever to do with the color of her new neighbor's eyes.

"I do have everything I need here," she assured herself. "I don't need anything more."

* * *

There was no break in the heat all that week. A flat, bronze sun rode through a cloudless sky. The usually constant breeze had all but disappeared. Heat sapped everything of its strength, leaving the pea vines limp and yellow, the roses brown and apathetic. The spinach gave up the final ghost. The rabbits lay on their sides with their ears, their only cooling system, drooping. When Melinda went to gather the eggs Monday morning, she found only one. The hens gave her a defiant look, daring her to complain.

Melinda refused to let the heat depress her and stubbornly devoted the week to bringing in the rest of her harvest before it withered away to nothing. With her battered sun hat and a liberal helping of sunscreen, she set about gathering radishes and peppers, wrinkled tomatoes, and the rest of the beans and cabbage. The pumpkins, carrots, celery, onions, potatoes, beets, and squash could wait until September when it started to turn cold. Some of the vegetables she scalded and bagged for her own freezer. The rest she stored in baskets in the cooler barn to be hauled to Dale Purdy's stand. It had been a good summer, and she hadn't lost anything but the lettuce, which had never been much of a success no matter how she babied it. She wished suddenly, intensely, that her grandfather were there to advise her. He had grown lettuce the size of fans in his patch of a backyard.

However, as she walked up and down the harvested rows with the wheelbarrow, she thought that, on the whole, he would have been pleased with her. City-raised as she was, she had managed her second harvest—at least so far—on her own, and it was even better than it had been last year. At the end of the week, she stood surveying the dark, deep earth beds with more than a little pride. She would make a go of this yet.

The next morning Melinda was attacking the weeds that lined her driveway, armed with a hand-held sickle and a spade (the weeds were too tall for her mower), when Jack came over. He crossed the street without looking for traffic—there never was any—and stood with his hands on his hips to watch as she struggled to master the rhythm of swinging the scythe. He said nothing, and finally Melinda turned to him, red faced and panting.

"Finding this entertaining, are you?" she asked.

Jack shrugged and looked off over the fields, squinting against the sun. "Sort of, yeah."

"I don't want to use chemicals on them, if that's what you're thinking."

"Wasn't thinking it."

Melinda returned to her labor, hacking at the tough weed stems. She wondered if these weeds might be important, vital even, to some ecosystem. Maybe she should just leave them. Who knew what habitat she might be destroying? She paused again, wiping perspiration from her brow and looking along the driveway, hoping to see some indication that a desperately important creature needed these weeds. No such luck. There was no sign of life, not even an insect. Glumly, she went back to hacking.

"I saw that you went over and helped Ryan Delaney move in." Jack leaned against a fencepost, his arms folded.

"Yes. And I saw you didn't." Melinda didn't look up.

Jack shrugged and rubbed the back of his neck. "No," he said.

There was a long silence broken only by the sound of the scythe and an occasional clang as it missed its target and hit the hard earth. Melinda briefly thought of calling her home teachers to help, but they were both in their seventies, and she couldn't very well haul them out here to whack weeds in this heat. Besides, they'd just bring their spray cans of Roundup. She supposed the whole town thought she was crazy for insisting on doing everything the hard way. She sighed. Maybe she was.

"I'm going into town later if you need anything," Jack said.

"No, thanks. I'm fine," Melinda panted.

"They're calling for more rain tonight."

"That's good."

Jack wiped a hand slowly down his face and gazed up at the sky with a tiny smile.

"There's a weed whacker over there in my garage if you want it."

Melinda popped upright. "You couldn't have mentioned this half an hour ago?"

He ducked his dark head. "I wasn't sure how you'd take the offer. I know how you feel about burning gasoline unnecessarily," he replied.

Melinda tossed the sickle onto the meager pile of cut weeds. "It's necessary," she said shortly. "Go get it."

Jack recrossed the street, not bothering to hide his laughter.

Saturday, Melinda began carting the full bushel baskets to the pickup to haul to the Purdys'. Somehow the baskets seemed heavier coming from the barn than they had been going in. She was struggling with a basket of tomatoes when she heard someone call her name. Melinda straightened with a hand to the small of her back. Ryan and Tanner were coming across the lawn. Tanner wore a pair of overalls with no shirt and a straw sun hat that turned him into a miniature Huck Finn. Ryan wore jeans and a white T-shirt. He had replaced his tennis shoes with scuffed boots.

"Good morning," Melinda called, resting her back against the tailgate. She hadn't had the chance to see Ryan all week. Her first thought was that his eyes really were as blue as she remembered.

"It's too hot to be doing that today," Ryan said. "We've discovered a great wading spot at the river, and that's where we're headed. Tanner wondered if you'd care to come along and help him catch some frogs."

Melinda smiled at Tanner, knowing perfectly well that he had wondered nothing of the sort. "Thanks. I'd like to, but I have a lot to do. I have to take a load of produce to Dale Purdy."

Ryan bent down, scooped up the heavy basket of tomatoes, and dropped it into the back of the truck as if it weighed as much as a pillow. "How much more do you have to load?"

"There are about eight more bushels in the barn."

Without a word, Ryan set off for the barn. Melinda followed, jogging to keep up with his long strides. The rubber boots she wore made speed awkward.

"You don't have to help me," she said. "I can do it."

"I know you can. So can I."

"I'd pull the truck closer, but some idiot put the septic bed right in front of the barn."

Ryan shrugged. "The sooner you're loaded, the sooner you can go frog hunting with us."

She would have argued with him, but she could see from the set of his jaw there was no point to it. She'd always thought of herself as tall at five-foot-seven, but he topped her by a good seven or eight inches. She couldn't even glare at him full in the eye.

He hoisted a basket of runner beans and started back toward the truck. She picked up another basket herself and waddled after him in her flatulent rubber boots. They had the truck loaded in no time. Ryan brushed his hands on his thighs.

"After you deliver your load, you're free to come wading, right?"

Melinda laughed. "I guess I suddenly am. I'll meet you back here in twenty minutes."

When she returned from the Purdys' stand, Ryan's blue Subaru was parked in her driveway, and he and Tanner were sitting on her front porch.

"Let me just change into some shorts, and I'll be right with you," she told them, breezing past. She pulled on knee-length cut-offs, toed into her oldest tennis shoes, and took a look in the mirror. Her face was a faint pink from the sun, and her dark hair was escaping from its braid again. "Don't I make a pleasant picture!" Melinda laughed, made a face at herself, scooped up a pail, extra sunscreen, towels, and a bag of Oreos (she indulged about twice a year), and went outside.

Ryan was waiting in front in the car with Tanner strapped into his car seat. Melinda climbed into the passenger seat, and they were off.

"We found this place by accident," Ryan explained as the little Subaru zipped past the Purdys' place, kicking up dust. "I was trying to find Side Road 13, which I was told led to the home of a Mr. John Ostler—we heard he had an air conditioner for sale. Some idiot kids in a Buick were driving on the wrong side of the road, and I ended up skidding into the river. No harm done, but a nice gentleman on a tractor had to pull me out. Eventually, I found Mr. Ostler living on Side Road 15, not 13, although someone had already bought his air conditioner. Still, it's a nice little spot in the river. Along here somewhere, I think."

He slowed the car and pulled over to the side of the narrow road, the tires crunching the dry weeds. A gravel lane veered off to the right and ended six feet later at the grassy bank of the river. Melinda could see the gouges where the Subaru's tires had been stuck.

"Yes, this is the place," Ryan said. "Lucky for me that tractor came along when it did."

"How are you getting settled at the ranch?" Melinda asked. She unstrapped Tanner from the car seat and lifted him out. Tanner squirmed from her grasp and ran for the water, squealing.

"Everything's fine so far," Ryan said, catching Tanner by his overall strap before he plunged headfirst into the brown water. "Hold on, bud; you can't swim." He tousled the little boy's hair. "The guys are great, and everybody's been very friendly—especially you."

As he smiled at her, the sun caught his hair, turning it more red than brown. Even his teeth were beautiful.

Melinda turned and waded into the water with her shoes on.

"It was frogs he wanted, right? It's not deep along here. It's probably only up to his armpits," she said. "Come here, Tanner, and let me hold your hands."

Tanner suddenly decided to play shy and buried his face in Ryan's pant leg. Ryan put a large hand gently on the blond head.

"It's all right. She's a nice lady. Do you want to look for a frog?"

After a short internal debate, his curiosity won out. Tanner let Melinda take his hands and help him into the water. He was instantly all smiles, splashing and laughing.

"Come over here where it's shady," Melinda said. "I bet we'll find some."

Tanner followed her obediently, tentatively at first and then with growing enthusiasm. The water was cool in the shade, but it was shallow. Where the sun hit the surface it was warm, and the pebbles at the bottom glowed amber and gold. Melinda kept a tight hold on the chubby fist and pointed out spots along the weedy bank where frogs might be hiding. Bursts of aster and rose verbena colored the banks. A family of jays chattered at them from the barbed wire fence lining the adjoining cornfield.

"I'm thinking of making a few changes around the place," Ryan called from the bank. He stood watching them with his thumbs hooked in his pockets.

"What sort of changes?"

"For one thing, there's an old barn Dad never used that could be fixed up. I'm thinking of buying some longhorn bulls and starting a stud service."

Melinda gaped at him. "You're switching to longhorns?"

"I'm not replacing the herd," Ryan explained. "Just expanding a bit."

"But longhorns?"

He chuckled at her expression. "What's wrong with longhorns?"

She tried to recall the scoffing remarks Jack had made when Dale Purdy mentioned buying a longhorn steer.

"They're lean and rangy. And it's impossible to fence them in. They can leap like deer."

"So I'll make the fences nine feet instead of six. And they may be lean, but fifty percent of their body weight is cuttable meat," Ryan argued. "Since they're so narrow in the head and shoulders, it makes birthing the calves easier on the cows, so they can be bred more often. And did you know a longhorn can bear calves for twenty-five to thirty years?"

"Is that so?" She rescued Tanner as he started to lose his footing. "But they're so fierce looking."

"They're resistant to bloating and pinkeye—and tansy ragwort, incidentally. They can also stand the heat and cold better than other breeds."

She waved a hand. "Okay, I surrender. You've obviously been doing some research."

"On the Internet," he replied, grinning. "There's an auction at the end of the month in Amarillo. I think I can get the barn fixed up by then. Do you want to come?"

Melinda tried not to sound too eager as she replied, "Sure, sounds fun. I haven't been to an auction in ages."

They paddled around the edges of the river for more than an hour, with Ryan directing their hunt from the bank. Melinda managed to find one sorry-looking frog and a host of water skaters. Tanner was delighted with the frog but uncertain about the insects, which moved in nervous little jumps. He clung to Melinda's hand, squealing and pointing, then snatching his finger back as the bugs moved.

Laughing, Melinda assured him they were harmless, but he wouldn't let her put one on his hand.

They played with the frog until the novelty wore off, and then Melinda let it go in the murky shallows. By this time Tanner had mud smeared all over him, including his hair, and Melinda wasn't much cleaner. She dripped over to the bank and lifted Tanner out to Ryan, who waited with a towel to wipe him off.

"How is it that you invite me to go wading and I end up soaked while you stay perfectly dry?" she observed, standing knee-deep in the cool water and squinting up at him.

Ryan grinned. "Why do you think I asked you along? No way *I'm* going in there!"

Melinda made a face at him and scooped up a handful of water to fling at him. He ducked out of the way, laughing.

"All right," Melinda said, holding up her hands. "Just help me out of here."

Naively, Ryan reached down to help her out of the river. As soon as their hands locked, Melinda jerked. He tumbled in headfirst with a terrific splash. Ryan rose up spluttering while Melinda happily climbed up the bank and picked up a towel.

"You should have seen that one coming," she remarked with a smile. "It wouldn't take a shrink to read my mind on *that* one."

Ryan scrambled up on the bank, shaking the water out of his hair like a setter. "All right, I admit I was gullible."

Melinda handed him a towel. Ryan reached to take it from her—and then pulled down hard. Melinda let out a yelp as she found herself on her hands and knees in the river once again. She got a mouthful of tepid water and spat it out. There was grit in her teeth and loose wisps of her hair stuck to her cheeks.

Ryan squatted down to Tanner's level, pointing solemnly at Melinda.

"Now, Tanner, don't you think that's more entertaining than some old frog?"

Tanner nodded in agreement.

Once they had dried somewhat, they got back in the car and attacked the cookies and some cans of ginger ale Ryan had brought. A pleasant drowsiness had settled over them by the time they reached Melinda's house.

"Thanks for the outing," Ryan told her. "I enjoyed it."

"I did too. You have a sweet little boy."

Her arms were full of damp towels, sunscreen, and the pail. As Ryan reached past her to open the car door for her, she could smell water and sunshine. Melinda slipped out and waved good-bye to Tanner. Dirt-streaked and drowsy-eyed, he waved back.

She watched through her screen door as the Subaru disappeared behind the lilac hedge. She couldn't remember the last time she'd relaxed and enjoyed herself so much. It occurred to her that she hadn't had an afternoon off in a long time. She went upstairs to shower and change into clean jeans and a cotton blouse. It was too hot outside now to work anymore, and she was tempted to return to her murder mystery and find out if the housekeeper or the nephew had murdered Edward Rutherford.

Better not. She'd had enough play for one day. With all the outdoor work she had done lately, the inside of her house had suffered a bit. She forced herself into action; she squared away the kitchen, scrubbed the bathrooms, threw in a load of laundry (her dedication to the environment only went so far when it came to hand washing her clothes), and was in the middle of sweeping the hallway when she heard a noise outside.

Curious, she leaned the broom against the wall and went to the back door. Tanner, now dressed in clean, white shorts and a T-shirt, was sitting on her back porch, happily eating an apple. Ryan was pacing across her back lawn with a lawnmower. She knew the ground was uneven and pitted, but he strode along easily, the mower munching steadily. He nodded at her in greeting but didn't stop. After a moment's hesitation, Melinda walked over and sat down beside Tanner to watch.

Ryan finished the entire lawn in half an hour. When at last he shut off the machine, there was a deafening silence that made Melinda's ears feel full of cotton.

She had taken Tanner to visit the rabbits as Ryan finished with the lawn. Now she led him back to the porch and leaned against the railing. Tanner, starting to feel the effects of his long day, curled into the porch chair and gave a jaw-cracking yawn. Ryan joined them, wiping his forearm across his brow. Sweat had darkened the hair at his temples, but otherwise he appeared as cool and fresh as he had that morning.

"You didn't need to mow for me," Melinda said. "I'm perfectly capable of doing it myself."

Ryan shrugged. "I know you are. I just felt like it."

"It wasn't even that long," Melinda said.

"Better than putting it off," he replied cheerfully.

"I have a non-motorized mower in the shed. It doesn't belch out carbon monoxide."

Ryan eyed her a moment, then turned and held out his hand. "Come on, Tanner, time for your nap."

Tanner stuck out his lower lip and began to thump his heels on the chair, but Ryan scooped him up, set him on his shoulders, and directed him to hold onto Daddy's ears. Then he gripped the mower's handle and nodded at Melinda.

"I apologize for the carbon monoxide, but I will point out that you do drive a pickup truck."

"Which will change as soon as there's a hybrid alternative."

"Heck, why not use a horse and cart?"

"I've thought of it."

"Aren't you carrying this organic thing a little far?"

"I'm trying to find ways to live in harmony with the earth, not in conflict," Melinda replied.

"Hmm. Well, you might try doing that with people, too," Ryan said.

She watched him disappear around the corner of the house, then looked at the lawn again. She felt ashamed of herself. He had helped her, and she'd jumped all over him. He was trying to be kind. But it had made her uncomfortable. She didn't need his help, and she didn't want him to think she did. It was sheer pride, of course, and she told herself she should feel grateful, not irritated. But it was irritating, all the same. She didn't need his help or anyone else's. She scowled at the grass a moment longer, then went inside to finish sweeping. The sooner she turned that patch of lawn into tall-grass prairie, the better.

CHAPTER 3

When Melinda arrived at church Sunday morning, she sat near the back and tried to pretend she wasn't watching for the Delaneys' arrival. They got there just before the meeting started. Ryan was startlingly handsome in a dark suit. He looked like he had stepped out of a black-and-white movie, and he appeared taller than he had the day before. He carried Tanner in one arm and a blue denim knapsack over the opposite shoulder, a slight improvement over the bright pink diaper bag that Caleb Martin, who sat in front of her, was hefting. Melinda wondered absently why diaper bags always had to announce their function with bold colors and cartoon characters. Was there a rule about color-coordinating with the gender of your baby? Would someone report you for using a blue bag for a female infant? What if you just used a nondescript canvas tote? Did Gucci or Armani put out designer diaper bags?

Ryan saw her and nodded an acknowledgment over the heads of the people between them, but it seemed to her that his manner was cool and his tight smile perfunctory. Tanner was charming, a miniature version of his father, right down to their matching ties. She wondered if he would come over so she would have a chance to apologize for being snooty. But to Melinda's disappointment—which she quickly tamped down—Ryan sat near the front by the side door, where he could, she supposed, make a quick exit if Tanner got noisy. She reached for her hymn book as the bishop stood to announce the opening hymn. She deliberately tried not to watch Ryan during the meeting and kept her eyes forward, but afterward she couldn't have said who had spoken or what the topics had been.

He wasn't in Sunday School, and Melinda imagined he was likely introducing Tanner to the nursery. She could visualize Tanner being shy and uncertain in this new building, surrounded by unfamiliar people. She didn't see Ryan at the break between meetings, either, and when she emerged from the flurry of farewells after Relief Society, she didn't see Ryan's car in the parking lot. She told herself it didn't matter, and she spent the evening preparing her enrichment lesson and listening to the clock tick in her quiet house.

Monday morning there was nothing urgent left to do, since the more delicate plants were now safely out of the sun. Rather than jumping from bed at six o'clock as usual, Melinda let herself lie contentedly in bed until eight, which was absolute decadence. Then she showered and pulled on a white cotton dress, fed the rabbits and chickens, checked on the pigs, grabbed a quick breakfast, and set out for the store in her battered Ford pickup.

For serious shopping, one had to go all the way to Amarillo, but there was a small plaza in Redcreek that had the essentials—gasoline, rented DVDs, and Subway sandwiches. There was even an abandoned steel shed that some enterprising person had converted into a bowling alley. Melinda tended to avoid the plaza as much as possible, because it was the only gathering spot for local teenagers for miles. In the past that hadn't been a problem, but since some well-to-do commuters had purchased estate lots by the freeway and built a pile of mini-mansions, complete with iron gates on the driveways, the number of kids had grown. The character and demeanor of the crowd had changed too. The subdivision kids (the apple stealers) were different from the local country kids, and somehow harder and sleeker. They wore a sort of invisible barrier around them and looked at their narrow world with a bored cynicism that disturbed Melinda. She always tried to do her shopping during school hours.

Word around town was that the stockyards were being moved to Redcreek, and most people speculated that the town would keep building up to become an actual city before long. Melinda would be sorry to see it happen. She liked the solitude and emptiness of her little part of the Panhandle. Now, suddenly everyone seemed to be converging on the quiet spot.

But not on her twenty-five-acre patch of it, she told herself firmly as she wedged the truck into a vacant spot in front of the grocery store. At least she could comfort herself with that thought. She hoped Ryan shared her feelings about development. His place was much larger and adjoined hers on two sides. She would hate to ever see it go to housing tracts.

She admitted that living in a sparsely-populated area had its disadvantages. The grocery store tended to become the social center of the county, and you met everyone there sooner or later, like it or not. A case in point: as Melinda walked into the store, she saw Danny Wilson, her least favorite of the subdivision kids, lounging with his friends against the magazine rack, his hands in his pockets. He always had an arrogant smirk, and the dismissive glance he gave Melinda made her feel like a fourteen-year-old who'd blundered into the wrong clique at school. She'd encountered him a few times cutting across her property, and once she'd been forced to confront his parents when she'd caught him trying to break into her truck. If he was embarrassed by the memory of the incident or by the fact that he was clearly cutting school today, he showed no sign of it.

Melinda passed him and his dark-dressed friends, untethered a grocery cart, and steered into traffic. Another least-favorite person, local gossip Carmella Ostler, was heading toward her like a ship under full sail. Carmella had an untold number of children, and she always dressed them all in matching T-shirts so that (she would explain, laughing) if one ever went missing it would be easy to describe what the child was wearing to the police. Melinda found the idea appalling. She ducked down the nearest aisle with much-practiced skill.

Having shaken her would-be assailant, Melinda browsed the aisles, dodging frazzle-haired mothers pushing shopping carts laden with milk, Cheerios, and three or four small children mashed in together. She was hoisting a sack of sugar into her cart when someone tapped her on the shoulder. She turned to see Ryan smiling down at her.

"Hi there!" she greeted him, wondering what had suddenly gone wrong with her breathing. Her lungs were acting funny.

"Stocking up on a few basics," he said.

"Same here. Try as I might, I can't seem to grow my own sugar." She waved to Tanner, who sat kicking his legs in his father's shopping cart. She glanced offhandedly at what Ryan was purchasing. You could tell a lot about a person by the groceries they bought. So far he had a bag of flour, two bags of disposable diapers, a box of oatmeal, a jar of salad dressing, and two boxes of lightbulbs.

"Listen, I wanted to tell you I'm sorry for snapping at you Saturday," she said quickly, before she could chicken out. She glanced up at him and away again. "It isn't easy for me to accept help from other people."

"I gather that," Ryan said drily. "But it was my fault too, for doing it without asking. I can't guarantee I won't mess up again in the future, but can we call a truce and start over?"

"I'd like that. Thanks." Melinda hesitated, not wanting to hurry away but feeling awkward. "Is Jenny staying on as your housekeeper?" she asked, fishing for conversation.

"Mark's wife? Yes, and I've asked her to tend Tanner for me during the day as well," Ryan replied. "He can come out with me once in a while, but sometimes cattle and small boys don't mix."

"You're speaking from experience."

Ryan placed a broad hand on his chest. "Hey, I wasn't just emotionally traumatized when Jack locked me in that stall. I have scars to prove it."

"Mmm hmm, I'm sure you do," she said, hiding a smile and moving on with her cart. Behind her, Tanner shouted, "Bye! See you yesterday!"

She looked back over her shoulder, frowning. Ryan wiggled his eyebrows at her.

"We haven't quite mastered the concept of time," he said.

Melinda laughed and returned to her shopping. She put a jar of olive oil, a tub of honey, a packet of black pepper, a box of gauze (pruning the raspberry canes had taught her a lesson last year), a box of cornstarch, and a bottle of shampoo in her cart. She debated for a while, and then treated herself to a chocolate bar. She stood in line at the counter behind a plump woman in a dirty blouse who was purchasing Pine Sol and two gallons of vanilla ice cream. Once again, she felt a tap on her shoulder. This time she turned to see Carmella Ostler. Her heart dropped. Trapped.

Carmella, wife of the famous seller of the air conditioner, was a short, loud, and unabashedly intrusive person. Whenever Melinda came into town, Carmella seemed to be there waiting for her. Melinda wondered suspiciously if perhaps the woman slept in her car in the parking lot, watching for her. She had impossibly blond hair piled on her head like a pyramid and shellacked with Bold Hold. Her narrow little eyes never missed anything. And Carmella made a point of remarking on everything she saw.

"Who was that gorgeous young man you were talking to back on the baking supplies aisle?" she gushed, loud enough for everyone in the line to hear. "Melinda, dear, don't let that one get away."

"He's my neighbor," Melinda replied, trying not to sound chilly. "Paul Delaney's son."

"Oh, is that him? I've heard all about him. They never got along, those two, you know." Carmella sighed. "Some children! It took his poor father's death to bring him home. Couldn't be bothered coming before now, I guess. Some people just aren't sensitive."

"Hmm. Well, he's home now," Melinda said, trying not to think of the way Ryan had looked when he'd told her about his wife. Not sensitive? Right.

"He's certainly not hard to look at, though, is he? How convenient for you, dear. Aren't you the lucky one, living between two handsome men? That doesn't happen every day, does it?"

Melinda didn't bother answering. She could imagine what Jack would say if he'd heard that remark.

Carmella played with the string of black plastic beads around her neck. "It would be wonderful if you finally settled on someone, Melinda. How long will it take for you to realize a girl shouldn't be on her own? And here you have two to choose from."

"I beg your pardon?" Melinda said, her expression freezing on her face.

"It isn't right for you to be out there on that farm all alone. You should be married with three children by now. You're not getting any younger, you know."

"None of us are," Melinda said drily.

Undaunted, Carmella went on. "But was that a child I saw with the Delaney boy? Is he married?" She wrinkled her nose. Melinda sighed.

"He's a widower," she said. If Melinda didn't tell her, she would manage to find out eventually anyway.

"Now, how come I didn't hear about that? Paul never was much of a talker. A widower, huh? Well, I guess that's all right then." Carmella giggled. "He'll be needing a wife himself, because a man can't raise a baby on his own. So it's the perfect arrangement for everybody. Though I would bet Jack Peyton will be more than a little disappointed."

Melinda scowled. She and Jack were hardly a couple. They went to the occasional movie together, but that was the extent of it. He had helped her fix her roof the first year she'd moved in, and sometimes she took him zucchini when the plants threatened to take over the garden. Once he had given her a lift when her truck had died. She shifted uneasily on her feet. Come to think of it, he had been very kind the day she'd discovered her steer dead in the paddock. And he did drop by to chat now and then for no particular reason. But that didn't mean there was any kind of relationship between them, did it? At least not on her side. Hadn't he just been neighborly? Had he said something to this woman that led her to believe . . . ?

Melinda couldn't walk away, because she was next in line at the counter, but she turned her back flatly on Mrs. Ostler and refused to contribute any more fodder for gossip. Carmella didn't even notice she was being ignored. She was already deep in conversation with the woman behind her about the Wright girl who had gone off to "that pagan university—you know, *Berkeley*."

Her shopping done, Melinda sat in her truck a moment, wondering what to do next. It was too early for lunch. She was too irritable now to enjoy browsing through the small bookstore, which was her favorite pastime when she came to the plaza. She had plenty of chicken feed and rabbit pellets, so that ruled out a trip to the feed store. She didn't need her hair trimmed. There really wasn't much else to do. She pulled the truck into the gas station to fill up before heading home. Tim Ostler, Carmella's mousy sixteen-year-old son, came out into the heat to pump gas for Melinda. Tim was nothing like his mother and acted embarrassed if you brought up the connection. He wore the regulation purple T-shirt.

As she was fishing in her purse, Melinda saw a blue Subaru pull in behind her. She felt a sudden flash of embarrassment. It wasn't reasonable for her to be mortified. Ryan didn't know about Carmella's comments, but Melinda was embarrassed all the same. She wished he had stayed in Wyoming. She wished she hadn't met him at the store today. She wished he wasn't so good looking. She wished she knew what Carmella had meant about Jack Peyton.

As soon as Tim took the money, she stomped on the gas pedal and sped off without glancing at the occupants of the Subaru. Ryan was likely headed toward home. Without really meaning to, Melinda turned south, away from the ranch. She drove along aimlessly, watching the heat shimmer on the flat horizon of the grazing range. She passed a newly tilled field and thought about how there was something indecent about the freshly-shaven earth, dull brown against the blue of the sky, lying exposed for all to see. It looked so vulnerable. The two-lane road stretched before her, empty. A jackrabbit exploded from the side of the road and went bounding across the ground, dodging for shelter under thick, rambling bushes as Melinda passed.

The rows of maples lining the fields drew her eye out over them, seeking the almost invisible horizon. She reluctantly let her spirits rise. There was something magic about the country, the way the heat shimmered like pools and made the distant hills float, the way a little water could turn bleak brown earth into a green and living thing. The golden colors of late summer were meltingly beautiful. When she rolled her window down, the air was fresh and caressing. And *hot*. She rolled the window up again. Still, it was peaceful, exactly what she had hoped it would be when she first came to Texas. She passed a crape myrtle in front of someone's house and thought maybe she'd introduce some crape myrtle into the forest she had planted on the back half of her property. Myrtle didn't really belong in a forest, but they were such pretty trees. She would have to read up on them.

The forest was her favorite part of this whole enterprise. Farming organically, trying not to harm the environment, was only part of what she was trying to do. Rehabilitating the earth, reestablishing ecosystems, and building up diversity of life were her main goals. She had studied environmental restoration projects in school and the concept sparked her imagination. Could land that had been farmed to the point of barrenness for decades be changed to support a forest—not just the trees and underplantings, but the animals, birds, and insects that were part of a healthy forest as well? She had vague plans to turn the project into her PhD dissertation at some point, but right now that plan was foggy and far away, and secondary at best. Right now building the forest for the sake of the forest itself was the thing. Just thinking about it made her spirits rise. And if something good could come out of the money from the divorce settlement, all the better.

Melinda stopped in Happy (a ridiculous, almost desperate name for a town, she thought) for a strawberry milkshake and then turned northwest and followed back roads until she started running into new subdivisions. Veering off the beaten path, she found herself at Buffalo Lake. Small and oval, it lay placidly reflecting the bright, cloudless sky. A few houses had been built farther along the shore, their small docks jutting out into the water to claim slices of shore for their owners, like clothes-pegs securing the houses to the line of gently moving blue. But here, where she stopped the truck, the shore was unclaimed and empty. She sat with her windows rolled down for a moment and simply gazed out over the water. An unexpected splash of snapdragons made a yellow stain along the shore. In the middle of the lake, a solitary figure was trying to windsurf, a triangle of vivid red that kept dipping and disappearing. She could see the optimistic windsurfer's white Honda parked in the distance. There was a sharp, damp smell in the air, and the sound of seagulls fighting drifted across the water.

Melinda watched the windsurfer and slurped the last of her milkshake. A fly buzzed in the back window. It wasn't a bee, so she ignored it. The sound only added to the hot laziness of the morning. She felt her tangled temper start to smooth out and settle. Jack had once told her that he'd come to this place often as a boy to fish for lake trout, but he'd never caught anything but stinging nettle. When school was out, the shores bustled with teenagers with boom boxes, and sometimes families came to picnic.

She sat up straight and punched the key into the ignition. Most people were at work or at home getting lunch ready now. She should be doing the same instead of sitting on hundred-degree vinyl, breathing in toxins, no doubt. She made a mental note to check how much sandpaper she had on hand, because she was planning to refinish her sewing table. And she had to remember to defrost the freezer and clean the rabbit hutches. Feeling much happier, she swung the truck back onto the road, pushing it to an exhilarating speed on the straight stretches. One thing she had discovered in the two years since her divorce was that it was no good wasting time. She never felt better than when she was busy.

When she got home, there was a note tucked in her screen door.

You're invited over to dinner tonight, six o'clock. I promise I'm not doing the cooking; Jenny is.

—R.

Melinda looked at it thoughtfully, reading it over a couple of times, then tucked it into her grocery bag and walked inside. She would go, if only to defy Carmella Ostler's comments that morning. She justified the idea of an evening out by hurling herself into an afternoon of intense hard work. The rabbits hardly knew what hit them; they were transferred in and out of the temporary holding pen and returned to scrubbed hutches in record time. By midafternoon the house was gleaming, the wet laundry was baking tidily on the line in the sun, and she had made a decent start on the cold frames she was building *and* popped a dish of potatoes in the oven. At six o'clock, Melinda was on the ranch house's doorstep, smelling faintly of sawdust and wearing a white blouse over a slimming, blue wrap-around skirt. She'd had a mental debate about the skirt. She didn't want to look too dressy, as if this dinner with Ryan had any particular importance or meant any more than their earlier picnics. *Oh well,* she thought as she heard footsteps. *It's too late now.*

Ryan came to the door. Melinda held out the covered casserole dish she carried.

"Scalloped potatoes," she said.

He grinned and took them from her, holding the door open with his elbow as she squeezed past him.

Apparently Ryan had invited the hired men to dinner as well, for the kitchen was crowded and noisy. Melinda could put a name to each face, but beyond that, she really didn't know them well. Jenny, her black hair shimmering to her waist, hurried over to take the casserole dish from Ryan. The kitchen smelled deliciously of peppers and hot cornbread.

"Come in and sit down. We're just about to eat," Jenny ordered, taking the bite out of her brusque commands with a smile.

Ryan put his hand lightly on the middle of Melinda's back and steered her into the chair beside his. As she sat down, he leaned forward to whisper in her ear.

"Thanks for bringing the potatoes. Jenny's got this thing about Mexican rice. About now I'd kill for some good old steak and potatoes."

"I'll start chasing a cow around the yard," Melinda whispered back.

It took some time to get everyone seated around the long, loaded table. On Ryan's other side, Tanner was strapped into a high chair. He banged his spoon impatiently on his tray. Peter Clegg and Dayton Bridger sat opposite Melinda, looking like they'd be more comfortable riding horses than sitting at a table. Dayton, hound-faced and unshaven, was typically as communicative as a fencepost. Peter, whose lean body resembled a thick, tightly woven rope, gave Melinda a bright smile and a nod of greeting. Jenny's husband, Mark, who was half Mexican and half Navajo, sat at the foot of the table. There was a chair for Jenny beside Melinda, but Jenny kept bouncing up to stir and serve and pour and hardly sat at all.

Melinda thought Jenny had prepared a ridiculous amount of food, but it disappeared surprisingly quickly. She could account for a great deal of it herself. It was a novelty to eat food she hadn't prepared. The table hummed with pleasant conversation about the ranch operations, the unseasonably hot weather, and the price of beef. For the most part, Melinda was content to eat and listen, but when Ryan commented on how many new houses had been built since he'd last visited, she had to join in.

"There's been talk of Redcreek incorporating all those new subdivisions where Black Cat Road meets the highway," she said. "It would increase our population by fifty percent."

"It makes sense with the stockyards coming," Peter Clegg remarked. "The property values will probably double. Redcreek would collect property tax on all of it."

"The stockyards will just attract more building. Think of the traffic it'll cause. You can hardly move on a weekday morning as it is, with all the commuters," Melinda pointed out. "It's just another reason to raise property taxes."

Ryan eyed her, his fork halfway to his mouth. "You don't sound too pleased with all the development going on."

"It's getting so you can't find open land anymore. It's all going to be blotted out with houses."

"And have you seen these houses?" Jenny said, nodding her agreement. She had finally settled in her chair like a hummingbird pausing at a flower. "Pink and blue and yellow, like building blocks. I saw one last week that had *three* garages. Why do you need three cars? You can only drive one car at a time," she added reasonably.

"Are you saying you're in favor of development?" Melinda asked, turning to Ryan.

"No, I'm not, actually. But I can see why the city folk want to move out here. You can't blame them; it's such a pretty part of Texas."

"Yes, it is. Precisely why I don't want any more of it lost to housing projects."

Jenny launched herself once again. "Lemon pie," she announced, setting what looked like a cloud in the center of the table. She shot Ryan a defiant look. "See, I make more than Mexican food."

"You're an angel," Peter Clegg declared. "If you ever get tired of Mark here, I'll marry you in a minute."

Jenny blushed visibly, and everyone laughed.

"What would your fiancée think?" Mark said to Peter.

Peter shrugged and shot a sideways glance at Ryan. "Maybe I'll join the Mormons, too," he drawled. "Then I could have all the wives I wanted."

The smiles around the table stiffened, and everyone looked at Ryan to see how their new employer would react to this remark. Ryan just grinned.

"Sorry, Pete, you're out of luck. We gave that up over a hundred years ago. Knowing your fiancée, I wouldn't recommend it anyway. Doesn't she wrestle steers in the rodeo circuit?"

"You've got a point." Pete sighed.

"Pie!" shouted Tanner, bringing the focus back around to the more important matters at hand. He flapped his spoon and sent rice all over the floor. Jenny jumped up to attend to it, but Ryan waved her back into her chair.

"I've got it. Sit for a change," he told Jenny. Deftly, he dealt with the spilled food and spooned some pie into a bowl for his son. Tanner dug into it with relish, soon abandoning the spoon altogether and attacking with both hands. The others turned their attention back to the food, grateful that the tense moment had passed.

When dinner was over, Jenny gingerly carried Tanner away for a bath. The three hired hands went out to do the evening chores, leaving Ryan and Melinda alone at the table.

"Thanks for inviting me. This was fun," she told him. "I knew Jenny pretty well, but not the others."

"It was nice having you."

Melinda rose and began carrying dishes to the sink. Ryan stood to help her.

"You don't have to clear away," he said. "You're a guest."

"I want to." She began filling the sink with water, but he shook his head and pointed to a door she hadn't noticed under the counter.

"We're high-tech here," he said wryly. "Dishwashers and everything."

"Let me fill it, then. It'll be fun for me; I'm not used to such luxury, so don't argue."

In the end, they both cleaned up, stepping around each other between table and sink. Several times they nearly collided and had to duck out of each other's way. It looked so much like a slapstick routine that eventually they were both laughing.

"Let's try something a little more effective," Ryan said after one narrow miss. "I'll bring the dishes from the table, and you stack them."

"Gotcha."

He turned to fetch a load and, realizing he was still holding a washrag, turned back to the sink just as Melinda was stepping away from it with a handful of utensils on their way to the dishwasher. Ryan yelped as a fork made contact with his wrist. Forks and knives went clattering to the floor in a wash of soapy water.

In openmouthed dismay, Melinda waited to see if Ryan was truly wounded. He ruefully examined his wrist.

"No blood," he announced. He lightly gripped Melinda's shoulders and moved her solemnly aside. "Shall we try that again?"

"Don't blame me. You said you were going to carry stuff from the table. I didn't know you were behind me."

"Shall I wear a bell?"

Melinda squatted on her heels and gathered up the utensils. A spoon had fallen under a chair, and she duck-walked a few feet to reach for it. Ryan, turning from the table with the casserole dish in his hands, stepped backward and brought his heel down on her index finger. Now it was Melinda's turn to yelp.

"What on earth are you doing down there?" Ryan leapt away. "Did I step on you? Are you all right?"

"It's a good thing you weren't wearing shoes," Melinda said sourly, making a fist and tucking it under her arm.

"Let me see it."

"I'm okay."

"Give it here." Ryan gripped her wrist and critically examined the damage. "You'll live." He kissed the wounded digit lightly, as if Melinda were no older than Tanner. When he released her hand, she curled her finger inside her fist and held it. He pushed her firmly into a chair. "Don't move, and no one will get hurt," he ordered.

It sounded as if he were robbing a bank. Melinda burst out laughing. Ryan struggled a moment, trying to stay serious, and then he began to laugh too.

"We've done enough damage to Jenny's domain. Come on, I'll walk you home," he said.

CHAPTER 4

The next morning, the doorbell rang. Melinda, who was headfirst in the hall closet looking for her hedge clippers, called, "Come in!" without straightening. The door behind her opened. She called over her shoulder in a muffled voice, "I'll be right with you."

"No hurry," came Ryan's voice.

She emerged holding up the clippers triumphantly and turned to see him watching her with an amused expression. He held Tanner in his arms, the little boy's face half hidden by a too-large, red cowboy hat.

"Oh, hi!" She greeted them, sitting on the stairs to pull on her shoes. "What's up?"

"I've got to go check the fence line on the northern boundary. Mark says it keeps coming down. I was going to ask if you'd like to come riding with me, but it looks like you're going out."

"I'm tackling the hedge by the vegetable garden, actually," she said, standing up and brushing the seat of her jeans. "I want to do it before it gets too hot."

"Can you do it later?"

She was surprised, but shrugged. "I guess I can. Why? What's up?" She grinned. "Just craving my company?"

"Actually, I wanted to bounce some questions off you."

She could read nothing from his expression. She nodded and set the clippers down. "All right, I'm game."

He must have known she'd agree, because he had two horses tied to her porch railing. He'd chosen a pleasant-faced chestnut for her. He assured her that the mare was so gentle you couldn't tell if she was asleep or awake. The mare had a broad white stripe that made her look more like a cow than a horse. Melinda rubbed the horse's long nose and wondered how Ryan had known to choose a gentle mount for her. She managed to climb aboard with a modicum of grace and tried to remember what she was supposed to do. She hadn't ridden since pony camp at age eleven. Even though the mare was small, Melinda felt enormously far from the ground. The mare turned a benign eye toward her and waited patiently.

The other horse was a tall bay with four white socks. Ryan climbed one-handed into the saddle and settled Tanner in front of him.

"Do you like to ride horses, Tanner?" Melinda asked, and Tanner smiled back and said, "Yes, ma'am." Then he touched the brim of his cowboy hat in a gesture he'd certainly learned from his father. Melinda began to laugh. Tanner settled back against his father's lean stomach as comfortably as if he were in a car seat.

"What a little charmer. I take it he rides with you a lot," Melinda remarked.

"Oh, yeah. He's an old hand at this, aren't you, buddy? He cut his first tooth on a saddle horn."

Tanner swiveled around to look up at his father.

"Go," he commanded. So they went.

For a while they plodded along in silence while Melinda caught the rhythm and settled down more or less comfortably. Ryan glanced over and shot her a broad grin.

"All right?"

She tucked her toes inward and sat up straighter. "Fine, thanks. Lead the way."

Ryan nudged his mount with his knees. He rode easily, flexing with the gait of his horse. They went up the gravel road and turned onto the Delaney property, passing the house and outbuildings. The feedlots were still empty, waiting for the summer's crop of calves, where they would be held until sold. Ryan pointed out the barn he and the men were fixing up for the longhorn bulls. It was set apart from the other buildings by a high-fenced corral.

"I'm putting cement walls between the stalls, floor to ceiling, so the bulls can't see each other, much less get at each other," he explained.

"Is that really necessary?"

He cocked an eyebrow at her. "I see you haven't been around bulls much."

It took them twenty minutes to reach the northern boundary of the property. Clumps of sagebrush added a dusty tang to the air that reminded Melinda of the bunches of herbs drying in her kitchen. The horses' hooves made cheerful, hollow sounds. She and Ryan rode without speaking, except to comment on the view or the occasional groups of cattle they came across, grazing on the browning grass. Paul Delaney had favored Black Angus, and Melinda had always thought they looked more intelligent than Jack's white-faced Herefords, though she wouldn't have told Jack so.

They reached a high wire-and-post fence—ships' masts in a prairie sea. Melinda could see signs of repair—broken posts, new wire stretched among the old, and several postholes.

"The fence keeps coming down. Every time we check it there are repairs to be done. It's only this stretch of fence," Ryan told her, looking glum. "Mark tells me they didn't have any trouble with it until about three months ago."

"Is the ground just soft or something?" Melinda asked curiously.

"No."

"Are the cows leaning against the posts?"

"Not that we've been able to observe. It isn't the normal damage you get with cows."

Melinda's eyes widened. "Is someone cutting the wire and deliberately knocking over the posts?"

Ryan's lips thinned. He rubbed the back of his neck.

"The wire, no, but the posts, maybe. I'm going to have Mark spend the night camping in that little hollow over there to see if we can learn anything."

"But who would do such a thing?" Melinda protested. Purposely destroying another rancher's fences was criminal. She couldn't imagine that any of the people she knew could be guilty of it. "Whose property is this behind yours?"

"Our land borders on Dale Purdy's," Ryan said, pointing. "And over there is Brian Fitzgerald's. If someone were doing this deliberately, they'd have to be coming by way of Brian's or Dale's property. I'd see them if they went past the house."

Melinda shook her head. "Neither of them would do such a thing."

"I didn't say they would. But someone could be cutting across their property. I don't even know yet whether this is vandalism." Ryan leaned his chin pensively on Tanner's hat. "I wanted to ask you, though, have you had any trouble at your place? Anything going wrong that you can't explain?"

Melinda stared at him. "There's something besides the fence, isn't there? Otherwise you wouldn't ask."

"I don't want to alarm you or start jumping to conclusions," Ryan said slowly.

"There *is* something, then."

He shrugged and looked away, over the open pasture. Taking off his hat, he let the breeze stir his autumn-colored hair.

"Again, it's not something I can say was done deliberately. It might have been accidental. One of Dad's horses died last night. She was all right when Dayton turned her out in the paddock for the night, and I can't find anything harmful she might have eaten. The vet came this morning, and he thinks—I can't believe I'm even saying it—but he thinks she was poisoned."

Melinda looked down at her horse's twitching ears and felt something turn over in her stomach. "But why would somebody do such a thing?"

"I don't know. Dad didn't have any enemies, and neither do I—that I know of. But the other day you mentioned your chicken coop catching fire, and then your steer dying from tansy ragwort even though there was none in the pasture."

Melinda's mind suddenly felt hazy. She realized she was gripping the reins too hard and that her mare was beginning to fidget. She forced her fingers to relax. "I never did figure out what started the fire, but I told you, I thought it was just teenagers messing around with matches. It happened about three months ago. And the steer, well . . ."

"Has anything else happened?"

"Not that I can think of." She ran one hand through her hair. "But with your horse being poisoned and everything . . . Do you think it's one person doing this? This is crazy. Who would want to do anything like this on purpose? What would be the point?"

"I don't know. I don't want to upset you," Ryan said. "I just needed to ask."

"I'm glad you did, but I honestly don't know what to say."

As they headed back toward the barn, Melinda glanced over at Ryan's solemn face. It was such a contrast to his usual cheerful expression. Impulsively, she asked, "Why don't you two come over for dinner tonight? It's nothing fancy, but there's plenty."

"There's no need to return the gesture."

"Nonsense. I'd like the company," she said, and realized it was true.

"All right then, thank you," Ryan replied with a slow smile. "What time shall we come over?"

"How about six? That'll give me time to tackle that hedge."

"Must be some hedge," he murmured.

* * *

Jack Peyton owned the pasture to the east of Melinda's property. Melinda's hedge was part of the dividing boundary. As she started to work, she glanced up and saw Jack striding along the edge of his field, and she paused to watch him. She hadn't really paid attention to his appearance before now, but as she watched him come along the fence line, Carmella Ostler's words floated into her head. Melinda had to agree with Carmella's description of Jack. He *was* handsome. He was well over six feet, with short, dark hair and a rough-cut look to his tanned face. A little taller than Ryan even. Jack had ranched all his life. Melinda knew very little about his ex-wife and children—they were gone long before Melinda came to live here, and Jack rarely spoke of them. It was funny she had never really stopped to take in his appearance before or to find out more about him. He was just part of the landscape, friendly but unobtrusive.

As if feeling her gaze, Jack looked up and spotted her. He lifted his hand in greeting. She waved back with her clippers and watched as he approached with long, easy strides. He paused a few feet away and leaned his arms on the top rail of the fence next to the hedge. The sleeves of his chambray shirt were rolled up to expose sun-browned, muscular forearms.

"Hi," she said, letting the clippers dangle at her side.

"Hey." Jack rubbed a work-worn hand over his jaw, looking down at her with light blue eyes. They weren't, she thought irrelevantly, as blue as Ryan's. He jabbed his thumb toward Ryan's house. "I saw you over there again."

"Yes. He isn't so bad, Jack. Haven't you gone over to see him yet?"

"I've got nothing to say to him."

"Maybe you would if you went and saw him. There's no reason why you two can't be friends."

Jack snorted. "Ryan Delaney was about as useless as a lawnmower on a beach. He didn't know one end of a cow from the other."

"I would wager he does now," she replied coolly.

"I give him six months. He'll have made such a hash of his dad's ranch, he'll have to file for bankruptcy."

Melinda's eyes narrowed. "What's with you? Maybe you two didn't get along as boys, but you're adults now, remember?"

"Be sure to finish before the heat of the day. You could bake your brains in this weather." He tipped his head in farewell and strode off again. Melinda shook her head as she watched him go out her gate and cross the road to his house. Quiet, low-key Jack. What was with him? Maybe Ryan *had* been awkward as a boy, but that certainly wasn't a reason to dismiss him as an adult. As she returned to her work, she wondered why she hadn't asked Jack whether suspicious things had happened at his place too. But that would mean explaining the reason she was asking. And when she thought about the reason, she felt ill. A burnt coop could be chalked up to simple mischief or youthful rowdiness, but a dead horse was beyond mischief.

Late that afternoon, Melinda returned to the house with the idea of throwing together a fruit salad to go with supper. However, when she stepped out to fetch her mail, she found a note taped to her front door. It was written in Ryan's large, neat hand. It said that Tanner had fallen ill and they would be unable to come to supper after all, but thanks anyway.

She stood a moment on the steps, holding the note in her hand and gazing up the road, and then she went inside. Quickly she changed into clean jeans and a BYU T-shirt, then packed food into Tupperware and walked up the narrow road to the Delaneys'. When she glanced toward Jack's house, she noticed his truck parked in the driveway. Jack said he had seen her come to the Delaneys' before. She wondered if he was watching her now from behind his living room curtains. The thought mildly alarmed her. Maybe Carmella wasn't so far off . . .

Ryan's short hair was disheveled, and the lines around his mouth had deepened. He simply stood in the doorway and looked at her with a peculiar expression on his face.

"I figured if Mohammed wouldn't come to the mountain," she said brightly, "the mountain would have to come to him. How's Tanner?"

Ryan's forehead creased as he led the way to the kitchen.

"I don't know. He was outside with me all afternoon because Jenny had to take today off. He seemed perfectly fine, and then all of a sudden he had a temperature and started throwing up. I don't think it's anything he ate. It's probably the flu. He's asleep in my room now."

"Can I see him?"

He led her into the back room. She stood in the doorway for a moment, gazing at the little boy in the big bed. He slept fitfully, with one hand gripping the patchwork quilt. His cheeks were rosy, his hair plastered damply to his head. Melinda glanced around the simply furnished room, noting the little personal things that made this Ryan's room: the comb on the dresser, the sweatshirt tossed across the foot of the bed, the framed photograph of a very pretty blond woman. Tanner's mother, she knew immediately. Melinda crossed to the bed, sat gently on the edge of it, and put her hand on Tanner's forehead. Tanner muttered something and tossed in his sleep.

"Yes, he definitely has a fever. Have you given him anything for it?"

"Children's Tylenol," Ryan said. "About twenty minutes ago. He managed to keep it down."

"It might be the flu, but it could be heatstroke. I've seen it before, this time of year. Small children are especially susceptible. You can't always identify it right away."

"That's true. I didn't think of heatstroke. What do you do for that?"

"Just try to keep him cool and get liquids down him if he can hold them. You don't want him to get dehydrated, whether it's flu or heatstroke. He should be all right in a little while."

"He had me worried. He's usually so healthy." Ryan sat on the other side of the bed and ran his hand gently through Tanner's limp hair. "Why didn't I put a hat on him? I usually do. I just didn't think of heatstroke."

"I don't think you need to worry, Ryan."

"But, I mean I forgot it was even a risk." Ryan sighed and rubbed his hand over his jaw. "I forgot the climate's not the same as Wyoming. You know, sometimes I wonder if I made a mistake moving back here. Maybe I should have sold the place and stayed put."

"Isn't that a little drastic?" Melinda asked, trying to keep the tone of the conversation light. "He'll be all right. You shouldn't blame yourself. And if it's flu, it has nothing to do with your living here."

"It's not just Tanner getting sick," Ryan admitted. "Somehow I thought it wouldn't take so much adjustment to come back here and take over where Dad left off. A ranch in Wyoming, a ranch in Texas, what's the difference? But somehow it's turning out to be more stressful for both of us than I'd anticipated." He gave Melinda a rueful look. "Tanner misses his grandparents in Jackson Hole. Jenny's been great, but I miss having Caroline's mother's help with Tanner. And, well, it hasn't been easy for me either, coming home after so long, even with Dad gone. Maybe *because* Dad's gone."

For a moment, Melinda sat quietly watching him, and then she asked, "Is there anything I can do?"

"You're doing it." Ryan reached out and touched her lightly on the arm. "You're listening to me whine at the moment. That's all I could ask for."

"Come get some supper. Fried chicken has a way of putting everything into perspective."

Ryan's eyebrows shot up. "Did one of your hens die of old age already?"

"I cheated and bought this one nicely wrapped in cellophane," Melinda replied with a grin.

Back in the kitchen, she dished up the food she'd brought and was pleased with herself as she watched Ryan eat with gusto.

"You've definitely put your frying pan to better use than I have." His eyes glittered at her over the rim of his glass. "You're something else, you know? Any other female I know, if I stood her up for dinner, would huff and pout and not speak to me again. You just show up with a picnic and a smile."

"You had a good excuse," she told him. "If you hadn't, I'd have done the pouting routine. I'm quite good at it." Melinda paused, then asked, "Speaking of pouting, what's up with Jack Peyton?"

Ryan's glass halted halfway to his mouth. "Jack? What do you mean?"

"I don't know what's wrong with him. Ever since you moved back, he's been walking around looking like sour pickles. He seems to be carrying a grudge over things that happened when you two were ten years old."

Ryan fiddled with his glass on the table, making wet rings. "Actually, the grudge he's carrying began when we were in our twenties."

"What happened?"

"He used to like Caroline," Ryan said slowly.

"Ah. I see."

Ryan shrugged. "I don't know how serious their relationship was, but I always suspected it was more serious on his part than on hers. Caroline's family lived down by the Purdys', and she and Jack would go out once in a while. Not what I would call steady, but Jack did seem to have his hopes up. After I got back from my mission, it seemed like things had broken off there, so I started seeing her. Then her family moved to Wyoming. Six months later I followed her and married her. I guess Jack's never quite forgiven me."

"He could have followed her himself," Melinda pointed out.

"True. Though I don't know if he would have been a serious contender. He's not LDS, for one thing. That would have been important to Caroline. But try convincing Jack of that." He shot her a grin. "Okay, I've told you my life saga. It's your turn."

"There's not much to tell," she replied, reaching for her glass. "I grew up in Albuquerque and got an undergrad degree in ecology from BYU and a master's in botany from Arizona State."

"That would be an advantage in farming."

"Farming isn't exactly what I originally had in mind for a career. But it all worked out in the end."

"The end?" Ryan asked, smiling. "That sounds final."

"You know what I mean. I don't anticipate ever doing anything else but staying here and working this place."

"And is that enough for you?"

His voice had dropped to a quiet purr. Melinda looked up from her plate and found him watching her closely. The intensity of that aquamarine gaze was too much. She looked down again.

"I have everything I need. I'm content."

"And that's it? No marriage, no family?"

She took a huge bite of salad to give herself time to think. She didn't know how much she wanted to tell him. Her breath was doing odd things again. She hunched her shoulders.

"I'm not ruling it out," she said finally. "I just meant that I've decided farming is the right occupation for me. And establishing my forest."

"Ah." He seemed to accept this. "I'd like to see what you're doing with this forest you talk about."

"I'd love to show you anytime. It's my pet hobby."

Melinda stood and began clearing dishes away while Ryan went to check on Tanner. When he returned to the kitchen, he reported that his little boy was sleeping peacefully and seemed somewhat cooler.

"I'm glad. The Tylenol must be kicking in. So maybe it is just flu."

"Well, in case it is heatstroke, I'll try to keep him out of the sun for the next day or two, especially in the early afternoon," Ryan said. "I've learned my lesson."

"And lesson number two is that if worst comes to worst, you could turn the whole acreage into a giant skateboard park and go back to Wyoming."

Ryan began to laugh. "True."

"And," Melinda went on, reaching for a towel to wipe the table, "lesson number three is that cold chicken and salad can cure anything. Even homesickness."

Ryan's eyes shone as he took the towel gently from her. His hand briefly touched hers.

"Thank you, Melinda," he said quietly. "Let me walk you home. Tanner will be all right alone for a minute."

"There's no need. It's not that dark, and I won't mug anybody, I promise," she responded.

"That wasn't the purpose," he said drily.

Melinda hesitated, then smiled. "What was the purpose, then?"

Ryan was silent a moment, then he reached out to touch her cheek. His fingers were like feathers dusting across her skin so lightly she barely felt them. Then he slid his hand to the back of her neck and pulled her forward and upward to meet him halfway.

His kiss was brief and gentle. When his hand slipped back to his side, her heart was racing. She found that she had nothing to say and no voice to say it with. She cleared her throat and tried to find her brain. It seemed to have gotten lost somewhere.

"You're wrong, you know," he said quietly. "This isn't the end. It's the beginning."

CHAPTER 5

Melinda spent a restless night mashing her hot pillow and hopelessly tangling her hair. Every time she began to drift toward sleep, the memory of Ryan's touch would bring her eyes popping open again. She told herself she was being foolish. She did *not* want another relationship. Hadn't she learned her lesson the first time around? What was she thinking? Two intervening years had dulled the raw pain of her divorce, but it was still there, nagging like a bad toothache. True, Ryan Delaney seemed to be an entirely different sort of person, but still, she'd promised herself that she would never get trapped like that again. Finally, as dawn began to send faint rays filtering through her window, she wrapped a quilt around herself and went in search of Agatha Christie to read herself into oblivion.

The next morning she was awakened by the phone. Groggy and irritable, she rolled off the couch and dove to answer it, sending Abigail streaking under the table in alarm.

"Melinda? It's Madge. Don't tell me you were still sleeping?"

Madge Farnsworth. Melinda rubbed her eyes, trying to focus as the nasal voice whined on. She had met Madge in college, and Madge, a talented illustrator, had gone on to become a respected and much-sought-after agent for aspiring artists. It was she who had taken one look at Melinda's botanical drawings and recognized her artistic abilities. Madge had urged her to push them beyond the realm of a hobby. She had talked Melinda into having her first and only art exhibition in Albuquerque, and though Melinda had given her little hope that she would participate in another one, Madge still called periodically to put a word in.

"It's not like it's the Louvre," Madge was saying now, her tone wheedling. "Just a little showing, a few dignitaries in penguin suits, that's all. No one you know will even see your stuff."

Melinda pinned the receiver between her ear and her shoulder and remembered she'd left her laundry in the washer all night.

"Madge, I'm not interested. I've got my hands full enough. Thanks all the same."

"All I need is seven or eight pieces. Chuck will fill in the rest. He has a ghastly collection of Carlysle. I've never liked Carlysle. Too heavy, like Rodin. I need something light and cheerful to break it up, and your stuff is perfect. Come on, girl, you've got to have something kicking around I could use."

Melinda smiled. It was typical of Madge to make it sound as if Melinda were doing *her* a favor.

"I really don't have anything. I haven't drawn or painted anything in ages."

"Give me some of your old stuff, then. It's just an exhibition, darling, to raise money for the Community Garden Club. Come on—that's *so* your cause. How can you not support community gardens?"

"You know I do."

"Well then. You're perfect for it. And it's not a sale; I'm not going to auction off your children."

Melinda hesitated, running through her collection in her mind. All she really had were amateur oil paintings and a few framed sketches. Nothing, certainly, to hang in a private gallery.

"What about that terrific wall hanging you did, the one of the marsh?" Madge interrupted her thoughts.

"That? It was practically the first thing I ever did. Besides, I have no idea where it is right now. Probably stuffed in a box in Mom's basement with the mice getting at it."

"All right, but promise me you'll at least think about it." Madge sighed. "You're too good to just go to seed out there on that lump of earth you call paradise."

"I'll think about it," Melinda lied, to get her off the line. Much as she liked Madge, she found her conversation wearying. She was fast running out of excuses not to paint again, and she suspected that sooner or later Madge was going to win the battle.

She hung up the phone and stood staring at it a moment. Why was she so dead set against the display? Like Madge said, it wasn't a sale, and she would get her pieces back afterward. It wasn't a lifelong commitment. The cause was right up her alley. She had to admit she missed her art, amateur though she was. Her fingers itched to hold a brush again. But somehow Melinda couldn't bring herself to get everything out and begin. Whenever she considered doing so, a deep melancholy settled on her chest that she couldn't shake. It felt as if painting were a bright part of her past that would never again bring the contentment or satisfaction it once had. It was ruined for her now. There was nothing left to paint. Shaking her head, she focused on her laundry and let all thoughts of Madge and oil paint crawl into a dark corner.

Friday morning Melinda drove out to the garden center and laid a supply of pine bark mulch for her front flower beds in the back of her truck. She backed the Ford into her driveway and began carrying the blue-and-red bags from the truck to the shed behind the garage. On her fourth trip, she looked up to see Ryan walking up the driveway with Tanner tagging behind. She tried to ignore the increased rate of her pulse.

"Need any help?" Ryan asked. "Those look heavy."

"Nope, this is the last one," Melinda replied, slamming the tailgate shut and hoisting the final bag to her shoulder. "Thanks anyway. How's Tanner feeling?"

Ryan followed her as she stowed the bag with the others.

"He's back to normal, thanks. Things are slow today, and we were just going for a walk."

Melinda looked at him thoughtfully, wondering how a five-hundred-head operation could possibly be slow.

"What are you up to today? Anything exciting?" he asked.

"Well, I promised myself I'd get my storm shutters on today. I've got a lull before the fall harvest, but if I wait until after that, it'll be bad weather." She pulled a face. "I'm afraid that's as exciting as it gets."

"I'll help you," he offered. "Then it'll go faster."

"Oh, I can't ask you to do that. I can manage."

"Where are the shutters?"

Melinda hesitated, then gave in. "Down in the basement. But only on one condition; you can help me do mine if you'll let me help you install yours."

"Deal," Ryan said, and followed her down to the cool basement, where they dug out the heavy metal shutters and lugged them upstairs together. Tanner played contentedly with Abigail, who, Melinda was surprised to see, cooperated—forgetting momentarily that she had a fiendish nature and becoming purring and docile. Melinda and Ryan finished the job by one o'clock. She had to admit it was a relief to have it done so quickly.

"Amazing! I thought it would take me all day," she exclaimed. "Let me throw together some lunch, and then we can take that walk you were talking about."

After a quick lunch of tomato soup and cheese sandwiches, they set off with Tanner astride his father's shoulders. As they left the house, Jack Peyton was just pulling into his driveway. Melinda waved, expecting him to cross the road to join them, but Jack only nodded at her, ignoring the Delaneys completely. Then he turned and went into the house.

"Well, so much for letting bygones be bygones," she muttered, hurrying to catch up with Ryan. He hadn't slackened his pace. If anything, he'd sped up when Jack had appeared.

The Panhandle as a whole was a marvelous place for walking, and late summer was a marvelous time to be doing it. The air was still hot but had a mild, prophetic taste to it, predicting cooler weather. The maples with their rough, grayed trunks were just touched with gold. The trees never turned too brilliant, like they did in pictures Melinda had seen of New England, but they would take on their own humble, rosy hue for autumn. There wasn't much traffic on the concession roads; their little caravan passed only an occasional car and one tractor rattling slowly toward home. The bearded farmer driving it waved a greeting, and Tanner, quite enthralled, waved back.

They walked until Ryan's shoulders got tired from carrying Tanner and then stopped to sit on a low rail fence beside the road to let Tanner play for a while. The little boy darted back and forth in the tall grass chasing grasshoppers, laughing when they escaped, and screaming in alarm when he actually caught one. Ryan hurried to rescue him and showed him how grasshoppers had sticky feet and little feelers on their heads. Tanner hesitated, then forgot his anxiety and hunkered down to examine the insect more closely, intrigued. When he was satisfied that the grasshopper really wouldn't hurt him, he stood and toddled after another one. Ryan let the prisoner escape. Brushing his hands together, he came back to lean against the fence beside Melinda.

"For such a curious little kid, he certainly seems to be afraid of a lot of things," he remarked, watching Tanner slide under the fence and bound away into some farmer's field. Melinda could see horses farther down but a safe distance away. They only blinked mildly at the intruder and returned to their grazing.

Melinda shrugged. "I don't know. Think how new and unusual everything is for him. Can you imagine what it would feel like to meet a grasshopper for the first time? They *are* intimidating with those unblinking eyes."

"The only things that really terrify me are snakes," Ryan said, tilting his head back to squint at the sun. "How about you?"

Melinda thought about this for a moment. "I don't know. I'm not fond of bees or hornets or anything that stings."

"Nobody likes to be hurt," Ryan agreed.

"No," Melinda said, nodding, gazing out over the tawny fields. "Nobody likes to be hurt."

Tanner had been around animals long enough to know not to venture too close to the unfamiliar horses. He squatted in the brown grass a respectful distance away and chattered to them in a singsong language of his own. Watching him, Melinda let herself wish, just for a moment, that he were hers. How would it feel to know that this little person with his angelic face and taffy hair belonged to you? What would it be like to take him to T-ball, walk him to school, watch him grow up? She had never given much thought to having children, but at the moment the idea seemed rather nice. She glanced at Ryan, leaning peacefully against the fence beside her, and pulled her thoughts back into place. To have a child, she would have to have a husband, and she'd been down that road already. Once was plenty, she told herself, and she climbed over the fence to go introduce Tanner to the horses.

When they finally returned home, it was nearly five o'clock. It only made sense that they should have supper together. Melinda produced bottled stew from the storeroom and whipped up egg custard with maple syrup drizzled over the top for dessert. Ryan inhaled appreciatively and shot Melinda a twinkling glance.

"Careful. I just may show up for supper every night," he warned.

"You're welcome to," Melinda replied offhandedly. "So long as you work hard enough to earn it every day. But Jenny's a wonderful cook."

"If you like Mexican food and nothing but. What are you planning to do tomorrow?"

"Finish building my cold frames."

"Do you need any help?"

She smiled. "I think I have it covered. But thanks."

"I could give you a hand, no problem."

"I know you could. But don't you have a ranch to run?"

"Well, yes, but building cold frames sounds more fun."

"They are, actually. I'm going to make a hotbed for some herbs, too, to see whether I can winter them over. It's a pretty simply concept. You dig a pit, fill it full of rotting compost and manure, cover it over again with soil, plant the herbs in it, then frame the whole thing with stacked bricks and put a sheet of glass over the top. Instant greenhouse with natural heating. You just prop the lid open a little whenever it gets too steamy."

Ryan shook his head. "You're something else, you know that? How in the world did you learn to build a hotbed?"

"From a library book."

"I'm impressed."

"With what, the fact that I can read?" she teased.

Ryan shook his head, watching her steadily. "With the fact that nothing fazes you. Anything you need, any problem you face, you just tackle it, and it all works out."

"Yes, well, it's not quite that easy," she muttered, embarrassed. "There are plenty of things that don't work out. And a lot of things faze me."

"Like what?"

Her brain scrambled for a reply. The things that really worried her, the things she really found truly daunting, no one could help her with. They were hers to deal with alone. But there was one thing she could and would accept help with.

"Apples," she said.

"Apples?"

"I have twenty-five apple trees that will all come ripe in September. Each tree produces about eight bushels of fruit. Last year the harvest nearly killed me. When they're ready to pick, I'll call on you—no hesitation. Deal?"

"Deal," he said, looking pleased.

"You won't be smiling when you have to face two hundred baskets of apples."

"Try me. I like apples."

Melinda wiped Tanner down with a rag to remove the maple syrup. He smiled smearily up at her. "You've been immensely helpful already," she told Ryan. "I really don't expect you to help with my harvest too."

"Too late, it's already a done deal," Ryan replied. "We'll see ourselves out now and let you get to your cold frames. You have to be finished by next weekend, because I'm taking you to that auction."

* * *

On Sunday Melinda quietly entered the church and chose a seat near the front, not far from the side door. She unobtrusively set her scripture case and purse on the bench beside her, subtly signaling that the space was reserved. When she saw Ryan and Tanner come in, she deftly scooped up the purse and case and set them by her feet. She put a pleasantly surprised expression on her face when Ryan paused at her bench.

"Hi there."

"Good morning," Melinda replied.

"Are you sitting alone? Do you mind if we join you?"

"Not at all," Melinda said, sliding over slightly. Ryan sat down next to her, plopping Tanner between them. Tanner wriggled around onto his knees to look over the back of the bench, and Melinda rubbed his back briefly.

"Good morning to you too, Tanner."

Tanner wrinkled his nose, grinned, and ducked his head against his father, peering out at Melinda with his gorgeous eyes.

As the meeting began, Ryan leaned over to whisper, "I have to give the opening prayer. Could you watch Tanner a sec?"

"Sure, if you think he'll stay with me."

"Of course he will. He knows you."

The words made Melinda feel ridiculously pleased. When Ryan went up to the stand, she gently pulled Tanner onto her lap and folded his arms under hers. Tanner obediently ducked his head but peeped around, forgetting to close his eyes. As Melinda listened to Ryan's prayer, she tightened her hold slightly around the warm little bundle of boy, pressing her nose into his soft hair. He smelled fresh and clean, an organic smell like strawberries. When Ryan returned to the bench, she was happy to find that Tanner was perfectly content to remain on her lap. He played with a small stuffed dog, leaning against Melinda as if sitting in an armchair, and hardly fussed through the whole meeting. With Ryan sitting close beside her, Melinda wondered (with some mortification) if her happiness were displayed too obviously on her face. The bishop kept looking down at her and turning away quickly to hide what she was sure was a smile.

* * *

Melinda put in a productive week and finished her cold frames, dug the pit for the hotbed, and planted red clover in the vegetable beds that had already been vacated. By the following Saturday, she felt a certain self-righteousness at the amount of work she'd accomplished. She was in high spirits as she got ready for the trip to Amarillo. She found herself debating over what to wear to the auction and laughed at her reflection in the mirror.

"He's not even going to notice what you're wearing," she snorted. "He's going to have his eyes on the longhorns." Nevertheless, she chose her outfit carefully: slim-legged jeans, an amber, cotton blouse, and chunky gold earrings that went well with her dark coloring. And for once, she left off the boots and wore flats. When Ryan appeared in the Subaru, she was waiting on the porch, feeling like a teenager waiting for her first date.

Ryan was wearing a chambray shirt with the sleeves rolled to his elbows. His hat had been thrown in the car's backseat. He reached over to open her door. She climbed in with a cheery greeting.

"Mark is going to meet us there. He's driving the truck," Ryan told her. "We can grab a burger at the auction for lunch, but I thought I'd take you to supper on the way home."

"Sounds good, thanks," she agreed. "Tanner's not coming?"

"I asked Jenny to watch him."

"How many bulls are you planning to buy?"

"Just three, I think. There's a fellow in Amarillo who has a couple I've got my eye on, but we'll see what's available. I'm going to design a Web site to advertise the stud service."

They sped along I-27 toward the city, the windows rolled down and the radio crooning Garth Brooks. The heat had let up a little. Melinda leaned back and enjoyed the sight of fields and trees rushing past. She and Ryan didn't talk much but just listened to the music in comfortable silence. They reached the outskirts of the town all too soon, and Ryan pulled the car into the parking lot of the fairgrounds. The livestock barns were surrounded by cattle trucks and horse trailers, pickups, and four-by-fours. Ryan opened her door for her and, taking her hand, led her into the largest of the steel barns.

Melinda had come to the auctions out of curiosity two or three times, but always just to look and not to buy. She had never been behind the doors at the back of the bidding arena where the holding pens were. Now she felt her interest pique as she followed Ryan inside. Instantly, she wished she hadn't ventured in. Behind the scrubbed, sawdust-covered arena, chaos reigned.

She found herself on a fragile-looking web of catwalks stretched high over the huge room of enclosures. For a moment a wave of vertigo hit her. She clung to the frail wooden railings on each side of her until her head cleared. The stench and noise were unbelievable. When she regained her balance, she opened her eyes cautiously and looked around.

Several other people were walking around on the catwalks, looking down on the sea of animals penned below. All were men, all wore cowboy hats and boots, and all carried clipboards, making notes and copying lot numbers as they studied the livestock. Melinda looked down at the maze of pens below and wished she hadn't. The cattle were crammed in so tightly they could hardly turn their heads. The pen that held sheep was so full it looked like a roll of quilted cotton batting.

Some of the poor animals were even standing on the backs of their neighbors, having been shoved there by the crowded conditions. The horse enclosures were the worst. A tapestry of bay and brown, black and gray, the enclosures seemed to stretch for miles. There was little movement—the horses were unable to so much as shift their weight. As she stared down in horror, one piebald mare lifted her head and whinnied. It was the most pitiful sound she'd ever heard.

She didn't realize she'd stopped walking until she felt Ryan's hands on her shoulders. He turned her to look at him, and his grim expression mirrored her own.

"It isn't very pretty back here. At least they aren't kept in here for long. Do you want to wait in the arena?"

She shook her head. "I'll come with you."

He took her hand again, his large palm warm and calloused against her own. She kept close beside him as they made their way over the web of walkways to the corner where the longhorn cattle were penned.

Thankfully, these pens weren't so crowded. For one thing, Ryan explained, there weren't as many longhorns as other breeds of cattle. For another thing, penning them tightly together would only result in them goring each other. Some of their horns had a spread of six or seven feet. Melinda gazed down at them in awe.

"I had no idea they were so big. I've never seen one close up before."

The bulls were each in their own separate pens, wedged into slots like letters in a mailbox, so they couldn't turn or go after each other. Ryan was studying them with a critical eye. "That one," he said, pointing to a large red-and-white spotted bull. Melinda thought the bull looked athletic, like a high jumper carrying the pole on his own head. The rangy body was antelope-like, lighter than other breeds she was familiar with, but she didn't like the look in the animal's eye.

"He's got to be close to twelve hundred pounds," Ryan mused.

"Are they all one breed? They all look so different," Melinda said, looking over the wide range of colors and markings.

"There are seven different bloodlines. They were brought by the Spanish in the fifteenth century and basically ran wild until a hundred years ago." Ryan was busy jotting down the tag numbers of the bulls that interested him. "I'm done. Come on, let's get out of here."

He grabbed her hand and they fairly jogged back the way they'd come. The door slammed shut behind them. The arena seemed sterile and silent in comparison.

"I had no idea," Melinda murmured.

Ryan gave her a crooked grin. "Do I know how to show my date a good time or what?"

"I can't wait to see where you take me for dinner," she replied drily. "The iron works? The state penitentiary?"

"Ah, I don't want to spoil the surprise."

The bulls weren't going to be up for auction until noon, so they wandered through the farmers' market on the other side of the fairgrounds and bought Polish sausages in buns to eat as they walked back. When Melinda refused fried onions, Ryan hesitated and then did the same.

Melinda found the actual auctioning very exciting. Every so often, a man would fling open the gate from the holding pen and drive a number of animals—a "lot"—into the arena. As the door clanged shut behind them, the animals would bellow and trot around the floor while the auctioneer rattled off their stats and began the bidding. Melinda had sometimes wondered why the animals pushed into the pen would run around rather than stand there looking lost. Now she knew; they were probably overjoyed to be able to move their limbs. She felt sorry for the calves, newly weaned, who milled around looking confused and heartbreakingly fragile. The dairy cows were being auctioned in a separate building. The animals in this arena were all beef cattle.

A second man prodded the beasts out a second door to herd them back to the holding pens after the bidding. It all went too fast for Melinda to follow, but she saw Ryan raise his number card several times while the bulls were being individually shown. When the gate banged shut behind the last bull, she turned to him in confusion.

"Did you get any of them? I couldn't keep track."

"Four. The two big reds, the smaller brown, and that tan and white splotchy one."

"The one with the backward-curved, handlebar-like horns? I thought he looked like a tricycle; he just needed colored streamers coming out of his horns."

"If you'd like to try putting some on him, go right ahead," Ryan said wryly.

"What did you pay for them? If I can ask . . ."

"They averaged just under four thousand each," he told her with what she thought was feigned nonchalance. "I'd intended to go for three, but when I got such a good deal on the brown one, I decided to go for it. The breeder has a good reputation. I'll go find Mark and tell him where to pick the animals up."

It was late afternoon by the time they finished the arrangements and headed back to the car. Ryan was in high spirits and talkative, full of plans for his new longhorn business venture. Melinda caught his enthusiasm and offered some marketing ideas of her own. She was so involved in the conversation, she didn't notice where they were going until Ryan stopped the car and she saw the elaborate sign overhead.

"Ricci's? But this is . . ." She stopped herself from saying *expensive.* He'd just spent sixteen thousand dollars on the bulls. He wasn't going to quibble over the price of a meal. She amended her sentence to, "I've always wanted to try this place but talked myself out of it." As he went to open her door, she suddenly realized something.

"We can't go in, Ryan. We smell like the livestock barn. And I'm in jeans and mucky shoes."

"We can duck into the restrooms and wash up first. The lights are low; no one will care." He touched her nose playfully. "You're still pretty, even when you're mucky."

All the same, as she made her way to the table she felt self-conscious, scrubbed with paper towels and smelling of hand soap. The waitress had placed them in a cozy corner—whether for privacy or to keep them at a distance from the other diners, she didn't know. The result was the same either way. Ryan's slicked-down hair looked black in the dim light, and the angles and planes of his face were cast into sharp relief by the floating candle on the table. As a final intimate touch, the waitress placed a wilting rose in a silver vase on the white tablecloth between them.

"Tanner's been whining to see that new Disney movie," Ryan remarked, sliding the rose aside so he could see Melinda better. "I thought I'd take him to the drive-in tonight. That way, if he falls asleep, it won't matter. Do you want to come?"

She grinned. "Is this turning into a regular thing?"

"Do you want it to?" His question was casual, but his eyes glittered in the candlelight.

She reached for her water glass. "Aren't you afraid you'll get tired of me?"

He shook his head, his gaze never leaving hers. "Not a chance. What do you say? Or does it make too long a day for you?"

"Not at all. I'd love to go," Melinda said, and realized he felt the same way. She didn't want their day together to end. The realization sobered her. She concentrated on the menu to avoid his gaze.

CHAPTER 6

They arrived home as it was getting dark and had just enough time to scoop up Tanner from Jenny's care and head for the drive-in. It was chilly sitting in the car with the window half rolled down for the speaker. Ryan had thought to bring a tartan wool blanket which, though scratchy, smelled deliciously of cedar. They huddled in the front seat with Tanner between them on his booster seat. He gave a delighted giggle as the speaker started to crackle.

"I love Walt Disney," Melinda told Ryan, passing him the popcorn. "It's been years since I've done this."

The screen burst into color and was overrun with cartoon figures dancing and singing enthusiastically about depositing garbage in the trash can. Tanner bounced excitedly on his seat and then grew still as he watched in fascination. Ryan glanced at the awestruck little face and grinned at Melinda over Tanner's head.

"The wonders of modern technology," he murmured.

Melinda grinned back and settled deeper into her seat to watch the movie. The animation was stunning and the plot a bit silly, but she found as it went on that she was immensely enjoying herself. The combination of the bright music, the salty popcorn, the warm blanket, and Tanner's head snuggled into her shoulder left her feeling marvelously content. As she glanced at Ryan's profile in the dark, he turned his head to look at her. Something in his expression made a funny shiver run up her spine.

"You look like a happy five-year-old," he said softly.

"I feel like one."

"You should get out more," he remarked.

"Don't talk," ordered Tanner. They obediently fell silent again.

The stars glittered in a black sky as they drove home after the movie. Tanner drooped in his car seat in the back and fell blissfully asleep, popcorn butter forming a messy ring around his mouth.

"I shouldn't keep him out this late, I suppose."

"Once in a while is all right," Melinda said, smothering a yawn of her own.

"Past your bedtime, too?" Ryan chuckled.

Melinda rolled her window slightly down and drank in the cool stream of night air. "No, it's that half ton of compost I dug in this week."

"You should have let me do it," Ryan said.

She would have replied, but another yawn cut her off. She closed her eyes and leaned her head against the seat, letting the air pour over her face. She didn't remember falling asleep, but some time later she woke with the back of Ryan's fingers lightly rubbing her cheek.

"We're home."

The car was stopped in front of her house. Tanner was still asleep, tipped against the car door with his mouth hanging open and his neck at an uncomfortable angle. Melinda kissed her fingertip and pressed it gently to Tanner's forehead. She stopped with her hand on the door handle.

"Thanks for suggesting the movie, Ryan. It was a lot of fun. I enjoyed the auction, too. The bidding part."

"And I was such stimulating company that you slept all the way home," he replied, grinning.

"Sorry."

"Give yourself a break. Sleep in tomorrow, at least until five," he suggested. Then he leaned across the seat to kiss her gently. "Good night, Melinda."

She watched him drive up the road and come to a stop in front of his own house. The red taillights went off, and she caught a brief glimpse of his silhouette as he entered the front door and turned on the light. He carried the sleeping Tanner draped against his shoulder. Then his door closed and all was dark. Melinda realized she was standing in her driveway in the middle of the night, shivering, and she took herself inside.

There didn't seem to be a question of whether they would sit together again at church on Sunday. Melinda knew her neighbors were taking note of this and caught more than one approving look from some of the older women. She also caught one or two envious looks from some of the younger women, which caught her off guard. She felt a flash of defensiveness. Why shouldn't she sit by Ryan? He needed a hand with Tanner (actually, he didn't; Ryan coped just fine), and he was just a friend anyway. She quickly squashed the inner voice that whispered, *Oh yeah?* She didn't want anyone jumping to the wrong conclusion (it seemed that for some of them, that was all the exercise they got). Sitting together didn't mean anything, really (then why did she look forward to it so much?).

By the end of sacrament meeting, she had tied herself into such a knot that immediately after the "amen," she jumped up and went down the hall to the restroom. Then she waited until Sunday School had begun before emerging. That way she had an excuse to tiptoe in late and sit at the back. Ryan, sitting at the front, glanced at her once, a slightly puzzled expression on his face, but he didn't turn around again.

* * *

September brought a cold snap to the air, a freshness to the breeze, and ripeness to the apples. Lots of apples, all at once. Melinda suddenly decided she didn't mind so much having help with her harvest.

One Monday morning, she and Ryan carried nested stacks of bushel baskets to the orchard and set about picking the apples. Melinda had only the one ladder, so they had to take turns. It was laborious but pleasant work, with the cold breeze setting the leaves to dancing. Melinda loved the feel of the swaying branches around her and the encompassing scent of approaching autumn. She looked down at Ryan's head below her, where he stood picking from the lower branches. Somehow everything seemed to fit together—the tangy smell of the apples, the color of the sun on his hair, the light brush of the breeze on her bare arms. She wondered how long she could stretch out the apple harvest.

Tanner had tagged along again. It didn't seem to Melinda that Jenny was doing much actual babysitting. Tanner was with his father every time she saw him. It was a nice thing, she decided, to see a man who enjoyed the company of such a small child. She thought with amusement of how her own father fled to his office whenever the grandchildren came to visit.

Tanner was very good about staying out of the way, happy to stand pushing blades of grass through the wire of the rabbit hutches. As a reward for his cooperation, Melinda made a batch of strawberry ice cream that evening. Tanner watched with fascination as the electric freezer churned in slow circles; he reached out a timid finger to touch the salt water dripping from the spout. When the ice cream was ready, both Ryan and Tanner dug into their bowls with such enthusiasm that Melinda was warmed by their obvious pleasure. It was, she thought, rather fun to make someone else so happy with such a simple thing.

* * *

It took until Wednesday to pick the apples. Ryan appeared each morning to help. When Melinda inquired whether his own work needed more of his attention, he only shrugged, grinned, and said that his men could manage for a while, that he'd rather be here. Melinda wasn't sure what to think. On one hand she was flattered and secretly glad for the help. She had to admit it was nice having someone show up every morning to lend some muscle to the heavier work, and Ryan's natural enthusiasm and optimism matched her own. The mountain of fruit didn't seem so overwhelming this year. On the other hand, she didn't want Ryan to think she couldn't cope without his help or that she was taking advantage of his generosity.

"Remember, you have to let me help you with your shutters as payback," she told him as they hauled the last bushel between them to the truck. "Though that will hardly make things even."

Ryan waved a dismissive hand. "No need. My shutters are up."

"But—then how am I going to reciprocate?" she protested, dismayed.

"You're not," he said, and as she drew a breath, he added, "And don't argue."

Thursday, with the apples done, Ryan returned his attention to his cattle, and Melinda set about making preparations for the winter. There was the chicken coop to weatherproof, rain gutters to clean out, and the squash and tubers to gather. She spent a feverish couple of days caulking, shoveling, forking, and hauling. There was plenty to do, even on a small farm such as this one. Melinda thrived on the feeling of energy well spent. She was a little glad, however, that the apples could sit for a while before she had to bottle them. She tumbled into bed each night exhausted to her bones.

Monday evening Jack Peyton came over while Melinda was in the front yard, escaping from her kitchen and cutting back her rosebushes. As she watched him approach, the thought occurred to her that, to her knowledge, Ryan and Jack had still not met each other face to face. She decided Caroline must have been something else, that a man would carry a grudge for so many years.

Jack dropped to the grass beside her and lounged on one elbow, watching.

"I see you got your beets and stuff in. You should have told me you were planning to do it, and I would have helped you."

"That's all right," Melinda said, surprised.

"I suppose Ryan Delaney helped you do it." Something in his tone made Melinda turn and look at him.

"He didn't, actually. I did it myself. Why would you think he did?"

"He helped you with your apples. I saw him. Every time I look over here, he's here."

She didn't answer. He pulled a blade of grass to twirl around his finger.

"I came over Saturday night to see if you wanted to watch the ball game with me. You weren't home."

She couldn't prevent the pink that crept into her cheeks. "I was out."

"With Ryan." It wasn't a question.

"He just helped me haul some baskets to Purdys'. You really should go over and talk to him, Jack. You have to meet him sometime." She snipped through a thick cane and gingerly tossed it aside, avoiding the thorns.

"I don't have anything to say to him."

"It was so long ago," she protested. "You should give him a chance. He's really a nice guy."

"I can see you think so." Jack stood up and came to stand over her. "But I'd feel a lot better if you didn't see so much of him."

"Why? I don't have any part in your feud."

"I'm just looking out for you."

"I don't need you to look out for me, Jack," she said quietly. "And I don't need protecting from Ryan Delaney."

"I don't know about that," he said enigmatically. "I just . . . well, you and I have been friends for a while, Melinda."

She stood and drew off her gloves. "And we still are, Jack. Ryan's moving here hasn't changed that."

He looked at her a moment, then nodded. "I hope that's true," he said in a low voice.

The mood had grown uncomfortably solemn. Melinda shrugged. "If it will make you feel any better, it'd be a help to me if you'd fetch some straw from Steve Myrup for my rabbits. Just a couple of bales."

"My truck and I are at your service," he said, grinning back. "And meanwhile, as soon as you're done mangling your roses, I'll take you to dinner."

She hesitated, then picked up her clippers. "All right, it's a deal."

Melinda changed into a flowered cotton skirt and white blouse. Jack, in a fresh shirt and saturated with Old Spice, arrived at six o'clock. He didn't ask where she would like to eat or tell her where he intended to take her until he cut the engine in front of Wimpy's Diner at the plaza. He had spoken very little during the short drive, though that wasn't unusual for him. He never spoke much unless he had something specific to say.

"Burgers okay?" he asked. "There's not much selection."

"My favorite," she assured him. She opened her own door, and they went into the dim, greasy-smelling restaurant and found a table in a snug corner. Instantly she was eight years old again and sitting in a McDonald's booth with her grandfather. The whole family had been visiting, but Grandpa had snuck her out of the crowded house and taken her on a ride in his truck, just the two of them. They'd delivered something to a neighbor, Melinda remembered, and run an errand or two, and then as a treat he had taken her out for a strawberry milk-shake and onion rings. She could still taste the saltiness and feel the stickiness of the ketchup on her fingers. She wondered if the restaurant still gave out paper placemats and crayons to kids. She missed her grandpa's old truck with the cracked vinyl seats that snagged her legs when she slid across them. The floor in front of the passenger seat had a hole worn right through it, and if you lifted the floor mat you could get a glimpse of asphalt zipping past, right beneath you like a waterfall. Grandpa had joked that if his brakes ever gave out, he could put his boots right through the floor and skid to a stop like Fred Flintstone. Her mother had declared the truck unsafe and forbidden her to ride in it, and the next time they'd gone to visit Grandpa, he'd bought a new car—a huge white Buick. It was like a living room on wheels, but it hadn't been as fun to ride in.

Wimpy's was empty except for a handful of older couples, all seated together and apparently celebrating an elderly gentleman's birthday—his ninetieth from the looks of him. The teenage waiter took their orders, writing meticulously on a notepad, and disappeared behind the swinging doors. Melinda settled back in the orange, plastic-covered seat and glanced across the table at Jack.

To her surprise, Jack looked distinctly uncomfortable. His lanky body was usually loose and relaxed, but now he sat bolt upright, the muscles in his jaw working, and his hands fiddling idly with the napkin dispenser. When he saw her look at him, he looked away.

"Anything wrong, Jack? You look tense about something."

"What? No, nothing. Sorry." He went back to fiddling, this time with the ketchup bottle.

Melinda frowned as the unwelcome words of Carmella Ostler came back to her. Surely Jack wasn't thinking seriously of, well, turning serious, was he? Was that why he seemed so ill at ease? They had been neighbors for two years. He had always been someone she could call on when the truck broke down or something very heavy needed lifting. He had been there for her when her steer died. Sometimes he had invited her over for barbecues. Surely he didn't think there was anything more to their friendship? She scanned her memory for anything she might have done to encourage him to think differently. Nothing came to mind. But she could still hear

his comment from earlier that evening—*I'm just looking out for you.*
There was something proprietary about that phrase that didn't set
well with her.

When the food arrived, Melinda reached for the salt shaker and
looked at Jack again. She was relieved to see that his usual relaxed
manner seemed to have returned. He ate his burger with enthusiasm and began talking, animatedly for him, about a horse he had
once broken in. Melinda decided that she had simply imagined any
discomfort on his part. Of course he didn't think of her as anything
but a neighbor. It was conceited and paranoid to think otherwise.
Feeling absurd, she attacked her milkshake and brought her mind
briskly back to the conversation.

He was more talkative than usual on the drive home. At one point
his hand hovered over Melinda's knee, but he withdrew it before the
gesture bothered her. When they arrived home, he pulled the car into
her driveway and simply sat, making no move to open her door or
walk her to the house.

"Thanks, Jack. It was fun," she said, reaching for the door handle.

"We'll do it again." He leaned over, and a startled Melinda turned
her head in time to catch his kiss on her cheek. It was quick and
friendly, certainly not romantic, but it was the first time he'd tried
such a thing. She didn't know what to make of it. She barely stopped
herself from blurting, "Look, we've got a nice friendship here. Don't
go ruining it!" Instead, she practically jumped from the car. She
waved good-bye from her doorway. She didn't linger to watch him
pull the car into his own driveway. She hurried inside, wanting to be
alone to consider this new twist in their relationship, and at the same
time not wanting to think about it at all.

* * *

The first frost hit in late September. Melinda loved this time of year.
Feeling like a bear getting ready to hibernate, she barricaded herself
in the kitchen to begin canning the bushels of unsold apples she had
saved for herself. She took pleasure in the crisp, red curl of a length-
ening apple peel and the smell of cinnamon and steam as she put up
applesauce and pie filling. She liked the sound of the bottles gently

clinking together in their boiling bath. The soft, hollow popping sounds the lids made as the jars sealed made her smile with approval. She loved to watch the rows of gleaming bottles steadily increase on her shelves: the fat, white apple slices; the crimson cherries; the emerald pickles; and the luminous, golden corn relish were like rows of gems glinting in the dim light of her storeroom.

When she was finished canning apples, she packed away the herbs she had dried, making the house and her hands smell like a pizzeria for a few days. She also treated herself to her favorite: sugar cookies flavored with crushed lavender flowers. (Her mother always said they tasted like soap, but Melinda found them appealing in a sort of nostalgic Victorian way.) She felt a certain smugness as her storage supply grew. So far she had managed the harvest as well as her grandpa could have done himself. Everything had brought fair prices at market, and she still had plenty for herself. And there were still the potatoes and carrots in the ground, snugly waiting for their turn.

Fall was a busy, contented time, and for some reason she enjoyed the process of harvesting even more this year. She told herself it was because of the fine crop and the good weather, as well as the greater sense of confidence in her own abilities compared to her first year of farming. But part of her had to admit it was also because of the new companionship of Ryan and Tanner Delaney.

Melinda no longer saw Ryan every day now that he was busy rounding up his calves to wean them and prepare them for sale. Though there were occasional early auctions, such as the one they'd attended, most calf sales happened in October or later. In late September, Melinda stopped by the Delaneys' for a hot chocolate and a chat with Jenny. Tanner greeted her like an old friend returning from an expedition. He gripped her hand and towed her into his bedroom to show her every Duplo creation he had made, which were all neatly lined up on his windowsill.

"Very nice," Melinda told him, bending down to view the toys from his level. She gave him a one-armed squeeze. "Very impressive."

"He is sulking today because he's not allowed to help with the calves," Jenny told her from the doorway.

"Poor kid. Why doesn't he come over and play with my rabbits for a while?" she offered.

Jenny's eyes lit up. "Oh no, he is a bother to you," she said, sounding wistful.

Melinda laughed. "I'd love to have him if you can spare him for an hour or two. It'd give you a breather."

"*Gracias,* Melinda. Tanner, you would like to go to Melinda's house, yes?"

"Yes." The little boy nodded vigorously.

Melinda and Tanner spent a pleasant hour playing with the rabbits. She hadn't named them, but Tanner insisted they be called something. So they chose some names for them, drawn from Tanner's favorite nursery tales and Disney characters. After the rabbits lost their appeal, they toured the orchard to look at the pigs and generally enjoyed each other's company. Tanner was a quiet and thoughtful child but fairly articulate when he needed to be. Now and then he would break into singing a tuneless, nonsensical string of syllables, and Melinda remembered her mother saying once that when a child sang to himself, all was right in his world.

Melinda enjoyed herself even more than she'd expected to. The feel of Tanner's chubby hand in hers, his wide-eyed delight at the small treasures they found, and his instantaneous laugh warmed her heart. For a moment, a brief golden moment, she let herself pretend she was his mother, that they belonged to each other.

When the afternoon drew to a close, she took him back to Ryan, along with an apple pie. Jenny had gone home, and Ryan was just getting off the phone with his first stud-service customer.

"I knew that Web site would pay off," he told her happily. He swung Tanner into his high chair and rummaged in a drawer for a pie server. "He's booked for this Monday."

"That's great news!" Melinda exclaimed.

"At least it will help finance this mad little escapade a while," he replied, the corners of his eyes crinkling.

"I haven't seen your Web site yet. What's it like?"

"I'll show you."

Ryan set the pie aside, and they went into the living room. He flipped the computer on, and they watched the monitor come to life. Ryan sat down and connected the computer to the Internet, brought up his Web site, then stood and gestured for Melinda to take the chair.

"Whenever I hear the word *Web*, I want to dust off the monitor screen," she remarked. She studied the bold blue title before her: "Delaney Longhorns, Redcreek, Texas."

"That tab is for those interested in artificial insemination," Ryan directed. "This tab is for the stud service. Scroll down to see the next part." He leaned on the back of the chair with his forearms and looked over her shoulder. Melinda leaned forward slightly and watched the image of Ryan's splotchy, handlebar-horned bull slide up the screen. But it zipped past too fast for her to read the writing below the picture.

"Too far." Ryan reached forward and put his hand over hers, guiding the mouse to the "scroll up" arrow. His palm was warm on the back of her hand. Every nerve in her body tingled at his closeness. His breath warmed her ear. She pulled her hand from under his and nodded vigorously.

"Very nice. Very interesting. I'm sure your business is going to do well," she said briskly. "How about that pie?"

After they'd eaten, she offered to show Ryan her fledgling forest, as he hadn't had a proper tour yet. She was pleased when he reached unhesitatingly for his jacket. Swinging Tanner between them, they walked up the road to her place, went around the house, and through the orchard to the back half of her property. She was only two years into her project, so the hundreds of saplings and seeds she'd planted had barely had time to do anything yet, but she was inordinately proud of them. She walked along, pointing out the overall plan of the planting, indicating which trees would go where and describing how the forest would expand, painting a vision of what it would look like someday. She had selected mostly hardwood trees, a healthy mix of maple, ash, oak, red cedar, and elm, with a few fast-growing tulip poplars and cryptomeria scattered amongst them. She had splurged on a few larger, older trees to give the forest a jumpstart, but most of the trees were tiny, barely more than spindly twigs. But you could see the general layout and catch a glimpse of what she envisioned.

"It's going to be beautiful," he declared, pausing beside a chunk of rock that rose out of the ground like a breaching whale. She had arranged a pecan tree artfully beside the rock, and when the tree reached maturity, the spot would be perfect for picnicking.

"Wait until the maples start to spread out and the birds start to move in," Melinda said happily. "Then the leaves will fall, and humus will slowly build up and enrich the soil. Then the understory will start to fill in, and we'll get other animals too—squirrels, rabbits, and raccoons—and maybe even larger predators if there are any left in this area to move in. I want to build up an entire ecosystem—birds, bugs, and all."

"I'm not sure I like the idea of larger predators moving in next door to my cattle," Ryan said slowly.

"We're not talking wolves or coyotes," Melinda assured him. "The biggest thing around here would be a fox. And they certainly wouldn't move in before the tree cover is well established. This forest won't really be what I'd call mature for another thirty or forty years."

Ryan chuckled and swung Tanner up over a muddy spot. "You're really looking forward, aren't you? You might not even be around to enjoy this forest when it's mature."

Melinda brushed a finger lovingly against a slender branch, feeling the tickle of its delicate leaves. "Maybe not. But someone will be here to enjoy it. In the meantime, it's an engrossing project."

"Was there forest here before the farmers moved in?"

"Around here? No. It's too arid. This isn't a restoration of the way it used to be. It's something entirely new. I'm changing the soil, cooling the ground, and maybe changing the climate on a local level. At some point, I hope it will be able to renew and sustain itself without human intervention. It's an experiment and not guaranteed to turn out as I picture it." Melinda shrugged, suddenly feeling a little sad. "I may not be around when these trees are at full height, but I do hope I'm around long enough to get a little benefit from the shade."

"Amen to that," Ryan said fervently, rubbing the back of his sunburned neck.

When Ryan and Tanner had returned home, Melinda took a pie to Jack as well, as a bit of an afterthought. He was watching football, so she stayed and had some pie and watched the rest of the game with him, though she really didn't understand it all and couldn't follow half of the action. He was sprawled over most of the couch, so she opted for an armchair at a safe distance, chiding herself even as she sat down for being so paranoid. He made no attempt to move closer, however, or to kiss her when she left. Perhaps she'd been worried over nothing.

* * *

A few days later, as Melinda was helping Ryan carry in a new child's bed he had bought for Tanner, she happened to glance at a pile of mail on his kitchen counter. The top envelope had Jack Peyton's name typed in the corner.

"Have things finally straightened out between you and Jack?" she asked conversationally as they maneuvered the bed through the doorway of the bedroom.

"Not yet, but he sent me a letter yesterday," Ryan answered. "He's offered me a pretty penny for this place."

Melinda stopped cold, staring at him, and nearly dropped the bed on her foot. "Jack wants to buy your ranch? The whole property?"

"He's offered me more than I think it's really worth." Ryan shoved the crib farther along the wall to make room for the bed. In a fit of domesticity, Jenny had wallpapered Tanner's room with red dinosaurs. The walls looked like they had the measles.

Melinda felt an odd surge of anxiety. Ryan hadn't said what he thought of the offer, and his face told her nothing. Was he considering selling? His words came back to her: *It's turning out to be more stressful for both of us than I'd anticipated.* Would he go back to Wyoming? She realized with a jolt that she didn't want him to go.

"Are you thinking of accepting the offer?" she asked carefully, keeping her voice even.

Ryan straightened and turned to face her. She deliberately kept her face impassive. If he decided to sell, it was his own business. She told herself it didn't matter one way or the other.

"Do you think I should?" he asked slowly, his voice low.

"It's up to you. I can't tell you what will make you happy."

He continued to stare at her, his hands at his sides. He gave a sharp nod. "I'm not deciding anything right away."

"That's wise," she said, and with a mighty thrust, she single-handedly shoved the bed into place.

They walked out into the living room, where Tanner was playing with Duplo blocks on the floor. Melinda dropped beside him. Her face felt stiff. She forced herself to smile. "What are you making, kiddo?"

Tanner held up a creation built of colored pieces. "Daddy," he said. "And me." He held up another piece.

Melinda picked up a third conglomeration of blue and white pieces. "And what's this?"

Tanner thought for a minute, then said, "Mama." Taking the pieces from her, he solemnly began to break them apart. Melinda grew still, watching him, then picked Tanner up and sat him on her lap, her arms about him.

"Why are you taking it apart?" she asked gently.

Tanner fidgeted and tossed the pieces to the floor. "All gone," he said, brushing his hands together in imitation of the gesture his father often made. It would have been comical if it hadn't been so disconcerting.

Silently, Melinda reached to pick up the pieces again and stuck them back together the way they had been before. Then she handed the toy back to Tanner. "All better," she said brightly.

Tanner contemplated this a moment, then smiled suddenly, the expression lighting up his whole face. With a giggle, he tossed the toy back into the pile and began scattering Duplo pieces across the floor with both fists. Melinda swept him up and tickled him until he turned pink with laughter, then released him and watched him run from the room in search of more toys to bring. She looked up at Ryan and found him watching her from the sofa, his face unreadable.

Before she could reconsider, she asked, "What does Tanner know about his mother?"

Ryan tipped his head to one side. "He's seen her picture in my room. I've explained who she is. I don't know if he understands any of it yet."

He stood abruptly and went to the electric keyboard against the living room wall. Melinda sensed that was the end of the discussion. She began to gather up the toys while Ryan ran his hands quietly over the keys, playing jumbled snatches of melodies she didn't know, seeming unable to light on just one. Finally he settled down to playing

"Lake Louise" by Kitano, a smoothly flowing piece that reminded her of summer sunsets. She knelt beside him, entranced by the beauty of the sound. She was vaguely aware of Tanner coming back into the room and sitting quietly beside her, likewise caught up in the peacefulness of the music. The gentle sounds washed over and through her. When at last the piece ended, Ryan's hands fell into his lap. He raised his head to look at her. There was something in his expression that made her look away, made her feel that she was intruding. She shook her head, unable to form words for how she felt.

"I had no idea," she said at last. "You should be performing in concert halls. What on earth are you doing out here in the middle of nowhere with a bunch of cows?"

Ryan broke into laughter. "Now *you're* beginning to sound like your mother." And he began to pound out a rollicking rendition of "The Teddy Bear Picnic," while Tanner jumped up and danced.

CHAPTER 7

"I thought you might like a little of the harvest." Jack Peyton stood with his boots planted wide apart on her porch, a large paper bag at his hip. "I have more than I need."

"Thanks. Come in." She led him back to the kitchen. "I'm in the middle of baking bread."

"I guess maybe I'll hang around until I can get a slice, then," he said good-naturedly. "It's been a while since I had home-baked bread."

Jack was so tall he had to tip his head in the doorway. He placed the bag on the table and lifted out a mass of yellowing lima bean vines and spread them on the table like tangled Christmas tree lights. Melinda could hear the beans rattling in their dry pods. He dropped into a chair and stretched his long legs out in front of him, rubbing the thighs of his jeans with his palms.

"Those look great, thanks," Melinda told him. She returned to the counter where the risen loaves were waiting under a light towel. She rubbed them with butter, put them into the oven, and began to set out plates, knives, glasses, a jug of milk, butter, honey, and home-made strawberry jam. Abigail, sensing that something scrumptious was about to happen, jumped up onto one of the chairs, and Melinda gently pushed her off.

"I haven't been over to your place for a while," Jack said, looking around admiringly. "You've got it fixed up nice."

"Thanks."

"If you want to get me a bowl, I'll shell these beans for you."

"Oh, no need. I'll take them out on the driveway and beat them on the cement." Melinda leaned against the counter with her arms folded.

"I saw you helping Ryan with the bed yesterday," he said suddenly, keeping his eyes on the bean vines. "I was going to come help you, but by the time I got the truck parked and walked down, you had it inside, so I walked back up again."

"You could have come in."

He looked up at her then, his eyes narrowing slightly. "You didn't need my help by then."

Melinda didn't reply, but her mind went to the envelope on Ryan's counter.

"How is he doing, anyway?" Jack's question was offhand, but Melinda felt her teeth clench.

"He hasn't decided about your offer yet, if that's what you're asking," she replied flatly.

Jack looked surprised, then his face slowly relaxed into an easy grin.

"You know about it then? Actually, I did guess he'd discuss it with you."

"And so you brought me lima beans to bribe me into telling you anything I heard," Melinda said.

"No, it's not that," Jack said. "I wanted to bring them to you anyway." He rose and came to stand close beside her, his shoulder touching hers. Melinda took one step away.

"But you thought you'd tap my brain while you were here."

"Not at all." He ran a hand through his dark hair, making it stick out over his forehead.

"What I want to know is," Melinda began, "why you want his ranch. Do you hate him so much you'll pay that kind of money to get rid of him?"

"I'm not trying to get rid of him. I've just had my eye on that place for a long time, that's all. I thought after Paul died, the ranch would be sold up, and I wanted to get my offer in. I was upset when Ryan decided to move back here instead."

This explained Jack's attitude of the past few weeks. But Melinda was still puzzled. "You have your hands full with your own herd. You're doing well, aren't you? You've never mentioned wanting to expand. Why his place?" she persisted.

"There's a good artesian well on it, for one thing."

"Don't give me that," she snapped, turning to face him. "Tell me honestly."

"You really want to know?" His voice rose to a hoarse roar. "I'm not expanding. It's not the land or the cattle I want. It's the house. I want to sell my house and move into his."

"The house?" She was baffled. "What's wrong with the one you have?"

He rubbed the back of his neck and knocked his boot heel against the floor.

"Well," he said in a softer voice, "it's only two bedrooms and about as old as the Ark. The wiring isn't up to code. The kitchen's the size of a bread box. There's mold in the attic. I'd like a nicer place, with more room. The renovations on mine would be too extensive." He paused, shifted uneasily, then blurted, "I'm thinking of remarrying."

"Really? Soon?" She heard the incredulity in her voice and blushed.

"Soon as I can talk the woman into it." A crooked smile came and went uncertainly across his lips. As she looked into his intense blue eyes, a funny tingling started crawling along her scalp. Surely not . . .

"What do you think your odds are of talking her into it?" she asked.

"I think pretty good—if I play my cards right. And if I'm patient." He stepped closer, lifted his hand, and brushed a wisp of her hair from her cheek in a gesture that was surprisingly gentle. "I get the feeling she's not quite ready, so I'll keep working on it. I want a decent place to offer her when the time comes."

"You're buying it for *me?*" she whispered in disbelief.

"Something like that. And for me too. For us."

"But Jack, I don't—I mean—that's . . . expensive!" She bit her lip before she could blurt, *"And insane."*

"I want to do it. And I'm not being underhanded about it. It was a fair offer, up front."

Melinda couldn't think of a single coherent thing to say. Jack turned and picked up the paper bag, folding it over and over in his hands.

"It's a very nice house, Melinda. If we put the three farms together—yours, mine, and his—it would be the biggest spread around. I could run twice as many head. There would be plenty of room for us and our children."

The last word made her physically jump, and Tanner's sweet face came instantly to mind. "I—I really don't know, Jack." She was still too stunned to gather her wits about her. Why hadn't she seen this coming? She felt as if he'd punched her in the stomach, the wind knocked out of her.

Before she could anticipate him, he moved close again, ducked his head, and kissed her. Caught off guard, she tried to back up and banged her heel on the cupboard. He smelled of Old Spice and fresh earth . . . and cattle. She was too shocked to move away. When he raised his head, he was smiling.

"Don't reject the idea out of hand," he said. "Think it over for a while. There's no hurry."

"Are you serious?" She stared up at his familiar, hopeful face and suddenly felt she didn't know him at all.

"It's not such a wild idea. Though it's taken me long enough to work up to it. Or hadn't you noticed?" he said, running a finger down her jawline to her chin.

"What made you say something now?"

He shrugged. "I've learned my lesson. I'm not letting Ryan Delaney beat me to it this time."

Speechless, she watched him go out. He was halfway down the driveway before she remembered he hadn't taken any bread. She moved stiffly to the oven to check it. The afternoon had taken quite the unexpected twist. She wasn't sure how to react. Her first thought was that it was utterly preposterous.

Her second thought was less certain. Why not Jack Peyton? He was well off, good-looking, sort of fun to be with, kind, and hard-working. She supposed he was steady and reliable. But even as she thought these things, she shook her head at herself. He might be an improvement over her first husband, but Jack wasn't LDS. Though she knew that the mere fact of being a member of the Church was no guarantee against unhappiness, she had learned at least one thing as a result of her disastrous marriage to Derek: nothing less than a temple wedding would do. At some point since the divorce, she had come to the decision that it was all or nothing for her. She could never compromise on that again; all she had to do was remember what had happened when she had allowed Derek to persuade her to turn her back on her beliefs. She had willfully chosen to disregard everything she'd been taught all her childhood, and she'd paid for it dearly. No marriage was promised to be perfect, but at least with the right foundation, the odds were better . . .

Melinda grabbed her braid and yanked it hard, squinching her eyes shut in fury. What did it matter? It was pointless even thinking about such things. She would never marry again. Jack could make all the plans he liked, but she couldn't risk letting herself get stuck in another nightmare.

Jack's plans. She opened her eyes and looked out the window at the pale sky. Combining three ranches into one. She could co-own most of the land around her. No subdivisions could threaten her then. She silently admitted that she could understand the appeal of the idea for Jack. For one instant she could picture the fields around her outlined with white rail fences, sprawling red barns, the new house, that glorious kitchen . . .

But it was Ryan's house. Ryan's kitchen. His father had built it. Tanner had dinosaurs on his bedroom walls. Even if Ryan willingly sold the house to Jack, she was sure she could never live in it.

"Forget it," she groaned aloud to her reflection in the pot on the counter. "You don't want another husband. You don't need another husband. You're fine just how you are. You're better off just being friends."

The words sounded hollow to her ears. And would she and Jack Peyton be able to stay friends for long, now that he had spoken his piece?

* * *

On the first of October, it snowed.

Snow always came at a different time every year, and no one could predict its arrival. But somehow snow on the first of October seemed awfully early to Melinda. Last year it hadn't snowed until the week before Christmas, and by March the temperature had risen back into the low seventies. Winter was never much to deal with in the Panhandle. But there was a cold, expectant taste to the air all day, and after supper Melinda looked up from the dishes to see thick, white flakes slowly drifting past the window. She dried the dishes and pulled on a fuzzy bathrobe, ready to curl up with a good novel. She had scarcely settled down when she heard a thumping sound on the front steps and the doorbell rang.

"How long has it been since I spent a cozy evening alone?" she mused to Abigail as she snugged up her robe and went to answer the door. It was Ryan, carrying a snow-speckled Tanner.

"Trick or treat!" Tanner dutifully said when his father prompted him.

Melinda laughed and opened the door wider to let them in. "You must be soaked. I'm sorry, I wasn't expecting trick-or-treaters until the end of the month, but I can have hot chocolate in a few minutes if you want to wait."

"That sounds worth the wait. But you look ready for bed. I don't want to keep you," Ryan said.

"No, no. I was just settling down to spend the evening reading, but this is better."

"It's crazy about the snow, huh? I wonder if it's a bad sign of what winter will be like." Ryan dusted the melting snow off his shoulders and deposited his boots in the hallway. He followed Melinda into the kitchen. Under his coat, Tanner wore tiger-striped pajamas.

"It's the only thing I could come up with for a costume on short notice," Ryan explained, laughing at Melinda's expression. "We're practicing for when we do this for real. This is Tanner's first time celebrating Halloween."

Melinda poured milk in a pot and set it on the stove. "Pull up a chair. This will take a little while to heat."

Ryan leaned back in a chair at the table, and his eyes fell on the wall hanging beside the storeroom door. "That's unusual," he said.

Melinda glanced at him, then at the hanging. "Oh, that. I made that when I was in college. I found it in the attic yesterday and decided to hang it up before the mice got it. I'd forgotten I'd brought it here."

He stood up and went over to take a closer look. "It's fantastic."

Melinda went to stand beside him, looking critically at the image she had created. She had woven the large, rectangular picture from natural materials she had found in a marsh—rushes, cattails, seed pods, dried flowers, bits of bark and twigs, bindweed, even a few feathers she'd found, with just a touch of shading from a charcoal pencil. The scene showed still water, standing reeds, and a bent-legged egret wading under the drifting leaves of an overhanging tree. Sunlight glinted greenly through the foliage, turning the water into smooth amber. Melinda had labored diligently over each detail, not out of love, necessarily, but out of a compulsion to excel at everything she undertook, a compulsion that had driven her since childhood. Even now, looking at it, she found faults, little loose pieces, bits of weaving that didn't lie flat enough, the wrong color for the egret's beak.

"It was an experiment."

"It's beautiful. You did this?" He blinked at her unbelievingly. "I knew you did art as a hobby, but I was expecting oil painting or something."

"Oh, I did a little of that too, and drawing. Botanical prints, mostly. Come here."

He followed her into the living room, and they stood silently a moment, looking at the long wall opposite the couch. Madge Farnsworth had called again the night before. On an impulse, Melinda had gone into the basement and attic to hunt out the bits of artwork she'd brought with her to Texas. She had peppered the wall of the living room with the results of her search: a few works in oils and watercolors, several in fine-tipped pen, landscapes, and close-up studies of flowers and fuzzy-leafed plants. The works were a bit dusty but none the worse for their time in storage. The room had become a small gallery of her achievements, dug from their hiding places and exposed to unsympathetic light.

She watched Ryan walk slowly down the wall, gazing at her pictures. She was surprised to feel a pleasant warmth spread through her when she saw the admiration on his face. Madge was always saying she possessed some talent, but it was nice to see that someone else shared the opinion.

"These are incredible." He had stopped in front of a nine-inch canvas in a marbled frame. "Here's an especially nice one. I've always loved birch trees."

"Me too. I painted that one not long after I moved here," Melinda said, coming to look at it with him. "Actually, it's the last painting I ever did. But I think it would look better in a wooden frame."

"These are very well done. Have you ever sold any?"

"No. It was just a hobby," she said glibly, skipping over the fact that her selling a painting to a handsome, admiring musician was what got her into her brief and stormy marriage. "I don't do it anymore."

"Why not?"

"Too busy, I guess," she said vaguely.

"You should keep it up. Look at this detail. You have a real talent for using light and shadow."

"You think?" She frowned at the wall again.

"You could illustrate botanical reference books or something. Like those Audubon bird-watching guidebooks you can buy, with pictures of all the different kinds of birds shown in detail. You could do the same sort of guidebook for plants. Maybe you could compile a guide to your new forest, chronicling the stages it goes through."

"There's a thought." The idea appealed to her on a few levels—as an artist, a scientist, and landowner.

"Hey, could you paint Tanner someday? If you don't mind," he added. He looked over at Tanner, who was jumping up and down on the couch, trying to see into the wide mirror above it. Melinda followed his gaze. Tanner was a perfect subject, she knew, with his white-light hair and angelic face. She knew she could paint him—and do it well—provided her talent hadn't left her. She felt a momentary panic, wondering if it had.

"Do you want to?" Ryan asked.

"He *is* such a beautiful little boy."

"You think so?" Ryan looked pleased. "It would be nice to have a portrait of him—but he wouldn't hold still for it."

"I could do it from a photograph, I suppose," she said hesitantly. "Consider it an early Christmas present."

"That's very kind. Thank you." He caught her eyes with his and held her gaze. "I want to tell you, I had my doubts about moving back here, but your friendship has made the transition much easier for us both. It feels like home now."

Melinda hesitated, not sure what to say. She found Ryan's friendship comfortable . . . and comforting. But unsettling too. "It's nice to feel needed," she finally said with a shrug.

"Well, we need you," he said quietly.

Melinda turned abruptly toward the kitchen. "The milk should be ready. Come and get it."

In bed that night, Melinda lay looking up at the ceiling in the glow of the bedside lamp and chewed over the evening. Ryan's words kept coming back to her. *We need you.* Three simple words that took her breath away. She couldn't remember anyone saying that to her before—not her parents, and certainly not Derek. The logical question that followed was, did she need them?

She scowled and pulled the blanket around her ears. Over the past two years, she'd come to consider herself a capable, independent, self-reliant person. She had determined to become such a woman when her marriage had ended. Wasn't that what Derek had flung at her the day they had parted for good? *"You're as clingy and as incapable of standing on your own as wet tissue paper!"* Well, she had proven him wrong since then, hadn't she? She didn't need anything from anyone, physically or emotionally. She had fought hard for her independence, the escape she had found in this place, and she wasn't going to let go of it.

A thought struck her, and she sat up, wrapping her arms around her knees. Was that why Jack's hopes of marriage disturbed her so much? Was it really that she was afraid of history repeating itself? (Surely Jack wouldn't be another Derek!) Or was it because she was afraid of losing her hard-won independence? Did she still feel, after all this time, that she had something to prove?

She flopped back on the pillow with a groan and blew her bangs out of her eyes. Was she really being honest? Was it really that? Or was it because the proposal had come from Jack and not from Ryan? She wasn't sure she wanted to know the answer to that question.

"You're being an idiot, Melinda," she growled aloud in the darkness. "You're not going to marry Jack or anyone else. You're not going to depend on anyone else again. And if you don't shut up and go to sleep, you're going to have a migraine tomorrow," she added, and flouncing over in bed, she settled in for sleep.

October progressed. The sun still shone high in the pale sky, but its heat was weak and watery. A cold breeze rolled across the fields, bringing with it the scent of damp, rotting leaves. The snow melted as quickly as it fell. The roads were awash with mud. The drooping Shasta daisies in the flowerbeds lifted their heads in bewilderment, as if to ask, "Well, so is this winter or not?"

Melinda saw Jack a few times, coming and going from his house, and she would wave a greeting from across the street. But she was careful to be busy with other plans whenever he dropped by, and once she even found herself hiding in the chicken coop, pretending not to be home on an evening she knew he would be coming over. She chided herself for being unwilling—all right, *afraid*—to face the whole marriage issue. She was irrationally angry with Jack for taking things down a path she hadn't anticipated. Why couldn't they be friends and leave it at that? At least he didn't press her for any response; he stuck to his stated determination to be patient. To all appearances, he acted as though nothing had changed between them. But she knew the unresolved matter was always there, in the background, waiting, and sooner or later she would have to face it. It was an unnerving thought.

* * *

Every fall, Swisher County geared itself up for a harvest celebration. Redcreek was fairly central to the entire county. Its main street was transformed one weekend a year into a county fair with game booths, craft vendors, and an open-air market. Melinda invited Ryan to go with her into town to check it out. They took Ryan's car because of the car seat, and with Tanner bundled in a nylon jacket and mittens, and with an extra diaper in the glove compartment, they drove into town that Saturday morning.

The road grew more crowded the closer they got to town. The locals drove casually, relaxed, knowing they would arrive at their destinations eventually. The out-of-towners, however, were impatient. One peroxide-blond woman in a green coupe was especially anxious, weaving between the two lanes without signaling. Two or three irritated drivers honked at her. When she cut in front of Ryan, narrowly missing his bumper, he gave an exasperated sigh.

"She's going to injure someone," Melinda said as they pulled up behind the coupe at a stop sign.

Ryan wordlessly undid his seat belt and got out of the car. Melinda watched in surprise and apprehension as he approached the woman's window and bent down, one arm resting along the roof of the car. She couldn't hear what Ryan said, but she saw him pull something from his pocket and give it to her. Then he returned to his car and climbed behind the wheel. The coupe sped off, and Ryan pulled up to the stop sign.

"What was that all about? What did you say to her?" Melinda asked.

Ryan shrugged. "I gave her a dollar."

"What for?"

"I told her that apparently she couldn't afford to get her signal light fixed, so I'd like to make a contribution."

"You didn't!" Melinda laughed.

"She wasn't pleased, but I think she got the hint. And she kept the dollar," he added, grinning. He pulled the car into a parking space and cut the engine.

The local farmers had brought truckloads of their produce to Redcreek to sell: round, fresh cabbages, mounds of enormous pumpkins, bushel baskets of apples, and heavy burlap sacks of potatoes. They spread out their wares on foldout tables on the sidewalks, and the air was filled with the mingling shouts of hawkers and the greetings of neighbors who hadn't had time to see each other during the summer working season.

Redcreek, population six thousand, doubled its size during the harvest celebration. Ryan had to park his car blocks away from the center of town, and they walked in, carrying Tanner to avoid having him crushed underfoot. Tourists up from Lubbock and down from Amarillo prowled the street, buying dainty pint baskets of fruit and tiny bags of fresh herbs that looked like potpourri. The locals, however, were easy to spot; they shopped more seriously, hauling home trunks full of apple baskets, fat squash, and potatoes. The grim-faced mothers from the grocery store had moved out onto the street to do their shopping, pushing baby strollers like grocery carts and loading their toddlers' laps with purchases.

Dale Purdy had a booth set up in front of the civic center. His wife handled customers while Dale operated a rented cotton candy machine. Melinda and Ryan had to laugh at the stocky man's appearance. The spun sugar drifted up from the spinning machine in cloudy wisps to cling to his arms and face, giving him the appearance of a colorful abominable snowman. He wiggled his fuzzy pink eyebrows at Tanner, who responded with such enthusiasm that Ryan was obliged to purchase a wad of the candy before they could move on.

"I need to get a bushel of rutabagas," Melinda said, pushing her way steadily through the crowd. "Mine didn't do well. And I'd like to get some walnuts. Steve Tucker said he was going to have some here. Do you want to get Tanner a pumpkin for Halloween? There will be good prices here."

"Pun'kin," Tanner said promptly, pointing a sticky finger.

Ryan smiled. "I'll get a couple."

They wandered the booths and selected what they wanted. After they had finished shopping, Melinda held Tanner while Ryan ran the load back to the car to stow it away. When he rejoined her, they continued down the street, moving more slowly and taking in the sights, now that their main objective had been reached.

"The Amarillo Rattlers are giving autographs in the park," Melinda said, pointing to a sign. "Want to check it out?"

In answer, Ryan took her hand and struck out through the milling crowd like an icebreaker, pulling her after him. The hockey team was surrounded by a mob, however, so they settled for browsing through the rows of tables that had been set up to display the handicrafts of local artisans. The crowd wasn't quite as thick here, but Melinda noted that Ryan kept hold of her hand anyway. They trailed up and down the tables, examining dried flower arrangements, grapevine wreaths, Mod Podge flower pots, and earrings made of Fimo clay. Melinda had to stop to study these latter items in detail. They were of every shape, from fish to eyeballs to Christmas wreaths. She held a tiny pair of radishes up to her ear.

"What do you think?"

Ryan grinned. "There's a fourteen 'carrot' necklace to go with them."

"I think I'll get them. I have to have *something* fashionable to wear while I'm gardening," Melinda chuckled. She paid the vendor and tucked the small paper packet into her pocket.

They were halfway through looking at the handicraft displays when Melinda spied Carmella Ostler at the next table. Carmella was pouncing on a plastic canvas bank shaped like a cathedral, as if it were a long-sought treasure. She exclaimed to her tired-looking companion, "Look, Ella, isn't it darling?"

When Ella didn't bother to reply, Carmella looked up and saw Melinda. Melinda watched the tiny eyes sweep instantly down to her hand, still clasped in Ryan's. A beneficent smile lit Carmella's face.

"Melinda, dear! How nice to see you again!" The short woman swept forward. Melinda watched Carmella's advance with dread and dismay, but Ryan pressed his lips together in quiet amusement.

"Isn't this just the most fun? Have you ever seen such wonderful stuff?" Carmella exclaimed, taking Melinda's other hand briefly in hers. "I know John will have a cow if I bring home one more country decoration, but isn't this just the sweetest little thing you've ever seen? I couldn't resist."

"It's very unusual," Melinda said earnestly. She thought it rather ugly, in fact, but there was no point in saying this to Carmella.

"I'm Carmella," the woman gushed now, turning to Ryan. "I don't believe we've met."

Ryan dropped Melinda's hand to shake Carmella's. "Ryan Delaney."

"Yes, I've heard all about you," Carmella said. "I knew your father, of course. So sorry for your loss."

"Ah. Thank you."

"And is this angelic child yours?" She reached to pat Tanner's cheek. He shrank back in alarm, clasping his cotton candy to his chest.

Melinda was thinking up all sorts of sarcastic things to reply. *No, we won him in a raffle,* or *No, you get one kid free when you buy two pumpkins,* but Ryan only smiled and said, "Yes."

"Well, I'm glad to see you've made friends," Carmella went on, giving Melinda a meaningful look. "I've always been particularly fond of Melinda. She's a find, I'm sure you know."

Ryan nodded gravely. "I'm sure you know a find when you see one."

Melinda's smile turned into clenched teeth.

"I certainly do," Carmella said, beaming broadly. She hefted the plastic cathedral under her arm. "Well, I'll leave you two alone. I know three's a crowd. I'll see you later, Melinda, dear. I believe we have a lot to talk about."

She sailed away with the plastic church while Ella hurried to catch up. Melinda sighed, wondering what Ryan had thought of the conversation. Ryan shifted Tanner in his arms.

"I suspect there's enough material there to occupy a herd of psychiatrists," he murmured and reached for her hand again. Snickering, Melinda let him take it.

They bought hot dogs in squishy buns from a street vendor and sat on the library steps to eat and listen to the municipal band wheezing on their platform. Ryan leaned back on the top step with his elbows, hooked one boot over the other, and watched the cheerful, shuffling crowd. "This brings back memories. One year Dad was the one to sit in the ducking booth. I remember it was about forty degrees. I sank him six times. He nearly skinned me alive when we got home." He nudged her with his shoulder. "I saw a sign tacked to a telephone pole. There's a dance tonight at the Baptist church. Wanna go?"

"To the Baptist church? I mean . . ." She stopped, blushing furiously.

"I don't think the roof will collapse if two Mormons go, if that's what you mean," he replied, sounding mildly amused. "It's just a dance. How about it?"

Melinda swallowed the last of her food and set about wiping Tanner off with a paper napkin. He was so sticky that bits of the napkin stuck to his face. "I don't know. I mean, thank you, but I haven't been to a dance since high school."

"Neither have I. It might be fun," Ryan replied.

"What would you do with Tanner?"

He shrugged. "I think Jenny and Mark have plans; do you know someone who could watch him?"

She thought a moment. "I bet if I asked Carmella, she'd get her daughter to watch him. She'd see it as a good cause."

He screwed his face up in mock dread. "Is the daughter anything like the mother?"

"Joanne? Not a bit. She's seventeen and rather shy. She and her brother are mortified if you mention their mother in public."

"If Joanne agrees to babysit, will you go?"

"Yes," she decided and went off to find Carmella without giving herself time to chicken out.

She found Carmella at a table loaded with baked goods and homemade jams. She was buying a pint of mint apple jelly the color of antifreeze. When she heard Melinda's request, her eyes widened, and she made little clicking sounds with her tongue.

"Now isn't that nice? Of course you have to go to the dance. If Joanne isn't free to babysit, I'll tend the little angel myself. What time—about sixish?"

"That should be fine. Thank you, Carmella," Melinda said, forcing her voice to sound grateful. She hated to ask anything of this woman, because it would only strengthen Carmella's conviction that they were the best of friends. However, she knew of no other babysitting candidates, never having had a need for a babysitter before. She firmed up the arrangements and hurried back toward the library, dodging tourists along the sidewalk.

She had taken leave of her senses, she was sure. She hadn't danced in years, and she would more likely than not make a fool of herself. Then she considered something else. What would Jack think? Just three weeks ago he had—well, not outright asked, but implied that he wanted to marry her, and here she was going to a dance with someone else. But then she hadn't committed to him. In fact, she argued with herself, she was just waiting for the right opportunity to turn him down in the politest way she could. She skirted around a sticky child who stood eating a slick ball of hand-pulled taffy and dropped onto the step beside Ryan.

"All arranged, six o'clock," she announced.

"Great. I'd better get Tanner down for a nap this afternoon, then, so he'll be pleasant company tonight."

They walked back to the car, and Ryan drove her home with Tanner strapped in back among the baskets of vegetables. Melinda spent the afternoon contentedly cracking walnuts, then showered and got ready for the dance.

At six o'clock, Melinda stood scrutinizing herself in the mirror, feeling foolish. She wasn't sure what was proper to wear to a country dance, but she'd finally decided on a denim skirt, a cream-colored blouse, and navy blue pumps. It didn't look too bumpkin-ish, but not too formal either. She'd pulled her hair into a bun, then reconsidered and fussed with it a while, finally ending up with a French braid. The new carrot necklace finished the outfit. She thoughtfully studied herself, wondering if she should have gone with the bun after all. She made a face. Why was she so worried about how she looked? It wasn't like she was going to visit the president, after all. It was only a dance in little Redcreek. Ryan had certainly seen her looking a lot worse than this.

There was the sound of a car pulling up outside. Quickly she grabbed her house key and sweater, made sure Abigail had water in her dish, and let herself out.

Ryan had changed into dark slacks and a tweed jacket that accentuated his dark hair. "You look very nice," she told him as he held the car door for her.

"Thank you. And you do, too," he replied. "Let's go show everyone what a stunning couple we make."

Melinda sat and watched him walk around the car to his side, his words ricocheting in her head. She wasn't sure what he had meant by such a comment. Probably nothing, she told herself. It was a harmless thing to say. *Just take it as a compliment and let it go at that,* she thought.

When they arrived at the Baptist church hall, things were already in full swing. There was no band, but a disc jockey was set up in one corner. Couples crowded the floor and lounged on folding chairs set around the edge of the room. A long refreshment table was placed against one wall, and the hall had been decorated with a country theme: bales of hay, dried Indian corn bouquets tied with jute, and gingham tablecloths. Some insane person had spent hours painting big murals of autumn scenes on butcher paper. In one painting, a pilgrim danced ring-around-the-rosy with two jolly turkeys. It beat chasing them around the yard waiting for them to have heart attacks, Melinda supposed. In another, a wicker basket lay with gourds, melons, and an incongruous goldfish spilling out of it (Melinda wondered who in Swisher County harvested goldfish).

Ryan hung Melinda's sweater in the cloak room and rejoined her. "Shall we dance? Or would you like something to nibble first?"

"If we don't dance now, I'll lose my nerve and never do it," Melinda responded.

"Good point." He took her arm and guided her onto the dance floor.

It wasn't as awkward as she had feared. Ryan proved to be a fairly adept dancer, and she followed his lead without too much trouble. She gradually relaxed and started to enjoy herself. They managed to get through several dances without crushing each other's feet or those of their neighbors. The DJ played a disorienting hodgepodge of music, from fifties oldies to soft rock and Euro-pop, and even some salsa. Melinda wasn't sure where all the people had come from. The population of Swisher County seemed to have tripled and packed itself into the room.

The music slowed as "Unchained Melody" began to play. Somehow she and Ryan naturally moved closer together, one of his hands firm on her back. His other hand was warm around hers. Something inside her wanted to rest her cheek on his broad chest. The thought jolted her like a swat on a skittish horse's nose.

"I'll take you up on that nibble now," Melinda said in a rush.

Ryan wiggled his eyebrows at her. "I thought you'd never ask."

Melinda pretended she hadn't heard him and led him off the floor.

CHAPTER 8

"I was so afraid I'd be the oldest woman here," Melinda confided to Ryan over red Kool-Aid and date squares. There were no chairs left. They'd wedged themselves into a corner next to a stand of dry corn-stalks. "I thought I'd be lost in a sea of teenagers. But there seem to be a lot of older couples. I just saw Sister Morrison dancing with her nephew, and she must be pushing eighty."

"Then you're at least second oldest," Ryan said, grinning.

She made a face at him. "Very funny."

A teenage girl approached them and stopped in front of Ryan, smiling up at him through droopy lashes. It appeared that she'd applied her makeup with a putty knife and donned what looked like her big sister's leather skirt and metallic red top in an attempt to look older. It hadn't worked.

"I'm Molly," she announced.

"How very nice," Ryan replied.

"I love this song," she purred. "Don't you?"

Ryan cleared his throat, and Melinda saw the muscles at the corner of his mouth twitch.

"Actually, I think the DJ is taking a break right now," he murmured.

The girl glanced over her shoulder and turned back to him, unabashed. "Oh. When he starts again, do you want to dance?"

"I would, thanks," Ryan said. "But I'm escorting this poor old woman tonight, and it wouldn't be very nice of me to ditch her."

Melinda set her drink down hastily and began to cough. Molly eyed her critically, trying to figure out the relationship. Ryan leaned closer and dropped his tone so that Melinda presumably couldn't hear. "They only let her out of the nursing home once a year to come to this dance. I can't bring myself to spoil it for her. She's been looking forward to it for so long."

Molly accepted this with a remorseful nod. "Maybe some other time," she said and moved off in search of different game. Melinda punched Ryan in the shoulder.

"What was I supposed to say?" he protested, putting his hands up in defense.

"You could have thought of something better."

"No, I couldn't. She terrified me." He looked sideways at her. "Most women terrify me. But you don't."

The DJ returned and the music resumed. Ryan caught Melinda's hand as she went to punch him again.

"If you're done nibbling, I like this song."

She promptly set down her paper napkin. Ryan led her back to the dance floor. It was a slow song she'd never heard before, guitar with orchestra backup. Couples crowded the floor around them. Melinda automatically moved to waltz position, but Ryan murmured, "You're giving away your age," and placed both hands on her waist.

Melinda hesitated, then put both of her arms loosely about his neck. She told herself she was being silly. Waltz position or bear-hug, they were only a few inches apart either way. What difference did the position make? But it did make a difference. Whether it was the stance or the slow music, Melinda knew that some dynamic between them had changed. He seemed suddenly taller, his aftershave stronger, the tweed of his jacket rougher under her palms. She was acutely aware of each breath he took, each light touch of his knee against her skirt. Her feet felt too big, and she could find no natural expression in which to arrange her face. She stared steadily sideways at the ghastly turkey mural on the wall and could think of nothing intelligent to say. Even if she could, it would be impossible to speak to someone only inches away. She wondered if he could tell how their closeness was affecting her and found the possibility embarrassing.

She dared a glance at him and found he was smiling gently, his eyes half closed, watching her. The dim lights made his eyes look gray.

"Something wrong?" he murmured. His breath stirred the wisps of hair at her temples.

"Not at all," she replied brightly. "What is this song?"

"'Cherish,' by Gold Dust. Like it?"

"Very much. It's soothing."

He arched one dark eyebrow. "You look anything but soothed, Melinda. From your expression, I'd say you look more like a squirrel about to get hit by a car."

"Do I?" She fumbled for a comeback. "It's these darn orthopedic shoes," she said.

Ryan chuckled and maneuvered her skillfully out of the path of an oncoming couple. Melinda saw with surprise that it was Danny Wilson, grasping a teenage girl who had black-and-white streaked hair and a Lycra outfit to match. It looked more like they were grappling than dancing. Danny's face was flushed, and he appeared unsteady on his feet. His companion was having a difficult time keeping him upright.

"Did someone spike the punch bowl?" Ryan murmured as they went past.

"Edith Bixby is supposed to be standing guard," Melinda said.

"It seems that Edith has been remiss in her duties."

Out of the corner of her eye, Melinda saw a commotion and turned back in time to see Danny, who had tripped, go sprawling to the floor. The teenage girl staggered on her thick-soled boots but kept her balance. Looking disgusted, the girl walked off the floor and left Danny lying there with the other dancers eddying around him. Someone reached down to help him up, but Danny brushed the hands away and pulled himself to his feet. The man who had tried to assist him must have said something Danny didn't like, because Melinda saw Danny whirl suddenly around and shove the man in the chest. The man went flying backward and fell. His date gave a shrill scream. The rest of the people on the dance floor realized something was happening, and all motion ground to a halt. The music stopped abruptly.

Danny was shouting at the man he had pushed. "Mind your own business, old man!"

Ryan started forward, but Danny, who had apparently decided not to cause further trouble, headed off the floor. All eyes watched him lurch around the refreshment table and out the door. There was a low murmur, the shifting of feet, and Melinda heard someone say, "Troublemakers." The man on the floor had been helped up and was holding up his hands and nodding to show that he was all right. The music began again, mid-song. After a moment, the dancing resumed, but the mood was more subdued now. When the song ended, Melinda started back toward the chairs, but Ryan caught her by the elbow.

"Let's go outside for some air," he suggested. She let him collect her sweater, and they went out of the hall.

The Baptist church was situated on an acre at the edge of Redcreek, surrounded by a rusting fence and tipped headstones dating back to the early nineteenth century, their engravings a mix of Spanish and English. A silky breeze stirred the cottonwoods. A cold, silvery moon rode high overhead, coming and going behind the clouds. Music poured from the building whenever the door opened. Butter-gold light spilled from the tall windows, vainly attempting to warm the ground. Melinda pulled her sweater close. The grass soaked her shoes as they walked around the building. One or two other couples lounged in the doorways and waved greetings as they passed. There was no sign of Danny Wilson.

"I hope he gets home all right," Ryan said. There was no need to explain who he meant.

"He lives in the subdivision by Black Cat Road. He probably drove here."

"He'd better not try to drive home in his condition."

"If he does, it won't be the first time," Melinda sighed.

"What's his name, do you know?"

"Danny Wilson. He's been trouble since his family moved here."

"It's so easy for kids to get on the wrong path, and so hard to get back on the right one," Ryan said. "Especially when they won't accept any help." He walked with his hands in his pockets, gazing up at the black sky. "The moon's so beautiful. Look how bright the stars are."

"It's because of the cold. Do you know much about stars?" Melinda asked.

"Only enough to know that some people have lucky ones." His eyes slid down to her. "Thank you for coming tonight, Melinda. I'm enjoying myself. I mean, other than that little moment."

"Me too."

"Are you? I'm glad. You need more enjoyment in life."

"What do you mean?" Melinda said. "I enjoy my life."

"You work too hard."

"There's no such thing," she replied.

He chuckled. "That's the sort of reply I'd expect from you." He turned and took her shoulders in his hands. "I've been wanting to tell you—" he began and then broke off as a teenage boy came running toward them across the grass.

It was Tim Ostler. He drew to a stop beside them, winded, his Levi jacket undone to show his purple T-shirt. His hair had flopped over his eyes. He bent over, with his hands on his knees, speechless for a moment as he caught his breath. Melinda felt a rising fear grow within her.

"What is it, Tim?" she demanded, taking the boy by the shoulders and forcing him upright. "What's wrong?"

"Joanne called and asked me to find you. She—she didn't have the number for the church, so she couldn't call . . ."

"What's happened?" Ryan asked sharply.

"Your little boy—she—you better get home," Carmella's son said miserably.

"Is he all right?" There was a catch in Melinda's voice, and she felt Ryan's grip on her elbow tighten.

"I don't know. She can't find him."

Ryan drove at a dangerous speed, his jaw set grimly. Melinda sat in silence beside him, gripping her hands together in her lap and watching the lights of distant houses move by. It was only fifteen minutes from Redcreek to Ryan's ranch, but the road seemed to stretch interminably before them in the dark. She tried to reassure the frantic voice in her head. *Tanner was fine, he had just wandered off someplace. They would find him. It would be all right. But why would he wander away at night? Couldn't Ryan drive any faster?* She hadn't realized what a fearful thing it would be to be a parent. Or how much she had come to care for the little boy.

When at last they reached Ryan's house, he jumped out, leaving the keys in the ignition. He was inside the house before Melinda could get her door open.

They found Joanne sitting at the kitchen table, her eyes puffy and her nose running from crying. She jumped up and threw her hands over her face when she saw Ryan's drawn expression.

"I'm sorry, I should have checked on him earlier. I thought he was sleeping. I put him to bed at eight like you said." The girl sobbed, agonized. "He went without a fuss, and I closed his door and went to watch TV in the living room. I guess I dozed off. I feel so awful, Mr. Delaney. I checked on him at ten o'clock, and he wasn't there."

Melinda watched Ryan put his hand out and squeeze Joanne's shoulder in a brief, gentle gesture of comfort. "It's my fault. I should have warned you that he sometimes gets up again after you put him down. We'll find him. He can't have wandered far."

Melinda checked the clock. It had been at least forty minutes. He could be anywhere.

"Where have you searched?" Ryan asked.

Joanne scrubbed at her face with her palms and grew calmer. "Everywhere. I went through all the rooms and searched the basement, even the attic. I thought maybe he went out in the yard, because the doors weren't bolted. I guess I should have bolted them, but nobody ever does. I didn't *think*. I called and called, and he didn't answer."

"I'll go check the stable," Ryan said. "Melinda, can you go through the house again? Check under beds, behind doors. Maybe he fell asleep somewhere."

Melinda nodded, and Ryan hurried out of the room. Joanne turned miserably to Melinda. "I'm so sorry. Nothing like this has ever happened before. I thought I'd better call you, but I didn't have a number, so I called my mom, and she said she'd send Tim after you. I'm sorry I had to ruin your evening."

"Don't worry about that," Melinda said, waving a hand at her. "That's not important. Listen, why don't you run and check the front yard while Ryan's checking out back?" Melinda hesitated, fear knotting in her stomach. "And Joanne, check the culvert, too."

Joanne froze, staring at Melinda with wide eyes. Then she fled without pausing to find her coat. Melinda put her hands to her temples. If Tanner had wandered into the culvert or the road, she couldn't bear to think about what might have happened. There were hundreds of acres out there, dark and cold and full of all kinds of dangers . . . But she knew it wouldn't do any good to stand there letting her imagination take over. Swiftly she began a thorough search of every room, checking in every small corner a little boy might hide. She was in the middle of checking in the laundry hamper in the bedroom when Ryan came in. She looked up hopefully, but he shook his head. His face was tight with concern, the muscles working in his jaws. He looked exhausted.

"He's not outside that I could see. I called Mark and Dayton, and they're on their way over. I'm going to check one more place. Sometimes he likes to crawl inside those old tires by the gate. If he's not there, we'll start combing the pasture. But I can't imagine he'd wander out there in the dark."

"Do you have a flashlight? I can get one from home."

"I have one." He headed toward the door, then looked back at her over his shoulder. "Say a little prayer, would you?"

When he'd left the room again, Melinda sank onto the edge of the bed and ran her hands through her hair, now loose and trailing from its braid. She realized that, instinctively, she'd already been silently praying for the past ten minutes. Her whole soul ached with it.

Where could he be? Had he wandered out to the road, where someone had picked him up? Would a barefoot two-year-old go that far in the dark alone? If anything happened to Tanner, she knew Ryan would fall apart. He was all Ryan had. An emptiness engulfed her, worse than any loneliness she had ever felt, even when she'd been with Derek. Ryan couldn't lose Tanner; he just couldn't.

"Please help me find him, Father. I need to find him *now*," she said aloud and stood up. If ever she needed guidance, it was now. She paused, hands on hips, listening intensely, half expecting a voice to tell her what she needed to know. Nothing. She felt a wave of irrational disappointment.

"All right then, I'll find him myself," she said. "If I were a little boy who didn't want to sleep, where would I go?" She'd play with her toys, she thought. But Tanner wasn't in the house. "What else would I want to play with?"

And then the thought slid neatly into her mind. Instantly she was outside and running across the yard. She heard Ryan shout behind her, but she didn't stop running. There was no sense in telling him her hunch until she was sure. But she *was* sure. She flew down the road, trying to avoid the potholes in the dark, her skirt hiked above her knees, her feet crunching on the gravel. Turning into her own driveway, she sped around the house, crossed through the backyard, and dashed through the sleeping vegetable beds that were huddled like mounded graves in the dark. She slowed as she approached the rabbit hutches.

The moonlight caught the glow of silvery hair, and a cheerful voice piped, "Hi, Minda."

She dropped to her knees in the damp grass beside the little boy, struggling to regain her composure. It would do no good to alarm and upset him now. He wore only his pajamas, though he'd had the presence of mind to pull on his Buzz Lightyear slippers.

"Hi, Tanner," she said, and was pleased to find that her voice was steady. "Did you come to visit the rabbits?"

Tanner nodded and held up a fistful of grass he'd pulled. "Thumper's hungry."

Melinda gently brushed off his fingers and picked him up. He rested heavily against her shoulder, his cold cheek pressed against hers, his arms wrapped around her neck.

"Are you sleepy, Tanner? I think we'd better go see your Daddy. Daddy's home now."

"Feed rabbits," Tanner said, rearing back and appearing to be on the verge of a full-scale protest.

"The rabbits need to sleep now. It's nighttime. Shhh," Melinda told him. "Come very quietly so we don't wake them up."

Tanner eyed the rabbits a moment, then nodded. He yawned and laid his head on her shoulder as she carried him around to the front yard. Ryan was jogging up the driveway. He saw her and slowed, holding out his arms. Melinda handed the little boy to him. Ryan wrapped his arms around Tanner gently, resting him against his chest, inside his jacket.

"Oh, Tanner, you gave me a scare," he murmured into the taffy hair. His voice held a tremor of relief and gratitude.

"He wanted to see the rabbits," Melinda told him. "He agrees it's time they went to sleep now."

Ryan lifted his face, the moonlight behind him, his expression lost in shadow. He reached out and laid his hand on her cheek.

"Thank you."

"I just had the feeling . . ." she began, then stopped. It had been more than a feeling. She had seen in her mind very clearly the hutches, the moonlight, the little boy. Sheepishly, she added, "I think I had some help."

He nodded, understanding perfectly. "I'm sorry to have cut our evening short."

"It couldn't be helped. I really did have a good time today," she said.

"Do you want to come up to the house for a while?"

She shook her head. "I know what you really want to do is tuck Tanner in bed and collapse into a chair," she said. "I'll call and see how he is in the morning."

He chuckled. "You're an angel. Not everyone would be so understanding."

She leaned up and planted a kiss on Tanner's already dozing face, then turned her head and impulsively kissed Ryan's cheek. "Be kind to Joanne Ostler. She's really upset about the whole thing."

"I know, poor kid. I don't blame her." He turned to go, lifting Tanner up against his shoulder. "I'm taking you to dinner Monday night. Sixish."

"Do I have any choice?"

"None whatsoever."

She smiled. "Good night, Ryan."

* * *

First thing in the morning, Melinda phoned the Delaneys'. Jenny answered on the second ring.

"The *chiquito* is just fine," Jenny informed her, sounding close to tears. "My husband told me when he came home last night that Tanner was fine, but I had to come check on him myself this morning. He ate a good breakfast," she added as if to further prove how fine Tanner was.

"I'm glad. Give him a hug for me," Melinda said.

"We are all very grateful, Melinda," Jenny said. "It was so cold last night, and if you did not find him—We are very blessed."

"Yes, we are," Melinda agreed.

"You want to talk to Ryan?"

"No, I'll see him at church. I just wanted to check in," Melinda said.

She'd barely hung up when the phone rang again. It was her mother.

"There you are. I let it ring and ring earlier. Where were you?"

"I was probably in the shower. What is it, Mom?"

"Thanksgiving dinner. You are coming, aren't you?"

"I don't think I can swing it this year, Mom."

"What? Why not? Everyone will be there, Melinda. Joan will be disappointed if you don't see Davey. He's grown so much!"

"I just saw everyone in the spring. I really don't think I can get away."

"Of course you can. It's Thanksgiving. Alice Moore is letting me borrow her oven so we can cook the ham and the turkey at the same time. She's not doing a big dinner this year, since Connie married that foreign fellow and moved away to California. She says it just doesn't feel right to be thankful this year. So I'm using her oven, and Aunt Denise is bringing her sausage rolls."

"It's a full day's drive to Albuquerque, and I'd have to turn around and head back a day later. It doesn't make sense to come so far for such a short time, and I can't leave the animals any longer."

"You're not part of the family anymore, is that it?" her mother asked bitterly.

"Don't be . . ." She bit her tongue. "Mom, I've explained this to you before. This farm is a full-time responsibility. I can't just walk away any old time I want."

"Can't someone watch your animals for you?"

Melinda hesitated. Jack had kept an eye on her animals last Christmas while she was away, but she didn't feel like asking him to help her now, circumstances being what they were. And Ryan had his hands full with his own responsibilities. And truth be told, she didn't want to go back to Albuquerque at all, even to visit. Although the risk was slight that she would run into Derek, there was still that chance. Derek's parents didn't live all that far from her own, and he'd probably be in town for the holiday. She'd managed to miss him last Easter, but going home for Thanksgiving was pushing her luck.

"I'm sorry, Mom. Maybe I can arrange to come at Christmas," she said, knowing she wouldn't.

There was a miffed sound from the phone. "All right. Fine. If a bunch of ratty chickens are more important than your own family . . ."

"Mom, you know that isn't true. They'll starve to death if I'm not here."

"That must make you feel so needed and important," her mother said. She hung up.

Melinda sat gripping the phone, visualizing herself swinging it like a lasso above her head and hurling it across the room. But there would be no sense in that, only expense. She carefully set the phone back in its cradle and went to get ready for church.

CHAPTER 9

When she arrived at the chapel, Ryan was already sitting in what she had come to think of as their bench. Tanner, who was coloring busily in a sketchbook, glanced up at her, very obviously none the worse for his little adventure. Melinda sat beside him and ruffled his hair affectionately. "Hey, buddy."

"Hi, Minda," Tanner said and bent back over his crayons. Over his head, Ryan and Melinda exchanged smiles.

"Hey," Melinda repeated softly.

Ryan began to say something, but at that moment the bishop stood to begin the meeting. Ryan closed his mouth again, but reached his arm along the back of the bench to place his hand on Melinda's shoulder.

* * *

When Ryan arrived Monday evening to take Melinda to dinner, Tanner wasn't in the car.

"I left him with Joanne Ostler again," he explained. "She jumped at the chance to redeem herself. She vowed she'd lie on the floor outside his bedroom door half the night so he couldn't get out."

"We're not going to be out that late," Melinda said. She shot him a glance. "Are we?"

He shrugged as he pulled the car onto the highway. "Maybe."

They drove into Amarillo, and Ryan took her to an Italian restaurant she had never tried. They sat at a window table with a pink cloth and red carnations in a crystal vase. They ate tortellini in cream sauce, scallops, steamed vegetables, and salty garlic bread. For once Melinda let herself indulge without worrying about cost. Ryan looked as at home in a dark suit and tie as he did in jeans and a ten-gallon hat. Even though she'd seen him dressed nicely every Sunday, Melinda thought he looked incredible tonight. From the giddy glances the teenage waitress kept giving him, she obviously shared Melinda's opinion.

When they had finished their meal, the waitress brought them a tray of desserts from which to make their selections.

"This is a great place. I'll have to remember it," Melinda said, debating between a sinful chocolate mousse and an exotic lime gelato.

Ryan ordered a scoop of the Italian ice cream and looked at her thoughtfully across the table. "It's perfect. This whole evening is perfect." His fingers touched the back of her wrist, burning her skin.

Melinda finally chose the mousse and settled down to enjoy it. "Yes, it is," she agreed. "The food is delicious, and the atmosphere is wonderful."

"The company too," Ryan murmured.

Melinda gave him a look, debating whether to comment on this.

"And what do *you* think of the company?" Ryan asked, leaning forward on his elbows.

She shrugged one shoulder and concentrated on her dessert. "I have no complaints."

"Ah. Well, that's reassuring," he said with a wry grin.

She arched an eyebrow. "What did you want me to say?"

He shrugged lightly. "I don't know. That I'm a charming and generous companion. That you've never been fed so royally. That this is the best evening you've ever had, and you're going to rush home to write down every detail in your journal." He cocked a dark eyebrow, his eyes glittering.

"You've got gelato on your tie," Melinda replied sweetly.

When he brought her home, he paused at her door and carefully took her into his arms. Their kiss was brief but full of warmth. She was mortified to find herself wishing it hadn't been so brief. But he lowered his hands to his sides and stepped back.

"I've been trying to find a way to tell you . . ."

"Tell me what?" she asked when he hesitated.

"I don't know if I can explain myself very well without sounding stupid," Ryan said with a crooked smile. "But after Caroline died, I told myself that I could either crawl away to lick my wounds and become a hermit, or I could pick myself up and go on living. It was a conscious choice I had to make. I think at the time I kind of resented the fact that the world could keep turning without her, you know? It didn't seem right that it should. But with Tanner to look after and everything, I decided being a hermit wasn't a viable option. I had to find a way to keep living—if not for me, then for him. It wasn't really the choice I felt like making at the time, but I made it."

"I know what you mean," Melinda murmured. She had faced the same decision, and she wasn't necessarily proud of her own choice. But she hadn't had a child to influence her.

"I knew that if this was going to be my choice, it wasn't enough to just survive. For both our sakes, and to be fair to Tanner, I had to make it turn out to be a good life. I didn't let myself look too far into the future. I took it one day at a time. But I kind of knew, deep down, that eventually, things would be all right again." Ryan rubbed his jaw, glancing at the car, the lilac bushes, the sky. "I guess what I'm trying to say is, it's only been a little over two years, and it's not completely all right yet, I know that. But, well, it's heading in that direction, you know? I think I will get there eventually. I can see how good life could be, if I'm just brave enough to reach out and grab it. There's hope."

Melinda couldn't imagine Ryan being anything but brave. She started to say so, but he laughed and shook his head. "I'm not sure why, but I just felt I should give you a status report—tell you where I'm at right now."

She nodded.

"You're a big part of all this, you know," Ryan added. "You're part of what makes me believe life can be all right again." He reached out to gently touch her cheek.

"Thank you for telling me," Melinda said. She paused, then added quietly, "I made a different choice. I'm still licking my wounds, I think."

"I got the feeling maybe that was the case."

"Someday soon I'll give you a status report on my own state, okay?" she said with a small smile. "Just . . . not yet."

He nodded and lowered his hand. "Okay. When you're ready." He turned to go, then stopped and turned back. "Oh, listen, we're going to Wyoming on Saturday just for a few days. I've got some final paperwork to do about the sale of the ranch there, and I want to take Tanner to see his grandparents. The guys will keep an eye on things while I'm gone. I'll call you when I get back, and we can get together."

"All right."

"And the week after that we can take Tanner trick-or-treating. Just around the neighborhood."

"Sure. I'd like that."

"I'd like to stop by the bishop's and the nursery leader's house. They're really the only other people Tanner knows around here. I'm not sure where Sister Matthews lives, though."

"I'll show you. And I can show you which houses to avoid."

He raised his eyebrows. "Avoid? Why, are there gang members and murderers living in Redcreek now?"

"No, but there are some fundamentalist Christian groups who don't hold with celebrating Halloween. And they also wouldn't welcome a Mormon showing up on their steps, even one with a harmless toddler in tiger pajamas."

"Okay." Ryan shrugged. "Fair enough."

His airiness caught her off guard. "It doesn't bother you that some of your neighbors feel that way about Church members?"

"The way I see it, you can either be about inclusion or exclusion, community or isolation. You can dwell on differences or similarities. You have to decide for yourself what you're comfortable with and then respect what other people are comfortable with."

Melinda pursed her lips. *Comfortable.* It was such an enticing word. One that fit precisely with how she felt around Ryan and Tanner.

"Well, I think trick-or-treating with you sounds like fun. I want to go."

"Great! I'll see you when I get back, then."

* * *

Ryan didn't get back from Wyoming until the day before Halloween. When Melinda checked with Jenny several days after Ryan had gone, Jenny only knew that there had been some trouble with the papers he had to sign, and so he'd extended his stay. When he finally called Melinda to report that he'd returned, she couldn't keep the relief out of her voice. Part of her had been worried he'd get back to Wyoming, back to Caroline's parents and his old home, and decide not to come back. *Of course he came back,* she scolded herself. If for no other reason, he had the ranch to look after.

"The buyer of my ranch had some difficulty securing the money," he explained. "But I gave him an extension, and he pulled some small miracles. In the end, it went through all right."

"How do you feel about it?" Melinda asked, expecting him to express some regret at having sold his old home. But his voice was cheerful.

"Relieved. It's all wrapped up and done, and I'm a wealthy man. And I never want to see any paperwork again. Are we still on for trick-or-treating?"

"You bet!"

* * *

Halloween night was the perfect spooky night. A light drizzle had fallen earlier but had cleared as it grew dark, and the air was crisp but not freezing. Deep, rounded clouds alternately concealed and revealed a tinfoil moon that just begged to be howled at. Tanner's face was painted in orange-and-black stripes to match his pajamas. His jacket had been stuffed underneath the tiger layer so that it wouldn't obscure his costume. He looked like a waddling orange. Tanner wasn't sure what all the fuss was about, but he was game for anything.

It was too far between houses to walk, so they took Ryan's car, even though it made for a lot of bustle, snapping the bulky tiger in and out of his car seat. Tanner soon got the hang of trick-or-treating and was enthralled with his good luck, getting candy from unexpected sources.

"Think about it," Ryan mused, as they walked up the Ostlers' driveway. "Every other day of the year you tell him not to take candy from strangers, but tonight it's okay. He must be confused."

"Actually, he looks pretty pleased with himself," Melinda remarked. Tanner had climbed the steps with his bag banging his knees and was hopping up and down trying to reach the doorbell. Ryan rang it for him.

Carmella Ostler had outdone herself. She was dressed completely in black, and her hair was sprayed green and done up in elaborate curls. She flung open the door, her witch's hat in her hand (for fear of smashing the curls, no doubt). She stuck her rubber nose in Tanner's face and cooed, "What a cute little kitty!"

Tanner shrieked in alarm. Melinda caught him just in time to prevent him from tumbling backward down the steps.

The witch began to cluck and pat her cheeks in dismay. "Did I scare him? Is he okay? You poor little honey!"

"He's fine," Ryan assured her. "All part of the Halloween fun. You have quite the costume."

Tanner had clawed his way into Melinda's arms like a cat up a tree. Secure in her grip, he glared at Carmella over his shoulder in open disapproval. Tanner's mouth opened, but before he could make any candid comments, Ryan clamped a hand over his mouth.

"I try to liven things up a bit. We don't get many trick-or-treaters, living out this far," Carmella said, modestly coiling a curl around her finger. "Here, give the poor kitty a little something extra."

Even a double share of sweets didn't pacify Tanner. He turned away, having none of it. Ryan fumbled for the bag Tanner had dropped, thanked Carmella for the candy, and they made a dash for the car.

Once safely out of earshot, Ryan laughed heartily, pounding his hand on the steering wheel. Melinda joined in, laughing until tears came to her eyes. She turned in her seat to grin at Tanner. He was still scowling.

"Nasty lady," he said.

After trick-or-treating, they returned to Ryan's house for hot choco-late. Tanner, still grouchy, was allowed to stay up a while longer as a peace offering. In an effort to cheer him, Ryan went to the keyboard and began to pound out some old show tunes. Tanner, still in his costume, listened a moment and then began dancing on his sturdy little legs, spinning in circles. Ryan glanced at him, smiled, and began to sing.

Leaning in the doorway, Melinda was entranced by Ryan's voice—lyric, smooth, and totally unexpected. She'd heard him mumble through hymns at church like everybody else, but as a soloist, his baritone was golden. After a while, he switched to a child's song. It was about woodland creatures, and as he sang about each one, Tanner acted them out with great concentration. He solemnly jumped up and down for the rabbit and hunkered onto his heels for the frog. He flapped diligently around the room for the robin and lay on the floor and wiggled for the fish. Finally, he lost interest and wandered off to find some toys. Ryan ran his hands aimlessly over the keys a moment and then found another melody.

"Put your loving arms around me, Belle . . ." he crooned.

Melinda knew the actions to this song. She slid onto the piano bench beside him and slipped her arms around his middle, resting her head on his shoulder. Ryan's hands froze mid-chord. After a pause, he began to play again.

"My kingdom for a kiss . . ." he sang.

Melinda reached up and placed a kiss on his cheek. Ryan paused again.

"The possibilities are mind-boggling," he mused.

* * *

Two days before Thanksgiving, Melinda spent the day baking cookies and breads to pack away in her freezer. She found baking made such a mess of her kitchen that it was better to bake a huge amount at once and freeze the leftovers for future use. That way she only had to deep clean her kitchen once. She would give some away at Christmas to the women she visit taught, and the rest she'd nibble on over the next few weeks. As she puttered, she imagined her family gathering for the Thanksgiving celebration. Her sister Joan's husband and her father would disappear into the den for a game of chess. Everyone else would crowd into the living room to listen to Chris play old favorites on the piano. He wasn't half bad, really. She had always considered him quite good, in fact—until she had heard Ryan.

There would be hot cider and the Chinese fire drill of getting Joan's children bedded down in the big bedroom. Her youngest sister, Ann, would read the children stories. Her father would have rented the video of *A Thanksgiving Treasure* for everyone to watch. The family watched it unfailingly every year. Her mother always got soggy-eyed at the appropriate moments.

The telephone rang, breaking into her memories. Melinda was surprised and delighted to find that the caller was her sister Ann. They gabbed for a few minutes about nothing in particular, reestablishing the rapport they had always shared, and then Ann trailed into silence. Melinda sensed she wanted to say something but wasn't sure how.

"So, what's up?" she prompted.

"What do you mean?"

"You know what I mean. You wouldn't be calling long distance if you didn't have something to say."

"I think I'm engaged."

"What! You *think?* You don't know?" Melinda laughed.

"Well, I haven't given him my answer yet."

Melinda thought guiltily of Jack. She'd been avoiding him for weeks, but she couldn't, in all fairness, put it off much longer. She pushed him out of her mind and focused on her sister.

"But you think you're going to accept?"

"I want to. But Mom's flipping her wig over the whole thing. Thanksgiving dinner is going to be a bloodbath."

"Ah. Why? Wait, first tell me whether this man has a name."

"Rod. Rodney Jarvis. Remember? I think I've told you a little about him, haven't I? We met at BYU, at the Cougar Eat."

"Okay, I remember. This is the guy you accidentally dropped your Navajo Taco on. But I didn't realize it was so serious."

"It's happened kind of fast. You'd like him, Mel. He's about six feet tall, and he's from Rhode Island. He's really smart, and he's studying physics. He's super sweet."

"Sounds good to me. So what is so objectionable about sweet Rodney Jarvis from Rhode Island?" Melinda asked in amusement.

Abigail leaped onto the counter to listen in. Melinda stroked the cat's ears.

"Oh, you know how Mom is. Nobody's good enough for her daughters. And she's also concerned that he's an only child."

"Oh." Melinda was puzzled. "I know Mom and Dad like big families, but I wouldn't think his being an only child would be so alarming. Is there something else?"

"He isn't very well-to-do. He's had to scrape to put himself through school. His parents aren't LDS, and they won't help him financially, because they didn't want him coming out to BYU."

"That shows he has determination."

Ann paused. "And he's got a criminal record."

"Aha." That was it. "Anything serious?"

"Burglary. A year in prison. But he was very young when it happened, and he hasn't done anything since. He was poor, you know," Ann said, as if this were very important for Melinda to understand.

"I see."

"He's been fine for years."

"Okay. And is he what you want?"

"Mom won't leave me alone long enough for me to decide what I want. Sometimes I wonder if I want to marry him just to spite her, and that'd be a stupid reason to get married."

"Yes, it would."

"But Melinda, I *do* love Rod."

"I see," Melinda said again, feeling like a stuck record. She rubbed Abigail's stomach, eliciting a rumble from the cat's throat. She could sound like a VW when she really got going.

"It isn't going to be an easy decision, Mel. Mom says it won't work out. But it seems to me that there are no guarantees, no matter who you choose. It's up to both people to make it work. I mean, you married a good, law-abiding citizen and everything, and look what happened. At least Rod is LDS." Ann's tremulous voice stopped dead, and then she quickly added, "I'm sorry if that hurt you. I didn't mean . . ." The air down the line trembled between them.

"I know," Melinda said after a moment. "And you're right. Marrying someone who doesn't have a criminal background is no guarantee you'll have a perfect marriage, and no one's saying that if you marry a poor burglar you will automatically end up miserable. Who knows? You'll probably fare better than I did. Whatever you decide, just promise me you won't do it just to spite Mom. Make sure it's what you really want to do." *And then stick to your guns. Don't let anyone talk you into anything you don't want to do.*

"I will. It's easier said than done. But it seems to me I'd rather marry who I want and be mostly happy than to marry someone Mom approves of and be mostly depressed."

Melinda couldn't help grinning at this very Ann-like statement. "Keep me posted on what happens."

"I will."

"Does Mom know you're calling me?"

"She said not to bother you with it, but I knew you were the one to talk to."

Melinda pressed her lips together. Of course her mother would think Melinda's input would be sub-par, considering the mess she had made of her own life in the area of relationships.

Ann sighed. "You're so lucky, Mel. You don't have to worry about anything like this. Your life is set and secure. You know what you want to do, and you're in control of everything."

Melinda nearly laughed in astonishment, and then she was taken aback by her astonishment. Wasn't it true? She was doing what she wanted. She was in control of everything in her life. But then she hadn't originally intended to end up alone on a vegetable farm in Texas, and she hadn't expected quiet Jack Peyton to pop into the picture. Or Ryan, for that matter. And where exactly did Ryan stand in that picture? Suddenly she felt like laughing again, this time hysterically.

"Well, it feels nice not to be the only black sheep in the family," Melinda said instead.

"Baaa. Maybe I should move away from everybody like you did," Ann said wistfully. "It must make life easier."

"I thought so once, but lately I'm not so sure," Melinda replied, smiling. "You're still you, even out in the middle of nowhere. You can't escape that."

"True."

"And Mom can still telephone."

Ann laughed shakily. "She can be pretty biting, can't she?"

"Sometimes. I don't think she does it deliberately."

"I'm getting a taste of what you must have gone through after your divorce. How on earth did you deal with it?"

Melinda rubbed a hand through her hair. "I tried to shut her out. To shut everybody out. To disconnect myself completely from other people."

"Is that possible?" Ann asked, sounding sad.

"Not for long," she admitted. "And I don't know that it was the right thing to do anyway. When you try to protect yourself from being hurt, you miss out on a lot, too." Ryan's words came back to her. *Community or isolation, inclusion or exclusion.* That's what it boiled down to, all right.

"Melinda, can I come visit you sometime?"

"Of course. You're welcome anytime," she said, surprised.

"I've wondered. I mean, I don't want to disturb you. You seem so comfortable and self-contained out there. You really don't need me to bug you."

"Yes, I do," Melinda said, and meant it sincerely. "I would love to have you stay with me. Is Rod going home for the holidays?"

"Yes."

"Then why don't you come here for New Year's? When I come for Christmas, you can drive back with me," Melinda told her. Then she realized she'd just committed to come for Christmas. Ah, well. "I've always found this farm a peaceful sort of place. It might be just what you need to help you focus and make your decision without distractions."

"Thanks, Melinda. You know, you're the only one I can really talk to about all this. Mom is no help, and Joan would be no better. You won't judge me. You know where I'm coming from."

"If that's so," Melinda said softly, "then it's been worth going through the whole thing. When you go to dinner tomorrow, eat a piece of Mom's pumpkin pie for me."

"I will. I love you, sis."

"I love you, too."

Melinda stood looking at the phone for a few minutes after she'd hung up. She had fooled herself into thinking that she could be totally independent and emotionally isolated from other people. She was irretrievably connected to so many people—her family, her friends. Maybe what she'd told her sister was true. Perhaps it was better that way, letting yourself love, even if it meant opening yourself up to hurt. It seemed that even pain had something to contribute.

She hesitated only a moment more and then reached for the phone to call Jack. It was time she stopped running.

* * *

On Thanksgiving Day, Melinda went for a drive to Buffalo Lake. It had been a while since she'd been there, and even her usual reluctance to burn unnecessary gasoline gave way to a fit of melancholy she refused to label homesickness. Melinda set her radio to a rock station instead of her regular country and rolled the windows down to let in a blast of frigid, bracing air. Once out on the back roads, she pressed the gas pedal down. The truck lurched up to sixty (any higher and the dashboard began to rattle). She relished the freedom, the feeling of her hair being whipped around her face, the squeal of the electric guitars on the radio. Her mother would have been appalled. Jack Peyton probably would have been, too. She regretted the disappoint-ment she'd heard in his voice when she had told him her answer, but with the conversation came relief. She was making her decisions based on what she really wanted, not just out of reaction to someone else. It was a glorious feeling.

A new song came on the radio—"Unchained Melody." An image of Ryan wearing his tweed suit automatically came to mind. She gently eased the truck to a steadier speed. She guessed that Jenny was spending the day at home and that Ryan and Tanner would be alone today. She hadn't prepared a Thanksgiving dinner for herself, but she had leftover ham in the fridge, and she could put together a salad. She decided that she would invite him over for dinner. He seemed to appreciate her cooking, and it would give her an excuse to see him. The realization of just how much she wanted to see him and Tanner—bright-haired, golden little Tanner—took her breath away for a moment. She turned the car and headed back home, chuckling at herself.

She was pulling into her driveway when she glanced at Jack's house across the street. An image of the cream-colored envelope lying on Ryan's counter jumped unbidden into her mind. She'd completely forgotten about Jack's offer to buy the ranch. Now that she'd turned down his marriage proposal, she was sure that Jack had withdrawn the offer. She wondered what Ryan would have decided if he hadn't.

CHAPTER 10

As soon as she arrived home, Melinda lit a fire in the fireplace and began unloading the fridge onto the counter to see what she had on hand. Abigail crouched under the table, watching to see if any of the food would be coming her way. When Melinda had dinner planned, she phoned the Delaneys' house without having to refer to the number written in her phonebook. Ryan answered on the second ring.

"Happy Thanksgiving," she greeted him. "Are you two all by yourselves today?"

"As a matter of fact, we are. Jenny left us a roast and potatoes; I'm just heating them now. She sprinkled chilies all over them, but they're close enough. I didn't dare do a turkey myself. I'd give us salmonella poisoning. What about you?"

"Actually, why don't you save the roast for tomorrow and come over for dinner?"

There was a pause she couldn't interpret, and then he asked, "Would we be intruding?"

"Not at all. I'm inviting you, aren't I? It's a last-minute thing, so it isn't going to be fancy. I should have thought ahead."

"That's nice of you. When do you want us?"

"How fast can you walk?"

"We'll be right there."

She felt irrationally pleased as she hung up and ran upstairs to change into a skirt. She was back in the kitchen, peeling an onion, when the doorbell rang.

"Come in!" she called. There were footsteps in the hall, but they didn't sound quite right. They were heavier and slower than Ryan's pace. She turned. Jack Peyton stood in the kitchen doorway.

"Oh, Jack! I thought . . . Hi," she finished lamely. It hadn't occurred to her to wonder what he was doing for Thanksgiving.

"I've been thinking ever since you called me," he said without preamble, taking his hands from his coat pockets and letting them hang by his sides. "I don't think I put things very well, and I want to ask you to reconsider."

She hadn't expected this. Melinda wiped her hands on a towel and turned to face him.

"There's nothing to reconsider, Jack," she said as gently as she could. "I've told you my answer. I'm sorry. I'm flattered you'd even think of it, but I can't marry you."

"Why not? We're great for each other. We get along so well."

"I explained already. I don't think of you in that—" she began, but Jack crossed the floor in one long stride and cut her off by pulling her into his arms so tightly she lost her breath. Before she could think or act, he bent his head and clamped his mouth down on hers.

For one reeling second she froze, pinned between his hard, lean body and the stove. Then her senses returned, and she started to struggle. His kiss only intensified. She felt as if her neck would break she was leaning so far back. She reached up, grabbed the hair on the back of his head and yanked. He jerked back, pulling her with him, and at the same moment she heard someone speak.

"I figured I'd bring the roast with . . ."

Jack swung around, releasing Melinda. She fell back against the stove and raised her hand to her bruised lips. They both stared guiltily at Ryan framed in the doorway.

Ryan had frozen midstep, looking from one face to the other. He held a large pot against the front of his leather coat. Tanner, the lower half of his face swathed in a purple muffler, peeked from behind his father's pant leg. For a moment, there was dead silence.

"Hi, Jack," Ryan said, his voice casual.

Jack stood with his feet apart and his fists on his hips, like a boxer squaring off. His chin jutted forward, and his eyes narrowed. Ryan looked ludicrous in contrast, with his red-checkered oven mitts and wide-eyed sidekick. Melinda could feel the electricity snapping through the air between them.

"Tables are turned this time," Jack growled.

Melinda stared at Jack, suddenly wondering if his proposal had merely been a way to get back at his old enemy. She wasn't sure what either of them would do in this situation, and she wasn't going to wait to find out. She spurred herself into action.

"Jack was just leaving. Happy Thanksgiving, Jack," she said briskly, gripping his elbow and towing him toward the door. Ryan stepped back out of the way, his expression wary. Melinda opened the front door and shoved Jack onto the porch.

"I'll have you know," she told him in a fierce whisper, "that I don't like being the pawn in your little game of one-upmanship. If you have a grudge with Ryan, fight it out with him, but leave me out of the middle!" She slammed the door, cutting off his angry glare, and covered her face with her hands, steeling herself. Then she strode back to the kitchen.

Ryan had set the roast down on the stove. He stood with his back to her and slowly drew off the oven mitts.

"I'm sorry," Melinda said flatly. "I didn't invite him. He just showed up."

"I know that. You wouldn't have invited me if you were expecting him."

"I just don't want you to get the wrong impression," she said. "He and I . . ."

Ryan turned abruptly. "You don't have to explain anything to me, Melinda," he said evenly. "Would you rather call this off? We can go back home."

"No. I'd like to have dinner with you," she assured him quickly. "I've been looking forward to it. All that with Jack . . . It doesn't matter."

"It looked like it did."

"He—"

"If it's all the same to you, I'd rather not talk about him," Ryan interrupted. "Let's just start over and have a nice friendly evening together." He squatted down on his heels to disentangle Tanner from his muffler and coat.

"All right," Melinda said softly.

After the unpleasant scene, the evening was strained and awkward. Ryan silently set the table while Melinda finished preparing salad and canned cranberry sauce. When they did speak, it was only about innocuous subjects—the weather, the cattle, the Web site, and how the bull business was progressing. They sat down to eat with Tanner perched on a stack of phone books on his chair. Melinda chewed the food that had suddenly grown tasteless, wishing she could rewind time. She wanted to clear the air somehow but was afraid to bring up the subject again. Jack was a touchy subject on the best of days, and mentioning him again might destroy what shreds of civility were left.

"The north fence was down again yesterday morning," Ryan said as Melinda served cookies after dinner. "This time I'm going to replace the posts with steel planted three feet underground and see what happens."

"That ought to do the trick," she agreed and knew she was nodding like an idiot.

"And a whole bin of grain was soaked with water in the stable," Ryan added grimly. "It wasn't rain. It was done deliberately. Someone poured water into the bin. The grain was starting to sprout when I discovered it."

Melinda frowned. "How could anyone get into the stable without being seen? You don't think it's one of your own men doing these things, do you?"

He shook his head. "I don't want to think so, but I'm beginning to wonder. Whoever it is, it's someone the dogs recognize, because they never bark."

"What would the motivation be?" Melinda leaned forward on her elbows, the tension between her and Ryan dissipating as they pondered the dilemma. "Do you think someone's trying to harm you or the ranch? Are they trying to frustrate you so much you sell out and go back to Wyoming?" She felt her heart give a lurch and struggled not to let her emotions show on her face.

"Maybe so. And the only person I know of who would have that motivation is Jack Peyton," Ryan said flatly. He eyed her a moment, then looked away. "He made me a higher offer yesterday to give me a little more incentive. Two thousand an acre. The land's worth only half that."

Melinda fell back in her chair. Why would Jack do such a thing? Did he really not understand that her answer was no? Did he think he could still convince her to marry him? She cleared her throat. "And are you going to sell?"

"I'm not planning to, but the matter's still up for debate," Ryan said. Melinda was confused by the sharp look he gave her as he rose and began to clear away the dishes.

"And remember," Ryan continued, "suspicious things have happened to your place, too. If it were only someone trying to get me to sell, they wouldn't also be targeting you. I mean, Jack hasn't made an offer on your place too, has he?"

"No, of course not. He knows I'd never sell." But the question made Melinda's face fall into a thoughtful frown. What was going on? It was all very confusing.

Ryan and Tanner left soon after dinner. Though his good-bye was courteous, he made no attempt to kiss her good-bye. Melinda chided herself for being disappointed.

* * *

On Saturday morning, Melinda found the doors of her rabbit hutches open and the cages empty. Scanning the vast vegetable garden, her hands on her hips, she puzzled over how all the latches could have come open. It was obvious that they hadn't; someone had opened them on purpose. She knew that she wouldn't find the rabbits, but she had to look anyway, to be sure. Grimly, she fetched a heavier coat from the house and struck out across her property, watching for flashes of movement in the furrows and peering into sheltered corners. The grasses and brambles growing along her fence line looked undisturbed. She couldn't distinguish any footprints that shouldn't have been there, though she admitted to herself that she probably would not have been able to recognize her own boot prints. She supposed that any caged rabbit, finding itself suddenly free, would head for shelter or for anything edible. But the garden was full of both shelter and food, and she saw no sign of furry life.

Who would do such a thing, anyway? She felt the anger rising to a boil in her chest as she strode along. It had to be Danny Wilson or one of his friends from the subdivision. They were always looking for trouble. She pictured Danny's face, flushed from drinking, and the way he'd shoved that innocent man who had only wanted to help him. She wished fiercely that the Wilsons had never moved to Redcreek, that the houses and subdivisions had never been built. She thought of Tanner's delight in the bunnies and wanted to cry. Shoving her hands in her pockets, she trudged through her back acreage, head down, discouraged, not paying attention anymore to where she was going but taking out her emotions on the ground with her heels. And then she looked up and stopped short.

At first she didn't understand what she was seeing. For a moment she was disoriented, staring stupidly at the gray expanse of a lake with tiny spindles poking through the surface at regular intervals. And then she realized she was looking at her baby forest, flooded under ten inches of water.

With a cry of anguish, she plunged into the water, feeling the iciness rush over the top of her boots as she slopped her way to the irrigation ditch on the west side of her land. The heavy metal gates were open. The water had reached a level where no more water could flow in, and the excess was beginning to spill over into the orchard and disappear into the grass. Her beautiful acres of seedlings looked like a rice paddy.

It took all her strength to bang the gates shut again, her hands nearly frozen. Melinda slipped as she tried to turn and fell to her knees in the muddy water. She stood, dripping and shivering, looking over her experiment now turned into an alien landscape, and tried to control the wail that rose in her throat. She hadn't left the gates open—she knew she hadn't. She never irrigated here; there was no need, especially not at this time of year. There was no way to know what damage the water had done until it receded and she could assess the state of her trees. The larger ones would be fine, but the smaller seedlings were all but engulfed by the water, just their tips showing. The waterlogged roots might rot, and there was a good chance the little trees would all simply tip over when the water soaked in and turned the soil to pudding.

There was no point in slogging around the place now, she told herself, swiping at her eyes with the backs of her hands. She'd only do more damage, not being able to see where she was stepping. There was nothing to do but go back to the house and wait to see whether all her effort and expense had been wasted. She trudged back toward home, feeling like she had just left the bedside of a dying friend.

When she reached the house, she changed into dry clothes and phoned Ryan. He answered on the third ring. "Can I come over?" she asked without preface.

He must have sensed the tension in her voice because he replied immediately, "Of course."

She didn't say good-bye, only hung up the phone and headed for Ryan's house.

When she knocked on Ryan's door, she heard him shout for her to enter. She pushed the door open and followed his voice to the kitchen, where she stopped short at the sight in front of her. Ryan lay on the floor with his head in the cupboard under the sink. Bits of piping and various tools were scattered about him like fallen leaves. Tanner, red faced with frustration, strained against the straps of the high chair.

"I see you've found a new hobby," Melinda said. Ryan's disheveled head peered out at her a moment, then disappeared back under the sink.

"Hi. I hadn't intended to take up plumbing as a hobby, actually."

Melinda gingerly tiptoed closer. "What happened?"

"Tanner decided to drop Silly Putty down the garbage disposal. Come in and sit down. What's up? You sounded upset."

Now that she had arrived, Melinda wasn't sure how to voice everything she was feeling. She sat down beside Tanner, who eyed her sulkily. Melinda put a hand softly on his hair, feeling like joining him in loud, sloppy sobs. "Is there a reason he's upset?"

"He's been trapped in that chair for half an hour," Ryan explained from the cupboard. "I don't dare let him run loose while I'm under here."

Melinda draped her coat over her chair, unstrapped the little boy, and lifted him out of the high chair. To her gratification, he clung to her neck in a fierce hug. "Minda!" She held him tightly on her lap, taking comfort in the warm, solid weight of him. Trying to keep her voice level, she told Ryan what had happened.

"What!" He sat up too suddenly and clonked his head on the drainpipe. He gave a yell and clapped a hand over the injured area.

Squinting at her, he said, "That's terrible. That's just the most awful thing." His mellow baritone was an octave higher.

"On top of it all, the neighbors are going to have something to say about me taking more irrigation water than my share," Melinda added miserably. "Taking water out of turn is criminal."

"Just explain to them what happened. They'll understand. They'll know it wasn't your fault."

"Of course it wasn't! Why would I kill my little trees? I've worked so *hard* on them, Ryan!" She felt the wail rising again and swallowed it down. "Do you think it could be those teenagers from the subdivision, messing around?" she asked hopelessly. "I mean, locals would know better than to fool with the gates."

"Melinda, I think you have to face up to this. Letting your rabbits loose could possibly be called mischief. But the flooding was an act of focused aggression, not something random." His voice was quiet, but it chilled her to the bone.

She knew he was right. And she knew of only one person who might carry that kind of a grudge against her right now, someone who might want to get back at her specifically. She felt tears threaten again and stood abruptly, hoisting Tanner onto her hip.

"I'll keep him occupied while you finish up," she said, quickly leaving the room.

* * *

Melinda and Tanner played Matchbox cars and fit-the-shape-into-the-plastic-ball for half an hour, and little by little, Melinda felt her ragged emotions soothe into place. Tanner seemed to sense her mood and played quietly, looking up at her now and then and once coming over to sit on her lap and lean against her for a moment. By the time the banging and clanking in the kitchen stopped, Melinda felt in control of herself again. The bedroom door opened, and Ryan looked in. Melinda, who was sitting on the floor surrounded by plastic shapes and miniature racing cars, looked up and had to laugh in spite of herself. Ryan's face and T-shirt were smeared with guck from the garbage disposal, and there was a purply-red bump growing on his forehead. His hair stuck out like a hedgehog's. He waved a towel at her.

"How are you doing?" he asked, glancing at Tanner, who was concentrating happily on his game.

"We're all right, aren't we, buddy?"

"I'll just wash up. You're a lifesaver."

The door closed before she could reply.

He reemerged ten minutes later, scrubbed and dressed in a fresh shirt and trousers, and dropped to the floor among the toys. Sitting cross-legged, he pulled Tanner onto his lap and roughed his hair.

"It's a good thing you're cute," he muttered into his son's neck, "or I'd sell you to the gypsies."

"I'm sure he didn't mean to break the disposal," Melinda said.

"Of course not. And it made such a terrific sound, didn't it?" Ryan chuckled and then turned his bright gaze to Melinda. "Thanks for watching him. You came at just the right time. What do you say we grab a burger at the drive-in, and we can talk some more?"

"Sounds good," she agreed.

* * *

"This isn't exactly the formal fare we had at Ricci's," Ryan remarked twenty minutes later, tearing open a paper-wrapped straw and pushing it into the lid of Tanner's vanilla shake. "Do you want to go home to eat? Might be nicer."

Melinda tipped her head to one side. "It can be nice enough eating in the car, depending on where the car's parked. Take the highway north; I'll tell you when to turn off."

Ryan good-naturedly pulled the car out and headed up the road. Following Melinda's directions, he drove north and then west until the ground began to slope downward. As snow began to appear in clots beside the road, he glanced at Melinda, but she just nodded toward the turnoff. They drove up around the bend and saw the empty shore of Buffalo Lake before them.

Ryan parked the car near the edge overlooking the water and turned off the engine. They sat in silence, gazing over the flat, calm expanse of violet water, the silent huddled houses farther up the shore, and the silver sky.

When Ryan spoke, his voice was subdued. "It's beautiful."

Melinda unwrapped her hamburger. "Eating in a car isn't so bad if you've got a good view to go with it," she said.

"I'd forgotten this place existed. It's been ages." He turned and looked at her. She couldn't read the expression on his face.

"Thank you," he said quietly. "Lakes are good places to go when you need peace, a place to settle your soul."

"Yes, that's a good way to put it. And that's what I need right now."

"In Wyoming, about five miles from our ranch, there was a lake. Well, more of a pond, really. But it was surrounded by trees and was just tranquil and secluded. Caroline and I would go there sometimes, especially if we'd had a disagreement and needed to talk things over. Conversations always seemed to go better at the lake."

Melinda kept her eyes on her burger. "Fought, did you?" she asked. Somehow she couldn't imagine it.

"Oh, every couple has things to iron out," Ryan said, crumpling his wrapper and pushing it back into the bag. "We never had anything major to solve, just wrinkles. I couldn't stand arguing with her. I'd feel just sick about it until we got things straightened out."

"You were an exemplary husband, then," Melinda remarked. "I doubt many men are that concerned about relationships."

His eyes widened. "You think that? Isn't that kind of cynical?"

"Realistic," Melinda replied, shrugging. "It's been my experience that when things go wrong, men just ignore the situation and hope it glosses over and goes away. They'd rather die than talk things out."

He shook his head. "I don't know about other guys. I just know I wanted things to be right between me and Caroline all the time. If they weren't, nothing was right in my world."

"That's a nice thing to say," she said quietly. "If all men thought that way, there would be a lot fewer divorces in the world."

He glanced at her and then away, gazing over the water. "If you can't get along and be happy here on earth, how can you expect to get along and be happy for eternity? Arguing and bickering is a heck of a way to spend your life. Imagine doing that for eternity!"

The thought sobered her. She couldn't imagine being stuck with Derek for eternity. Why hadn't she contemplated that when she'd first agreed to marry him? If she hadn't been able to imagine being with him forever, why hadn't that clued her in right away that he wasn't the right person? But she had to admit that marriage to the right person—to someone like Ryan—had its attractions. In fact, it sounded beautiful.

She opened her mouth, about to tell him about her own marriage, about Derek. But whether she would have gathered the nerve to tell him everything, she didn't know, because Tanner chose that moment to smear ketchup on the inside of his window and all over himself, and they spent the next few minutes mopping it up with baby wipes. The distraction rather ruined the flow of the conversation, and they never quite got back to it. But she knew sooner or later she would work back around to it, if not today, then someday. Ryan needed to know.

After their meal, they walked along the deserted shore of the lake, Tanner contentedly swinging by his hands between them. Ryan pulled up the collar of his jacket against the cold breeze off the water. "Have you heard from your family lately? Did they have a good holiday?"

"They did, thanks. Everyone's well. My sister is in the doghouse, which is a refreshing change. Usually I have the honor."

"Oh?" He chuckled. "What's her claim to fame?"

"She's thinking of getting engaged."

"And why is that a problem?"

"He's an impoverished ex-burglar."

"Oh. I see." He paused. "Well, maybe he's reformed."

"She believes he has. My mother will take more convincing."

"I wish her happiness." He paused, then glanced down at her. "Are you feeling up to talking about things some more? About what happened to your trees, I mean."

As she was brought back to the matter at hand, the sick feeling returned to her stomach, and she took a deep breath. "There's nothing to do but wait until the water goes down and then see what the damage is."

"When you go out there, I'll help you."

"Thanks. I'd appreciate it."

Ryan pursed his lips. "Once you find out what the damage is, Melinda, I think you should make a police report. They might be able to figure out who was behind all this."

"I think it might be Jack."

Ryan looked alarmed at such a blunt assertion. "Jack! Why do you think that?"

"We had a falling out recently. It may have been his petty way of getting back at me." Melinda gazed over the water and waited for his response. When he didn't speak, she looked up. Ryan was looking down at the top of his son's head.

"A falling out?" he finally said.

"Yes."

"You didn't look like you were fighting to me, at Thanksgiving." He still didn't meet her eyes.

She shook her head. "I didn't initiate that. Never mind, though. I'll just say I have my suspicions. He's upset with me. He might have lashed out in the way he knew would hurt me the most."

"That's a terrible thought. Is he the only person you suspect? I mean, is there anyone else who might want to hurt you?"

"Well, Danny Wilson might, I guess. I called his parents when I caught him breaking into my truck. But that was ages ago. I don't think he's still upset about it. I mean, I'm sure he's been in worse trouble since then."

Ryan was silent a moment. When he spoke again, his voice was low and careful, as if he were tasting each word. "Melinda, if we think that Jack *is* the one who did this, if he's capable of doing something that hurtful . . . maybe he's capable of other things, too. Like the chicken coop fire and the tansy ragwort."

Melinda shook her head. "Those things happened before our . . . falling out."

"True. I know it doesn't make any sense, but it's something to consider. Things have happened at both our places. I don't know whether or not all these events are related. If it's a coincidence, then we each have a separate vandal acting against us, and that sounds pretty unlikely to me."

"I agree."

"It seems more likely to me that all these things are related and that the same person is behind everything."

"Yes, I agree with that too—though we could be wrong," Melinda said. "Remember, some of these things happened before you ever moved here."

Ryan nodded, frowning in thought. "True. So if it is one person, whoever it is has something against both you and me. You first, and then me when I arrived."

"That sounds unlikely, but I guess it's possible."

Ryan shook his head. "Not Danny Wilson, then. He has nothing against me." He hesitated, then cast a glance at Melinda. "Jack, though. He has something against me, and now you say he has something against you too."

"But that brings us around to the same argument. These things started happening before our falling out," Melinda protested.

Ryan nodded. "And it's hard for me to believe that Jack is still so upset over Caroline after all these years. He got on with his life. I could understand him holding a bit of a grudge, maybe, but so upset as to poison my horse? I can't believe it."

Melinda tried to follow the twisting path of logic in her mind, trying to puzzle it out, but the same thought kept surfacing. If Jack *were* capable of hurting her so personally when he claimed to care about her, what would he do to Ryan, his longtime rival and perceived enemy?

"There could be another reason Jack would target you," she finally said. "Maybe what I said the other night was right. Maybe he wants you to get frustrated with everything going wrong so you'll sell and go back to Wyoming. Maybe he's afraid you're not going to take his offer, so he's pushing you."

"Why would my property be so important to him?" Ryan asked, baffled. "It's small. It's not even that great a range. It's certainly not worth what he's offering."

Melinda hesitated, not sure she wanted to tell Ryan that Jack wanted the house, not just the land. Then she would have to explain why. It seemed terribly conceited to say that Jack was willing to buy a new house in an attempt to please her.

Ryan gave a sudden, mischievous grin. "Maybe," he said, nudging her with his elbow, "he's just trying to get rid of the competition."

She hid a telling smile. "Oh, is that what you are?"

"Can't you tell? I thought I'd made myself clear enough."

A warmth spread over her as his words drove all other thoughts out of her head.

They drove back to Ryan's house, and Melinda made hot chocolate for them. It was becoming something of a tradition. She sat at the table by the window, embracing the warm mug with her hands and watching the horses moving in the paddock by the stable. She knew she should leave soon, but she was too warm and snug, and she didn't want to think about the walk home in the cold air. She glanced over to find Ryan watching her, a slight curve hovering on his lips.

"What are you thinking?" he asked.

"Nothing really. I'm just depressed. Not relishing the idea of going out in the cold."

"Then stay a while." Ryan stood and went to where Tanner sat, his head resting on the table, and scooped him up in his arms. "Nap time for this little guy. I'll be right back."

Melinda listened as Ryan tucked Tanner into the child's bed in the back bedroom. She heard warm, comforting sounds. She wondered briefly what life would have been like if she and Derek had had a baby. Would he have left her for that woman if they'd had a family?

Most likely, she told herself bluntly. And then she would have been left to raise a child alone. It was a good thing it hadn't happened. She stood abruptly and put her mug in the sink, then started clearing away the evidence of their hot-chocolate making. She heard Ryan come out of the back room, but when she heard nothing further, she glanced behind her.

He stood leaning against the kitchen doorframe, his hands in his pockets. He had a peculiar look on his face as he watched her. A funny prickling started at the back of her neck, similar to the one she'd had that night with Jack, but not identical. She picked up the dishrag from the sink and began to wipe the already-clean counter.

"Tanner all tucked in?" she asked.

"Mmm."

She felt him move to stand close behind her. Melinda deliberately kept her back turned, rinsing the rag out under the tap.

"So, it's taboo in your family to be courted by poor, reformed burglars, is it?" Ryan asked suddenly.

She nodded. "Yep."

"What about fairly wealthy ranchers?"

"A bit better, but not much." She tried not to smile.

"What would happen if your sister married him? Would your family shun her or something?"

She laughed and heard her voice go unnaturally high. *Don't lose your grip,* she told herself sternly.

"No, nothing like that. But it wouldn't be a pretty picture," she explained. "In my family, everything needs to be proper. What's proper is to marry someone of your own background, who comes from a good family—preferably someone with no jail term in his past."

"And what about you? You never found any appropriate, law-abiding man of a good family you could stand? Is that why you've never married?" His tone was amused.

Here was her chance. Now that it was here, Melinda wished it hadn't come, because suddenly Ryan's opinion of her was very important to her. But she would not run. She set the rag down and moved away to wipe her hands on the towel that hung from the fridge handle.

"I was married once," she said. She turned to face him at last, her hands on her hips. "Three years ago. It lasted about a year."

She searched his face, but his expression remained still.

"I didn't know," Ryan said gently.

Melinda shrugged. "I didn't tell you. I've been meaning to, but there didn't seem to be the right moment." When he didn't speak, she hurried on. "There was a short period in my life when I drifted a bit from the Church—not far, but far enough that I lost sight of some of the things that had always been important to me. Like family. And my goal of marriage in the temple to a worthy priesthood holder. Somehow I let Derek convince me that I didn't need those things, that we could be happy without them. He wasn't a Church member, you see. I'd only been married to him a short while when I really realized what I'd done. What I'd lost. And how I'd hurt everyone. My family. Myself." Her voice caught in her throat, and she stopped.

"Oh, Melinda . . ."

"Anyway, it didn't last long." Melinda went on ruthlessly, determined to have it all out. Or at least, most of it. "Derek left me for someone else."

Ryan looked at her in silence a moment, and then he moved closer and went to put his arms around her. Melinda moved quickly away, shaking her head.

"Please, don't. I'm fine."

He stopped as if she'd slapped him. "I was just trying to show you I care. You're hurting."

"I'm *not* hurting," Melinda said evenly. "It ended two years ago. I've gotten over it."

They stood staring at each other in the silent room.

"Hogwash," Ryan said.

Her jaw dropped. "Excuse me?"

"He must have hurt you badly. It explains a lot—the tough, independent act."

The strain on Melinda's emotions suddenly shifted, yanking her from uncomfortable vulnerability to a much more secure irritability.

"Listen, I don't need a diagnosis." She bristled. "And I don't need your sympathy either."

He looked startled, then frowned. "Oh, that's right," he said, his voice suddenly taking on an edge. "You don't need anything from me, do you?"

"What do you mean?"

"Every time I try to do anything for you, you throw it back in my face. 'I can do it myself.' 'I can do anything you can.'" His voice rose in exasperation. "If that's so, why did you come running over here when you found the flood this morning?"

"I wanted to talk it over with you," Melinda protested indignantly. "I wasn't *asking* anything of you."

"Exactly. You think you're so blasted self-reliant that you don't need sympathy or help or—or love. You don't need anybody in your life but yourself. You'd better be careful, Melinda, because someday you're going to wake up and find out that nobody else *wants* to be in your life!"

"I'll have you know that Jack Peyton doesn't share your opinion. He asked me to marry him!" Melinda retorted.

Ryan's face went blank. Melinda instantly regretted her hasty words. It wasn't what she'd meant to say or how she'd meant to say it, hurling it at him like a challenge.

"I thought you had a falling out." He sounded like his shirt collar was too tight.

"We did," she flustered. "Oh, it doesn't matter. I wasn't even going to tell you."

"But you just said that you suspect him of being behind all this."

"I said I thought maybe he was holding a grudge. You're the one who said he might have done the other things as well."

"But . . ." He threw his hands in the air in frustration, and she could see him struggling to keep his voice down. "How could you even consider marrying him? It's idiotic."

She felt her temper flare like water hitting hot oil. "I'm not an idiot."

"You are if you even consider for a minute marrying someone you don't trust."

"I didn't say I—"

"Even if he's completely innocent, Jack can't bring you any closer to your goal of a temple marriage than your first husband could," Ryan added. "You'd be making a mistake. Again."

"Look, just drop it, will you? It's none of your business, anyway." Melinda reached for her coat and headed for the front door. She expected him to follow her, to say something to stop her. He didn't. She let herself out into a wind so cold it brought tears to her eyes.

CHAPTER 11

Melinda didn't go to church the next day. She couldn't bear the thought of sitting beside Ryan in sacrament meeting—or worse, having him choose not to sit beside her. For the next couple of days, she kept inside as much as possible to avoid bumping into him or Jack, knowing she was being cowardly. She vacillated between anger, indignation, shame, and remorse. She had said everything wrong and left Ryan with the wrong impression. He must think she was the stupidest person in the world—to say all that about Derek, talk about her suspicions of Jack, and then turn around in the same breath and make it sound like she was contemplating marrying Jack. At the same time, Ryan didn't need to say those things about no one wanting to be in her life . . . She was beginning to feel like a mole cowering in a burrow when the phone finally rang one evening.

"It's me," Ryan said shortly. "I won't take up much of your time. I just wanted to tell you about something I learned today."

"What?" Melinda said, wishing her heart wouldn't race so idiotically at just the sound of his smooth voice.

"I got to thinking about Jack's offer for the ranch. The only thing separating my property from the highway is Dale Purdy's place. I talked to Dale, and lo and behold! Jack made him a handsome offer, too."

"Dale's place? He wants to buy Dale's farm?" Melinda couldn't take it in. Where would Jack even come up with that kind of money?

"I was suspicious, naturally, so I went to the county land office this afternoon. Your neighbor Jack has petitioned to have his whole property rezoned for development."

She couldn't feel the receiver; her hand had gone numb. "That's—I can't believe it. Jack wouldn't develop his land. He's dead against housing projects, same as I am."

"All I know is what I learned at the office. They say they posted a sign notifying the public and asking for any objections, but I haven't seen any sign like that. He must have taken the sign down. That's against the law."

"But how could that be?" Melinda argued. "Jack's trying to buy *more* land, not sell it to developers. He said he wanted to join our three properties together." She stopped cold at her own words. It made too much sense. A shiver ran down her backbone.

"Uh-huh, you see what I'm thinking. Land zoned for housing is selling at about ten times the price of land zoned for agriculture," Ryan went on.

"And you think Jack is trying to buy up a bunch of land, have it rezoned, and then sell it to developers?"

"I could see him making a lot of money at it."

"How can you say that?" she protested, knowing deep down even as she spoke that he was right. "Jack has been my friend ever since I moved here. He knows what I think of development and how much my place means to me."

"Such a friend that you suspected him of flooding your forest?"

She didn't have an answer to that.

"You told me you had a falling out and that you think he might have opened those ditch gates," Ryan said. "You concede he might be capable of doing the other things. I just thought you should know what I found out. It's the only thing that would explain everything that's happened to both of us: the steer, the chicken coop, the wet grain, the fences, my horse. Maybe he was hoping to scare you or frustrate you into packing up and selling. And if that didn't work, he always had Plan B; he offered to marry you as a backup. If I were you, I'd be mighty skeptical about his marriage proposal, Melinda."

She felt her face go stiff. Even though she knew his argument made sense, part of her had to protest against it. "Are you saying that you think the only reason he asked me to marry him was so he could get his hands on my land?"

"You said it yourself. He knows how much the farm means to you. So he knows where to hit you the hardest. Think about it. He's seen how successfully you brought in your harvest by yourself, and the work you've put in on the new forest, all the expense you've gone to. You braved it out when the steer died and the coop burned down. He knows you aren't going to give it all up and go back to New Mexico just because things get a little tough. So he's going about it another way to get what he wants. He's deceiving you, Melinda."

Melinda closed her eyes and felt tears sliding down her cheeks. She helplessly let them fall.

"So when he says he loves me and wants to marry me, I shouldn't believe him. Of course, he couldn't possibly mean it," she said bitterly.

"I'm sorry. If you don't believe me, you can go down to the land office and see for yourself. Jack applied for rezoning. I wouldn't doubt he's already made arrangements with a developer to sell everything he can buy up." Ryan's voice was irritatingly quiet. "I'm sorry, Melinda, but I had to tell you what I found out. I don't want you to be hurt again."

"Yeah, well, thanks a whole lot."

"Melinda . . ."

"You're about to be sympathetic again," she said and hung up.

She went into the kitchen, opened the fridge, and closed it again. The counters were as immaculate as always, and there was nothing to clean or put away or fiddle with. She sat down at the table, got up again, and finally went up to her room and put on her nightgown. She lay on her bed on top of the covers and stared up at the darkened ceiling. Her pulse thudded in her throat. Her fingers plucked at the yarn ties of the quilt. She hadn't been this angry in years. Her brain searched for the reason behind it. Was it just because of what Ryan had said about Jack? Was it because she had been foolish enough to believe that Jack really cared about her and that his flooding her field had been the vengeful act of a spurned and disappointed man?

She felt herself break into a sweat. Had she narrowly missed getting hurt again, like with Derek? Because she *did* still hurt, despite what she had said to Ryan. She still hurt like crazy. Guilt and humiliation still rang through her head whenever she let her guard down. If she had been a better wife, if she hadn't married so young, if she had been less clingy . . . But it was stupid to think this way. It wasn't her fault Derek had grown up in an abusive home and had carried that abuse into their marriage. She couldn't be blamed for that, at least. But he had left her for Sophie Nobrega, the size four Venus who played first violin in the same symphony Derek played in—and wasn't that at least partly her fault? If she hadn't been so dependent and smothering . . .

But no, she knew that she wouldn't have repeated that mistake again, not with Jack at least. Her heart wasn't intertwined with Jack's. Although she had liked him as a neighbor, she had never been in any real danger of accepting his proposal. Provided Jack had actually intended to carry it out and marry her, of course. Maybe he would have tried to get her to sign her property over to him first and then broken off the engagement. Maybe he would have just dazed her enough to coax her gradually over to his side. Maybe he would have actually gone through with it and married her, and then divorced her to get his hands on half of everything. He could have tied things up in court, making it impossible for her to hang onto the farm and forcing her to sell to him in the end—though that would be a lengthy way to go about getting what he wanted. She felt cold chills snaking up and down her spine. Did he love her at all, or had it all been a trick? She forced herself to stand back and examine the situation. Which scenario was more believable—that Jack Peyton loved her or that he wanted to use her to get her property? She'd had a narrow escape, all told. *Well, not that narrow,* she reassured herself. She hadn't ever intended to accept his offer.

But it *had* been nice to think that someone loved her . . .

She got up and went into the bathroom. Staring morosely at the red-eyed reflection in the mirror, she felt a wave of self-contempt. How gullible she was! How furious she felt! She wondered bleakly if her friendship with Ryan could ever return to what it had been. Never mind her friendship with Jack. That was as good as over; she knew that now—knew that Ryan was right. She remembered with remorse how she'd cut Ryan off, spoken so nastily to him. He hadn't deserved that. He was just being kind and concerned. He'd never been purposely cruel to her and never would be. She was sure of that. He was as different from Derek as a man could be. There wasn't an unkind bone in his body. He'd offered her help and friendship. And she'd stomped all over him.

Melinda rubbed her cheeks vigorously until they were as red as her eyes. What an idiot she was! Ryan's companionship had become so important to her, more than she'd realized before. It had snuck up on her, but there was no more denying it. She hadn't intended for this to happen, but it was there, staring her in the face.

"Admit it," she told the mirror. "Ryan Delaney is about the best thing that's ever happened to you, but after this he'll probably never come near you again."

She tossed her head in disgust at her reflection. She had sworn at the time of her divorce that she would never let herself get emotionally tied to anyone again. And what good had that done? Ryan had paid her the least bit of attention, and she had fallen apart like a Slinky. She wasn't sure what she wanted anymore.

Conscientiously she brushed her teeth, went into her room, meticulously read a chapter from her scriptures without absorbing a word, and turned off her lamp. Then she told herself to go to sleep, and she did.

* * *

The next morning Melinda went out, alone, to inspect her forest. She was relieved to see that the water had receded, though it had left thick, cookie-dough mud that clung like to her boots. The larger trees seemed to have survived, but about forty of the smaller seedlings had fallen over, their leafless branches splayed in the mud and their small roots exposed. Some had drifted several feet from their original locations, and a couple had even ended up in the orchard, where the pigs had trodden them into the ground. But all in all, she supposed, it could have been much worse. Melinda tramped through the forest until her boots were so caked with mud that she could hardly walk. She tucked the salvageable trees back into the soil and tried to prop them upright. The roots might still rot, being stuck back into such wet earth, but she might be able to save some of them. She sent a prayer of thanksgiving skyward that the damage hadn't been as bad as she'd feared.

She'd been working steadily for about two hours when the snow began. Melinda finished with the last of the seedlings and headed back to the house, mud-streaked and looking forward to a hot shower. Thick, wet flakes turned the air opaque and blocked everything beyond the driveway from view. When she emerged from the shower, steamed and in better spirits, she saw that two inches of snow already covered the ground and bent the hedges. Melinda fixed herself a breakfast of eggs, toast, and bottled pears and tried not to think about the slush forming around her sodden, replanted trees. The snow could crush them in their weakened state. The food was bland and dry in her mouth, but she forced herself to eat and not waste any.

After she finished, she bundled up in a ski parka and clean boots and went out to check the chickens. Melinda thought the empty rabbit hutches in the open shed looked sad, and she wondered if she should confront Jack or not. She had no proof he had been the one to take the rabbits, after all. Maybe she was being unfair and jumping to hasty conclusions. In the cold light of day, it all seemed so improbable. What if she and Ryan were wrong about everything? If she accused Jack and was wrong, she'd lose him as a friend forever—if she hadn't already. Maybe it *had* been Danny as she'd first thought, out for a walk, cutting through the Purdys' property. Maybe she would just replace the rabbits and let the whole thing go. She wondered if Ryan would ever let Tanner visit the rabbits again. Maybe she wouldn't even bother replacing them. They were good for fertilizer, but if she was honest with herself, she'd admit she was never going to eat rabbit.

But what about the things Ryan had learned at the land office? Could she rationalize that away too?

Melinda took a broom and swept off her porch, then knocked the snow from the sagging lilac hedge. The snow was wet and clung heavily to her boots and clothing. Once in a while she glanced toward the Delaneys', but the flakes were falling too thickly to see that far. When she went inside, wet and cold, to fix lunch, the snow had risen to six inches and was steadily piling higher.

The Panhandle wasn't used to such weather, especially so early in the year. By midafternoon the phone lines were down. The radio blared travel advisories for the northern part of the state. Melinda curled up for the afternoon with her novel and a bowl of popcorn, like a bear holed up in a cave. She secretly believed that humans were meant to hibernate like bears—grow fat and grouchy and sleep all winter. She told herself she was glad the phones were down because then she wouldn't feel bad when Ryan didn't call.

"I said I wanted peace and quiet. Now I've got it," she muttered to Abigail, who was stretched out beside her, watching her intently in hopes of catching bits of popcorn if they dropped. Abigail mewed in sympathy.

It snowed solidly for four days, as if the county had decided to get its annual fifteen inches of snow all in one go. Melinda ordinarily would have reveled in the coziness of it, the feeling that all around her the world was growing muffled and soft while she was warm and dry indoors. It was an ideal time to do things she usually didn't take time for. But somehow her heart wasn't in it. It was *too* isolated. The phone started working again, but it didn't ring, and she kept music going on the CD player to mask the sullen emptiness of the house. She baked apple pudding and cobbler until the place smelled rich with cinnamon, but she put the desserts away in the fridge untouched, because it didn't seem like that much fun to eat by herself. She started on the pile of novels she had collected and always meant to read, but the plots seemed dry and the characters annoyingly dense. She sorted through the drawers of her sewing table and alphabetized her thread by color. When she caught herself digging out the knitting she'd started two years ago and never finished, she knew she was depressed. She gave up shoveling the driveway after three days, and from then on she let the snow pile up. She had nowhere to go anyway, and she had enough supplies to keep her through the winter if need be.

On the fourth day of the storm, she went into the basement and pulled out her art supplies, a plastic toolbox filled with bottles of linseed oil, small brushes, stiffened rags, and dried-out tubes of old oil paint. There was also a supply of watercolors that still seemed usable, and a pad of thick, somewhat battered watercolor paper. She brought the supplies up into the kitchen, arranged everything on the table, and stood looking at them. Then she went to the sink for water, sat down, and began mixing the colors, her hands moving tentatively at first, then with growing confidence.

When at last she had everything ready, she picked up a charcoal pencil and lightly began to sketch the outline of a small child's head. Stubby nose, round face, and wide-set, almond-shaped eyes. She tried to capture Tanner's wonder at seeing a grasshopper, his joy in finding the frog, the enchantment of his first drive-in movie. Then she picked up a brush and began to fill in the lines with soft color. As she worked, Melinda's tightly drawn face slowly relaxed into a contented smile. The knots in her shoulders and back loosened as the tension left her. All her tangled thoughts of Jack and Ryan, rabbits, and trees smoothed away and were momentarily forgotten.

The painting flowed from under her hands with easy familiarity, and with it, she felt herself made refreshed and whole. Drawing and painting had always been almost a religious experience for her. With the flow of the paint, she felt a corresponding flow of warmth within her, a sense of approval and love from some higher source. It was like praising God with the work of her hands. It was something she had abandoned for a time during the tumultuous period of her life, as she had abandoned so many other crucial things. But it was a relief to discover now that Derek hadn't managed to destroy this part of her, at least. And the warmth and love that flowed back into her with each brushstroke felt like cool water flowing over parched earth. She wished she could tell Ryan how it felt. She thought that, of all people, he would understand. Her tears flowed as she worked; not hot, bitter tears this time, but cool, healing ones, and she let them come.

On the fifth morning, the sky was a sheet of cloudy steel, but the snow had stopped. She looked out the window to see the world transformed, white drifts smoothing over the landscape. She felt as if she'd woken up on the moon. She couldn't remember it ever snowing this much at once before. Along the driveway, where she had piled the shoveled snow, the drifts were three feet deep. The trees in the orchard looked frosted with whipped cream. There was no sign of movement or life beyond the trail she'd blazed to the chicken coop. She was all alone in a silent, padded cell.

At noon, her doorbell rang.

Melinda knew who it would be before she opened the door. Ryan stood on the step, a ski hat pulled low over his eyebrows, blowing clouds of frozen breath around his pink face. His gloved hand held the rope of Tanner's sled. He stamped the clinging snow from his boots and blustered inside. Tanner's face inside the hood of his snow-suit was as red as his dinosaur wallpaper.

"Isn't this amazing?" Ryan panted, leaning against the door while water dripped off him onto the polished floor. "I've never seen such snow in these parts. This is more like Wyoming."

Melinda didn't reply but carried Tanner into the family room to sit in front of the snapping fire while she removed his suit and boots. Once freed, he curled up in her lap, where she sat on the floor. His light hair was frizzy from the hood and stood out like a halo. She wrapped her arms around him and rested her cheek against the fuzzy head, feeling the cold come off him like iced steam.

Ryan followed them into the room, leaving his coat, hat, gloves, and boots at the door. He seemed taller than she remembered, his eyes nearly the color of Navajo turquoise. He dropped to the floor beside them and leaned on one elbow.

"I didn't expect you," Melinda said in a low voice. She smoothed Tanner's hair back from his forehead.

"I wondered if you were all right." He turned toward the fire, the orange light dancing on the planes of his face. "I've been feeling bad about the last time we spoke, and I wanted to apologize. I was out of line. I can't judge what another man's motives might be for asking you to marry him. I was jumping to conclusions, with the development thing and all. It seemed like a good case against him at the time, and I'm still not ruling out the possibility. But I can certainly think of other good reasons he may have asked you."

Melinda, who had been fantasizing about the speeches she would make when the opportunity arose, suddenly went blank. She merely nodded and said, "It's all right. You were trying to help me. I shouldn't have reacted the way I did."

"It was justifiable. I was attacking the man you want to marry."

"I never said that," Melinda replied.

"Said what?"

"That I wanted to marry him. I just said that he wanted to marry me."

"Then you aren't going to accept his proposal?" He turned toward her.

Was there a hopeful tinge to his voice? Melinda cleared her throat. "In point of fact, when you and I spoke, I had already turned him down. Cold. It was never really an option. That was the falling out I told you about. I thought maybe he'd flooded my trees in retaliation."

He was silent, thinking this over. She gazed into the fire and continued to smooth Tanner's hair, heedless of the static she was causing. His hair floated out like an aura.

"And while we're talking," she added, "I'm sorry I bit your head off when you—I'm sorry about the sympathy bit. My divorce is a touchy subject."

"The fact that you *did* react so strongly just proves I was right," Ryan said. "It does still hurt, doesn't it?" At her expression, he grinned and held up his hands. "Okay, truce. I just came over to say I was sorry. Now I have."

"Thank you. I'm sorry, too."

"And besides, Tanner was starting to get cabin fever, weren't you, buddy? He hasn't been able to ride out with me in this weather." He poked his son in the ribs. Tanner laughed and kicked his feet at his father.

"How are your food supplies holding up?" Melinda asked, smiling.

Ryan ran a hand through his hair. "Well, the refried beans are holding out all too well. Jenny really does need to expand her repertoire. I've got to make a trek to the store soon. I know I'm supposed to keep a year's supply of things on hand for emergencies, but with the move and everything, I haven't stocked up very well yet. And all Dad had on hand was four bags of dog food. At least he made sure he provided for the dogs." He chuckled deep in his chest. "I suppose we could resort to eating that. I read the labels; there's more chicken and beef in dog food than I usually get for my dinner."

"I always wondered why no one came up with cat-flavored dog food," Melinda mused. "I mean, when you think about it . . . No offense, Abigail."

The cat gave her a slit-eyed, haughty look and turned her back on them. Ryan laughed, a hearty, contagious sound, and Melinda joined in. When at last they sobered, Melinda shook her head. "I've got plenty of stuff if you want to borrow anything. I can fix up a care package for you."

Without waiting for his answer, she transferred Tanner to his lap and went to the kitchen pantry. She began pawing through the shelves.

"There are bottled peaches and applesauce. What does Tanner like? I've got bottled stew, spaghetti sauce, vegetables. Do you need any toilet paper?" She emerged from the room with her arms full and collided with Ryan, who was standing behind her in the doorway. Silently he took the things from her arms and put them on the table. Turning back to her, he took her by the shoulders, pulled her against him, and kissed her lingeringly. For a moment, Melinda hesitated, and then she let herself respond, pressing closer. He was here, he still liked her, and it was going to be all right. His hands moved to her cheeks, cupping her face, tipping her toward him. When he released her, Melinda stepped away, swallowing hard.

"So, do you need toilet paper or not?" she said shakily.

"Not," Ryan said lightly. He leaned against the table as she loaded a plastic laundry basket.

"How are your diapers holding out?"

"Fairly well. Why, do you have some?"

"No, but I have some good flour-sack cloths that are the right size."

"It's okay. I guess now is a good time for Tanner to start his toilet training. I've been putting it off." He moved up close behind her and gently put his hands on her shoulders. She could feel the heat of him behind her. Every tiny hair on the back of her neck sensed him.

"Melinda, listen . . ."

"I have some candles, too, in case the power goes out," she said.

He turned her to face him. "Do you think it will?" Ryan bent to kiss her again. His strong arms wrapped around her. Melinda felt a small surge of panic as she felt her own arms, almost of their own accord, move in answer around his neck. It had been years since anyone had held her like this, if indeed anyone ever had. She couldn't remember Derek being this gentle, this ardent. He had certainly never evoked this fiery sensation within her. Ryan's lips were still cold from outside, his breath hot as it mingled with hers. It was an odd sensation, intriguing, and the sudden intensity of her own feelings made her stiffen involuntarily. It was an automatic reflex, like shielding herself from a blow. Instantly he released her.

"I'm sorry," Melinda said. She looked up at his face, so close to her own, and willed her arms to go back to her sides.

He gave a crooked smile. "Too friendly?"

"No. But let me get used to the idea," she said.

"I promise my police record is clean. Do you want to see my bank account?" he asked, laughing now.

"Very funny." Melinda moved away and went in to the family room where Tanner was contentedly wrinkling through a stack of *National Geographics*. She scooped him up and settled in an armchair. Tanner snuggled against her and held up a foldout photograph of charging elephants to show her. She could have easily belonged in the picture herself, her adrenaline was surging so strongly.

"All right, I guess I'll have to accept that for now," Ryan said, resuming his seat on the floor in front of the fire. "But you can't hide behind the two-year-old forever."

"Would you guys like pot pies or chicken for supper?" Melinda replied. The feigned, everyday sound of her own voice soothed her jangling nerves.

After supper, Tanner fell asleep in the armchair with the picture of the elephants spread over his stomach like a blanket. Abigail perched watchfully on the back of the chair like an attentive nanny. Melinda and Ryan went into the living room—her museum, he called it—and she gave him the portrait she had done of Tanner. She had found a battered gold frame that complemented Tanner's fair coloring. She had painted the picture from memory. Now she could see that she had made his eyes too far apart and his mouth was the wrong shape, but Ryan viewed it with awe.

"It looks just like him. It's wonderful! I'm glad to see you've taken up painting again."

"I should be thanking you for giving it back to me."

"How so?"

She fished for the right words. "I like to paint happiness, to paint innocent, beautiful things. Painting and drawing brought me such joy before. I guess you could say Derek, my ex, soured it for me. He bought a painting at my first exhibition . . . my *only* exhibition. That's how I met him." She forced a tight laugh. "You might say I married him out of gratitude."

"What happened?" When she hesitated, he added, "I promise not to be the least bit sympathetic."

She smiled, then sobered. "He was a violent man. I found that out soon enough. I should have left him right away, but I kept thinking—well, actually I don't know what I thought. I didn't really think that I could change him. But maybe that somehow I sort of deserved it, for marrying the wrong person, the wrong way, against everything I believed. It was my way to atone for the mistake, I guess. I'd gotten myself into it, and now I had to put up with it. Of course, I didn't say this to myself in so many words. And I can see now how stupid it was to stay."

"So you just lived with it?" His voice was low.

"I learned to shut off my feelings—*all* feelings—in order to keep the pain out. And it was easiest not to think about it if I kept busy."

"You couldn't keep busy all the time," he said.

She smiled. "Try me."

"But you'd wear yourself out."

"If I was tired, I couldn't feel anything else," she replied lightly, shrugging.

"That can't be healthy."

"Are you turning into a shrink on me? You see, that's why I've never told anyone about what it was like living with him. I knew they would either get all drippy and sympathetic about it or they would start in about how I needed to get in touch with my inner child or something."

"You never told anyone about it?" His eyes widened.

"No."

"Not even your family?"

"It would have been too humiliating. My family would have seen it—*does* see it—as a failure on my part. 'You should have been more careful about who you married.' 'Maybe if you'd been a better wife, he would have acted differently,'" she mimicked. "In the end, he went off with someone else, and I was saved having to explain anything. And I just kept the emotions turned off. It didn't hurt so much that way. Not the best solution, maybe, but it worked."

"Shutting out the pain means shutting out everything else too," Ryan reasoned. "Including happiness. If you can't feel sorrow, you can't experience joy. They go hand in hand."

"I've kind of come to that realization lately," Melinda answered.

"It must be difficult going through something like that without having anyone to talk to about it. It would be very isolating."

"I grew to like isolation," Melinda said, shrugging. "It's safe."

"It's also lonely. That's something I can talk about with authority," Ryan said softly. His eyes bored into hers. She dropped her gaze to the small picture cradled in his strong hands.

"It's taken a while for me to figure out that isolation isn't the answer," she said. "There has to be a happy medium somewhere between being overly clingy and being coldly independent. And now . . . there's Tanner, who's so good and innocent and bright, in my life . . . and you . . . and I guess I'm beginning to think it's all right to let myself feel . . ." She trailed off, feeling foolish.

But Ryan only nodded solemnly. "I think I know what you're saying. Thank you for telling me, Melinda." He brushed her cheek with the backs of his fingers. "And thank you for the painting. It means a lot to me."

Melinda tipped her head to one side. "A bit too much like a Renaissance cherub, though, don't you think? I guess that's how I picture him."

"I think it's perfect."

"But the mouth is all wrong, now that I see him."

"Melinda, it's perfect. Why do you have to find faults where there are none?"

She went to sit on the ottoman. He sighed and sat on the couch opposite and gazed at her.

"You really are too hard on yourself," he said. "Loosen up. Let yourself be human. Enjoy life."

"You just want me to let my guard down so you can take advantage of me," Melinda replied, grinning and batting her eyelashes.

"Me? Never."

She sobered and eyed him thoughtfully. "You're right. You would never. You're the kindest person I've ever met."

"Now you're getting silly."

"Anyway, who says I don't enjoy life? On the whole, I love my life."

"Do you?" He shot her a sideways look.

"Don't you love yours?" she countered.

"Sure, I love cleaning out irrigation ditches and chopping cockleburs. I love weaning bawling calves, cleaning out garbage disposals, and having to drive for twenty miles to find a gas station. I love having my kid collapse of heat exhaustion. I love spending every day alone with a bunch of stinky cows and every evening alone with a two-year-old whirlwind."

Melinda laughed. "Is it really that bad?"

He nodded. "Yes, it is. And on top of it all, it'll be March before the roads clear, and I can't get to the grocery store."

"Don't be dramatic. Besides, I told you, I've got all this stuff you can have. Or are you too proud to let me help you?"

"I don't mind you helping me." He placed the painting to one side, stood, and went to the window. His hands in his pockets, he stood looking out at the rolling drifts glittering in the sun. "But I would feel better if you would let me help you a little."

"I do. You helped put up my shutters and pick apples."

"Anyone could have helped you with that. You know what I mean."

"Yes," she said after a moment. "I think I do."

"After all," he reminded her, "you're the one who told me it was nice to be needed sometimes. I'd like to try it."

For a moment they silently mulled this over.

"I don't know if I'm ready for that," she finally said. "I honestly don't."

"Well, give me a status report now and then, so I'll know if you change your mind." Ryan shifted on his feet. "I'd better get Tanner and head home. It's starting to snow again."

They went into the family room and stood looking down on the sleeping boy, his eyelashes long on his cheeks, his hands gripping the elephant picture in his sleep. Abigail shot them a defiant look.

"You can't wake him up," Melinda protested in a whisper. "He's so sweet looking."

"I can't very well leave him here. Who knows when I'll be able to dig my way back here? It'll probably be three feet high by tonight."

"I've *never* seen it that deep." She sighed. "I guess if you have to go . . ."

"Don't you want me to?" His eyes glittered.

Melinda laughed. "After four days of isolation, I was starting to talk to the houseplants."

"There's nothing wrong with that."

"They were starting to talk back," Melinda said.

Ryan chuckled and pulled her into his arms. He didn't try to kiss her, only held her in a warm, engulfing hug. Melinda relaxed into it and wished it would go on forever. But a moment later a sleepy voice behind them said, "Daddy?"

Ryan's arms moved reluctantly away.

"I guess we'll be going."

Melinda saw them to the door and watched Ryan bundle his little boy into his snow things. As they trudged away into the snow, she felt a void rushing over her.

CHAPTER 12

It was after dark when she heard a commotion outside. Going to the window, she saw a fire engine rush past, scattering slush and gravel, heading west. Wondering, she slipped her shoes on and went onto the porch. The night was alive with noises. The sky was stained crimson and yellow, like an old bruise that blended with an eerie red glow on the horizon, beyond the lilacs. For a moment she thought she was seeing an especially brilliant sunset. However, with a sense of disbelief, she realized something at the Delaney ranch was on fire. Something big.

She didn't even pause to get her coat. She was off, sloughing through knee-deep snow. Drifts dragged at her feet. She repeated a desperate mantra in rhythm with the pounding of her heart: *Don't let it be the house. Let them be all right.*

The front lawn was deserted. Rounding the house, she saw two fire trucks parked beside the barn, the new barn Ryan and his men had built to house the longhorn bulls. Flames had shot through the roof, half devouring it, hissing menacingly at the streams of water from the hoses. It was an unearthly sound, alive and overwhelming. Silhouettes darted back and forth against the surreal scene. The smoke rose in dark, billowing clouds. There was a terrible stench. In the flickering light, all movement was jerky and distorted. She recognized Mark, his face blackened with smoke. He stood watching the fire hoses with a grim expression, his hands tucked under his armpits. She hurried to him.

"Where's Ryan?"

"Dunno. Here somewhere."

"Who has Tanner?"

He waved a hand toward the house and then moved off in response to someone's call. Melinda whirled and ran for the house, colliding with moving figures, ducking out of their way.

Jenny was in the kitchen, rocking Tanner on her lap. Tears streamed down her cheeks. When Tanner saw Melinda, he scrambled off and ran to her, holding up his arms. She gathered him up and looked over his head at Jenny.

"I just saw Mark. He's all right."

"The fire engine is finally here?" Jenny asked.

"Yes, it pulled up a few minutes ago. It looks like they're already getting the fire under control."

"It takes too long," Jenny declared. "We're too far from town. If they had come sooner . . ."

"I'm sure they came as fast as they could," Melinda soothed her. "They'll take care of it. It won't reach the house."

"They couldn't save the bulls," Jenny said grimly, mopping at her face with a shredded tissue. "They're all gone."

Melinda felt like she'd been hit in the stomach. She actually felt the air go out of her lungs in a whoosh. "Was anyone else hurt? Was it just the one barn?"

Jenny shook her head. "No, no, I think everyone else is all right. But the bulls . . . The fire was so big!"

"I'll watch Tanner with you for a while. I don't think I could be any help out there. They look like they have it pretty much under control. I'd just be in the way."

Wound tight but having nowhere to direct their adrenaline, the women paced the kitchen. Jenny walked from window to window, looking out, the distant orange light washing over the tight planes of her face. After a while, Tanner fell asleep on Melinda's shoulder. She put him on his bed, and he turned onto his side with his fist pushed into his mouth. Melinda stretched out beside him, tracing his tiny profile with her finger and listening as the ruckus outside gradually died down. There was the sound of vehicle doors slamming, men calling to each other, and a truck driving past the window.

The Mickey Mouse clock glowed eleven when she finally heard Ryan's voice in the kitchen. She rose carefully so as not to wake Tanner and padded in her stocking feet to join Ryan.

Jenny and Mark were just leaving. As the door closed, Ryan turned to face her. Melinda felt her heart give a lurch at the strain and filth on his face, the sweat having tunneled tracks in the soot, striping his skin. His eyes were bloodshot. His clothes were so black she couldn't guess their original color. Wordlessly he opened his arms, and she went into them, heedless of the dirt and smell of smoke. She pressed her cheek against his chest and listened to the thudding of his heart.

"I'm so sorry about the longhorns," she murmured. "Oh, Ryan, I'm sorry."

He put a hand on her hair. "I'm just glad no people were hurt. The smoke was so thick, and the flames spread so fast. Mark practically dove in before I could stop him. If anything had happened to him . . ."

She tipped her head back and kissed his chin, tasting ashes. "You're a wonderful, caring person. Now, go shower and get a suitcase packed, because you and Tanner are coming back to my house."

His eyebrows shot up. "What for?"

"Because I'm not convinced that fire was an accident, and I'm afraid someone might torch the house next. And I'm not risking losing either one of you. I don't want you here by yourselves. Don't argue, because I'm going to win this one. Besides, it stinks over here."

To her surprise, Ryan conceded that it might be a good idea and went to follow orders. She woke Tanner and bundled him into his snowsuit, turning him into a blue-eyed sausage roll, blinking in confusion. Melinda packed the things she thought he'd need in his pillow case, unable to locate the diaper bag. Ryan emerged from the shower looking cleaner, but still the worse for wear, and he still smelled of the disaster.

The barnyard was empty of vehicles now. The ruins of the barn stood like wet, black streaks against the starry sky. Water lay in silver puddles in the moonlight. Melinda kept her eyes averted from the mess as they walked in silence through a night that seemed frozen after the chaos of the fire.

She put Ryan on an air mattress in the spare room, which she'd never had much use for, and offered to bunk Tanner down on the couch, but Ryan shook his head.

"He can sleep here with me. He won't know where he is when he wakes up," he said. When Melinda left him, Ryan was stretched out on the sleeping bag on the mattress, still in his clothes, cradling his sleeping son gently against him.

Melinda didn't sleep well. The next morning she was up early to cook a splendid breakfast of bacon, eggs, pancakes, and fried potatoes. She firmly believed that whatever happened in the world, you could face it better on a full stomach. Upstairs she could hear the shower running; it was odd to think that Ryan was up there in it. She wondered how he felt, being swept off to her house the night before. But she couldn't have left them there alone after the arson. And it had to be arson; she knew it.

Her mind skittered away from thoughts of who had set the fire. The pounding of little feet in the upstairs hallway told her that Tanner was awake. She went up to meet him. He was wearing only his pajama shirt and diaper. His face was pink and heavy with sleep. He threw himself into her arms and squeezed her around the neck, then wriggled loose and scampered to the kitchen, crying, "Brefkast! Brefkast!"

Tanner was well into a stack of pancakes with strawberry jam when Ryan came downstairs. He wore a plaid shirt and jeans, and he sported a day's beard; his eyes were still bloodshot, but his face didn't look as weary and grim as it had the previous night. His hair was slicked down, making him look like a rain-soaked camper. He ruffled Tanner's hair and sat beside him.

"What's to eat, little woman?" he drawled in a fair impression of John Wayne.

"Good morning. I guess I don't need to ask if you slept well."

"Hardly a wink."

"Bacon, eggs, pancakes, hash browns."

"Sounds great." Ryan jumped up before Melinda could move, fixed a plate, brought it to her, and then served himself. Melinda watched him settle across from her and tried to remember whether Derek had ever served her first in anything.

"You been up long?" Ryan asked, reaching for the jug of orange juice.

"I'm always up at five-thirty or six." Melinda poured maple syrup over her pancakes. "And I couldn't sleep very well either. Ryan, do you think it was Jack? Even if we were right about him doing the other things, don't you think this was too extreme? Why would he do such a stupid thing? He'd have to realize that he would never get away with it."

"He's getting panicky. It's likely that he has a deadline he's got to meet with the developers. After I left your house yesterday, I went and made it very clear to him that I wasn't interested in his offer. I told him I'd never sell and that my decision was final. He slammed the door in my face."

"Ryan, we need to tell the police what we suspect."

"I know. I told the policemen who came last night that I'd come to the station this morning to finish making my report. I think you should go with me to tell them what's happened to you too."

"Stolen rabbits are hardly in the same league as your bulls."

"More than that has happened." He drained his juice in one go and reached for the pitcher again. "I'm glad you asked us over last night. If I were home alone this morning, I'd just be sulking."

"I didn't ask you; I ordered you."

"Well, it was nice of you anyway."

Melinda pushed aside her half-eaten breakfast. "I'll just see to the chickens and pigs, and then we can drive into Redcreek together."

* * *

Melinda felt sick to her stomach as she told the gray-haired police officer at the station her experiences. She had never made a police report before, and she felt as if the officer's shrewd eyes were looking right through her. She stated things as simply as she could and tried to leave conjecture up to him. But when he asked her bluntly if she knew of anyone with a grudge against her, she had to be honest.

"Jack Peyton, my neighbor across the street." It felt funny to state the words aloud, almost a traitorous thing to say in front of this stranger. She told him briefly about Jack's proposal and poor reception of her answer. "He's the only person I know of who has anything against me."

"Well, we'll check it out," the officer said finally, closing his notebook. "We'll need more than your suspicions to go on, of course, but thank you for coming in. We'll keep in touch. Please call me if you think of anything else. The same goes for Mr. Delaney."

* * *

"Do you think the police investigation will turn up anything solid?" Melinda asked Ryan as they drove home.

"I think their investigation of the petition at the land office will be a good start."

"It's so disconcerting to think that someone you've known for two years could do something so terrible. To find out you don't really know somebody as well as you thought you did."

He shrugged. "Sometimes people hide who they really are."

Melinda pursed her lips thoughtfully. If she was sure of one thing, it was that when it came to Ryan Delaney, what you saw was exactly what you got. She had never met a more genuine person. It was refreshing to find someone you could trust, she thought, and she realized that she did trust him, completely.

"Will your insurance cover the loss of your bulls and barn?"

"It should. I have to meet with the guy this morning to look things over. But they'll likely wait until the police reach their conclusions to make sure I didn't set the fire myself."

"Of course you didn't."

"Thanks for the vote of confidence," Ryan said. "But they don't know me. They have to check it out."

"I suppose."

He ran a hand wearily through his hair, spiking it. "It's going to be a massive cleanup. There's still a lot of the structure left that we'll have to tear down before it falls on someone."

"I feel so bad about the bulls."

Ryan's lips tightened, and he gave a jerky nod. There wasn't anything to say in response. He reached over and touched her hand briefly, then returned his hand to the steering wheel.

They went back to Melinda's house, and she found some empty spools for Tanner to stack and knock over while she cleared away the dishes from breakfast and Ryan made some phone calls. When he was finished talking on the phone, Melinda cleared her throat. "Off topic, I've made a decision."

"Which is?"

"Madge—she's an art agent I know—wants me to display some of my work at a reception at a private gallery in Albuquerque. It's not a sale, just a fundraiser for a community garden project. I've decided to do it."

"I can tell that this is a milestone decision for you," Ryan observed, his face creasing into a smile.

"It is. Madge has been hounding me for a long time. I guess it's time to reward her a little."

"I'll have to go and see it. We could go together."

"To Albuquerque? It's a day's drive."

"So?" he asked mildly. Melinda felt a goofy grin spread across her face. She was touched that he would consider going so far just to see her bits and pieces in a gallery. She rubbed her hands together.

"I still have to decide what to send. I thought maybe the one of Tanner, for starters, if you'll lend it back. I like that one."

"Sure. That would be fine." Ryan glanced out the window at the blank whiteness beyond. "It's snowing again, I see."

Curious, Melinda went out on the back porch and leaned down to poke a measuring stick into the snow at the foot of the steps. Looking thoughtful, she returned to the kitchen. "Want to know what it was?"

"Do I dare ask?"

"Two and a half feet. I think that's a record. But mind, the wind piles it up against the house."

Ryan gave a low whistle. "I don't remember it being that deep before."

For a while they lingered at the kitchen table, talking quietly about a wide range of topics: the ranch, the bulls, the snow, Melinda's painting, memories of her grandfather. Both were reluctant to let the brief interlude end and return to the pressures and responsibilities that were waiting to be dealt with. Slowly, the talk turned to the past, and Melinda found herself telling Ryan about the crisis of faith that had followed her divorce, about her struggle to realign her values and find her footing. Ryan told her, simply and without fuss, about his own climb back to the world of the living after his wife's death, how his beliefs had grown stronger, and how caring for Tanner had pulled him through. Listening to his gentle voice and the tranquil flow of his words, Melinda felt herself grow peaceful, as if she were hearing beautiful music, a song she hadn't heard before and yet already knew the lyrics to, deep inside. She could sense her soul beginning to hum the familiar chorus. And while she listened, a part of her grew more and more astonished and impressed that this man could sit here at her table after losing so much of his investment and property only the night before and discuss with her the deepest convictions of his heart.

When the telephone rang, Melinda felt like she was coming up too quickly from a deep sea dive. For a moment she looked around, feeling disoriented. Then she scrambled to her feet and went to answer the phone, resenting the intrusion into their conversation and childishly crossing her fingers in hopes that it wasn't her mother. But the distressed voice on the other line belonged to a much younger person. The mellow bubble of the last hour's respite was irreparably ruptured.

"Oh, Melinda! You're home!" There was the hiccupping sound of crying.

"Who is this?" Melinda glanced at Ryan and raised her eyebrows.

"It's Joanne Ostler. I've been trying everyone, and no one was home, and I—"

"Slow down, Joanne. What's wrong?"

"My mom. I think she has appendicitis or something. She was fine last night, but this morning she woke up with a terrible pain in her stomach, and now she's lying down, and she can hardly move, and she threw up." The need for oxygen finally stopped Joanne.

"Calm down. It might just be the flu or something. Do you want me to come over?" Melinda asked.

"I called the hospital, and they told me to bring her in."

"I'll get the truck and drive her there," Melinda offered.

"I can drive." She had to smile as Joanne's voice changed instantly from panic to indignation. "I've been driving the farm truck since I was twelve."

"Then what's the problem?"

"It's the kids. Tim's at work and Dad's in Memphis, and I need someone to watch my brothers and sisters. Is it all right if I bring them over to your place? I don't know how long it will be for."

"Of course. Bring them right over," Melinda said and felt her stomach drop into her shoes. How many Ostler children were there? Six? Seven? So much for her peaceful interlude with the Delaneys.

"Thanks, Melinda. I didn't know what else to do."

Melinda hung up and rolled her eyes at Ryan. "Brace yourself. The Ostlers are coming to visit."

They arrived twenty minutes later, stamping into the house and shedding wet coats and boots all over the hallway. Joanne wisely sped away before Melinda could change her mind. Surveying the motley lot, she silently cursed herself for not insisting on driving Carmella to the hospital herself.

Melinda herded the group into the kitchen, where they all gathered around the table with glasses of chocolate milk. Tanner sat happily among them and looked at the sudden crowd with interest, like a king surveying his subjects.

The subjects turned out to consist of seven children, three girls and four boys, ranging from a gawky twelve-year-old to a pudgy toddler. Melinda knew them only vaguely but didn't feel like tackling introductions. She couldn't possibly keep them all straight anyway.

"Dad's gone to see his parents in Tennessee, and he was supposed to be back this morning, but they delayed his flight because of the snow," the oldest child informed her. "And then when Mom got sick, we didn't know what to do." The girl looked close to tears, and the other children looked at each other, the younger ones uncertain whether to cry too. Melinda didn't know what to say, but Ryan put a hand on the girl's shoulder.

"She'll be all right. Try not to worry," he told her.

"That's right," Melinda chimed in. "I have lots of things we can do while we're waiting to hear about your mom." At the moment she couldn't think of a thing. "So we'll just have a nice time, and everything will be fine. Have you had breakfast?"

They had, but they wanted more. Ryan stirred into action, frying up more eggs and fixing plates. Melinda shepherded the children into chairs, dragging in an armchair from the living room and perching a child on each arm as well as the seat. As she passed Ryan, she caught his eye and gave him an optimistic thumbs-up.

One of Melinda's guests refused to eat, with a shake of her blond curls.

"Aren't you hungry?" Melinda asked, bending down to peer into the little girl's face. It seemed a trifle pink.

"No," replied the child, and was promptly sick all over her plate. The other children delightedly began making mock gagging noises.

"Oh, swell," Melinda muttered, running for a towel. "Not only a comedy troupe, but a troupe with the flu as well."

One of the children piped up. "Oh, no, that's just Carma. She does that all the time when she's nervous,"

Melinda grimly eyed Carma. Ryan hunkered down to look the little girl in the eye.

"You don't need to be worried. Your mom will be fine. The doctors will know how to help her. And we're happy to have you here."

Carma stared at this stranger's face and apparently decided to believe him. She gave a sharp nod and squirmed away from the table.

By noon Melinda was sorely regretting her hospitality. The Ostler children proved to be a noisy, energetic lot. The spacious house felt suddenly cramped and crowded. She could feel a headache rapidly coming on, and she was rather at a loss as to what to do with them all. They lounged on every surface, bored and irritable. She knew that a fistfight would erupt at any moment if she didn't come up with some activities soon. Melinda scrounged up a book of crosswords from the basement, but only Carma was interested. She coaxed the other kids to sit around the table with a Monopoly game, but it was missing half its pieces, and they made only a halfhearted effort to play, pronouncing it a boring game. Ryan went back to the ranch to survey the damage with the insurance inspector and check in with his men, leaving Tanner to play with the rest of the kids. Tanner apparently decided to exercise squatter's rights and refused to share or play nicely with the younger Ostlers. He spent the afternoon clinging territorially to Melinda's side and threatening tears if any of the other children approached her.

Melinda, who was certain now that she had never liked children and was glad she'd never had any, decided to make roll-out sugar cookies to keep them all occupied.

This diversion lasted exactly an hour and left her pristine kitchen a sticky mess. Someone dropped an egg, and the little ones ran through it. Flour powdered the countertops, and bits of dough escaped onto the floor. The only cookie cutter she had was a circle, and this, the children declared, was also boring. In desperation, Melinda bundled them all up, including Tanner, and sent them out in the backyard to play fox and geese until they were so cold that she had to let them back in. They left the backyard demolished, their tracks having torn it up like a war zone.

By the time Ryan returned, the group had moved to the basement. The children were spread out on the floor making cardboard cowboys and horses, with glue and colored pencils scattered everywhere. Ryan looked tired but satisfied. Melinda was surprised to see Danny Wilson with him.

The teenager stomped the snow off his boots but hovered inside the front door, reluctant to enter farther. His face was red from the cold, and the one eye showing from beneath his floppy hair wouldn't meet Melinda's. Melinda shot a questioning look at Ryan, and he took her elbow to bring her closer.

"Danny came to see me a few minutes ago. You'll be interested to hear what he has to say."

Danny turned a deeper shade of red and coughed before speaking. "I was out walking my dog last night, and I cut across the field behind your place."

Melinda raised her eyebrows. Danny's subdivision was two miles away. Whatever he'd been doing out in the snow last night, she was pretty sure it wasn't walking a dog. She doubted he even had one. Ryan caught her look and shook his head slightly. Melinda said nothing but waited for Danny to continue.

"I saw Jack Peyton crossing the road, walking from Mr. Delaney's farm back to his place. He was carrying a gasoline can."

Melinda's jaw dropped, and Danny hurried to finish.

"It was late; I don't know what time. But it was dark. At first I didn't think anything of it. I figured he was just borrowing gas from a neighbor, you know? But then I saw the flames."

"You're certain it was Jack Peyton you saw?" Melinda asked.

"Yeah. I went running down to Mr. Delaney's place to see where the fire was. I would have gone for help. But then I saw Mr. Delaney come out of his house, and he saw the fire, so I, well . . . There was no need to sound the alarm then, was there? I mean, he already knew."

Melinda ran her fingers through her bangs. "So you got out of there before anyone asked what you were doing, is that it?"

Danny chewed his lower lip and glanced at Ryan.

Melinda relented and put her hand on Danny's arm. "Thanks for telling us, Danny. Really, it's very good that you told us. But we're going to need you to tell the police what you saw."

Danny ducked his head in a hesitant nod. "I know. After I got home and got to thinking about it, I figured somebody should know what I saw. That's why I came today." He finally shot her a look, half defiant, half fearful.

Melinda smiled at him, and after a moment, the boy smiled back, relieved.

"Thanks again," Melinda said softly.

Ryan took Danny in his car to make his report. He was gone longer than Melinda expected. Afternoon was waning into evening, and the Ostlers' boredom was reaching a fevered pitch when he came back, this time without Danny.

"Jack Peyton has been arrested," he announced, drawing Melinda aside from the strewn puzzle pieces she had been sweeping up. "The police took Danny's statement and sent a couple of officers around to interview Jack. Apparently he got hedgy and wouldn't answer their questions, and then he tried to bolt. Not the best way to convince people you're innocent. The empty gas can was still on his back porch, if you can believe it."

"Oh, Ryan, it really was him, then. We were right."

"It looks that way. Danny's statement helped clinch it."

"I owe him an apology," Melinda said. "I've been thinking he was guilty of all kinds of things."

Ryan smiled tiredly. "Well, I'm not so sure he's clean as the driven snow, if you know what I mean. But he's redeemed himself."

"Yes, he has."

"I hope Tanner hasn't been a handful. I didn't mean to be gone so long. I would have left him with Jenny, but she's busy helping Mark, and frankly, she looks a bit rattled today."

"He was no problem," Melinda told him, feeling rather rattled herself. "We've been having a good old time."

The phone rang then. It was Joanne Ostler informing them that it had indeed been appendicitis. The doctors had operated, and Carmella would be all right but wanted Joanne to stay at the hospital. Tim could manage himself at home just fine, but would Melinda mind keeping the kids overnight?

"No problem," Melinda mumbled again, hating herself.

Ryan, with many apologies, headed back to the ranch to help with the barn cleanup. Melinda threw together cold cuts and hard rolls for supper, and the eight-year-old announced he couldn't eat meat because he was a vegetable. A fight broke out among the others over whether the proper term was *vegetable* or *veterinarian*. Melinda put a stop to it by giving the budding vegetarian a piece of toast instead. This brought tears from the five-year-old until he got toast too. After supper, the youngest two had a very messy bath.

It was completely dark by this time, and there was no sign of Ryan returning. Muttering to herself, Melinda tucked Tanner onto the air mattress and spread everyone else out on the living room floor with blankets and cushions. The youngest Ostler, a chubby little boy with a face like Winston Churchill's, didn't like this idea and began to cry. Melinda bounced him in her arms a while, but he didn't appreciate this either, and Tanner, feeling exiled in the spare room, decided to throw a jealous tantrum. Finally, Melinda resorted to bribery. Both boys eventually fell asleep with cookie crumbs ringing their pouting mouths.

The older children, excited by the adventure, didn't want to sleep. This Melinda solved by giving them flashlights and comic books, once again scrounged up from the basement. Sometimes there were advantages to being a packrat.

With calm finally descending on the house, Melinda started scrubbing the kitchen floor. She listened to the giggles and whines coming out of the living room and decided she could easily wish at that moment that Carmella Ostler had never been born, or at least not in Texas. She wiped down the counters, gathered up the box of cereal that had been knocked over, and rescued Abigail, who had peanut butter in her fur. When the rustling and whispering in the other room finally simmered down, she figured it was safe to go out for a minute to double-check the chickens for the night.

The snow had stopped. The sky was clear enough to let a few stars glitter against the blackness. The fresh air was marvelous after the stuffy, noisy house, like fresh apple cider in her throat. She sucked in great gulps. The snow was soft and deep, and Melinda was breathless by the time she'd waded the fifty yards to the coop.

After making sure that everything was in order, she leaned against a maple tree and breathed deeply for a while, savoring the night and the contented, settled rustlings of her hens. Her house no longer felt familiar to her. The invasion of the Ostlers had made everything seem foreign. It was like falling asleep at school in one class and waking up to find that it had ended, everyone had left, and another class had started. She had no desire to go back inside.

The back door opened. Ryan looked out, his form silhouetted against the kitchen light. He disappeared back inside and reemerged wearing his coat and boots. He trudged along the path she had made to join her under the tree. He leaned against the trunk beside her with his hands pushed into his pockets. They stood in silence a while, looking up at the stars, and then he said, "Glad you're single?"

"Oh yes," she said fervently and laughed. "I'm definitely not the type to have seven children. Actually, Carmella has nine, counting Joanne and Tim. Can you imagine? It's hard for me to even think about it."

Ryan looked at the night sky. "Nine isn't so many. I knew a family in Wyoming that had thirteen."

"Really?"

"I think I'd like about nine myself," he mused. There was a bright note to his tone, and even in the dark she could tell he was wiggling his eyebrows at her.

"How's the cleanup going?" Melinda asked, pointedly steering off the topic.

"Well, it'll take a while, but at least we got started. It isn't pleasant."

"Have you heard any more about Jack?"

"The police called not long ago. Jack has a court appearance tomorrow morning. The officer told me that they called in someone from the Tucker Housing Development Corporation this evening. The officer wouldn't tell me more than that, but it looks like the police are on the right track. They'll dig out the truth of it in the end."

"What do you think will happen to Jack?"

"If he's found guilty? Jail time. I don't know how much. It depends on whether they can prove that he was behind the other things as well—the horse, the steer, the other damage. It would be easier if he would confess to it all, because it might be hard to prove. I think I may be in for some compensation on top of the insurance money. You might be, too, if you want to pursue it."

Melinda shrugged. "If he's not in jail for long, what's to keep him from going ahead and selling his own land to developers when he gets out?" The question had been worrying her.

Ryan rubbed the back of his neck. "I think the developers might be leery of dealing with him after they've been hauled in to swear an affidavit. Corporations tend to run from possible scandals and don't like to deal with known criminals."

"But he could find another developer with fewer scruples, couldn't he?"

"Just because Jack has applied for re-zoning doesn't mean he'll get it." Ryan thought a moment and then said, "I wonder how the rest of our neighbors would feel if they knew what he was planning. There should be a town meeting on it or something, don't you think?"

Melinda's mouth fell open. "Why didn't I think of that? I'll bet a lot of people around here feel the same way I do about housing projects. We could convince the planning commission to refuse the re-zoning proposal, couldn't we? Then none of the developers would be interested in buying."

"Of course."

"All we need to do is find out who heads the commission."

Ryan held up a hand. "I already found that out. It's John Ostler."

Melinda laughed. "For real? Considering the hospitality his children are enjoying, he may just be in the mood to listen to my side of the argument, don't you think?"

"I'd say you have pretty good odds." He paused a moment. "There's also another point in our favor: even if Jack somehow got approval for re-zoning, the developers still might not be interested since he has only the one property to offer them. The developers will be looking for a clean sweep of the area. Without my land and the Purdys' land, they don't have access to the highway."

"Either way, I'm glad you turned down Jack's offer," Melinda admitted. "Before all this happened, I mean."

Ryan chuckled. "It seems to me we just had this conversation, only with reversed roles."

"For a while I wasn't sure what you would decide. I knew that you missed Wyoming, and Tanner missed his grandparents."

"True. But there's more of an incentive to stick around here." Ryan put his arm loosely around Melinda's shoulders and gazed up at the bare branches of the tree, silver with frost.

"Really?" she teased. "In spite of the heatstroke and the stinky cows and Pizza Palace not delivering?"

"Are you trying to talk me into going back to Wyoming?" He laughed.

"No," she replied honestly. "Not by a long shot."

He bent his head to kiss her lightly.

"I'm not in any hurry to run away from the prettiest neighbor in Swisher County."

Melinda punched his arm. "Stop it with the compliments."

"Won't work?"

"Not necessary," she replied and returned the kiss more emphatically.

After a moment, he pushed away from the tree. "Come on, let's go back inside. There's no sense in freezing to death." As they waded back to the house, he asked, "How did you survive today?"

"All right," she replied, glossing over the desecrated kitchen and the peanut-buttered cat. "Carma must still be nervous, because she threw up twice more. Carmella should get her into therapy. There were a few skirmishes with the other kids, but Tanner was a breeze," she fibbed cheerfully.

"Thanks for watching him."

"I enjoyed it. He's sweet most of the time. If all kids were like him, I could see having thirteen of them myself. Now that things are settled, I suppose you could go back to your house," she added reluctantly. "You'd probably be more comfortable there under the circumstances."

"I'm sure I would," Ryan said. He paused with his hand on the doorknob. "But I'm going to stay."

"I was hoping you would," Melinda said.

CHAPTER 13

Melinda awoke the next morning at five, her back creaking and her head aching. She tiptoed into the bathroom to steal a quick shower. When she got out of the shower, pandemonium had broken out. Melinda dashed downstairs in her bathrobe. To her chagrin she found that the Ostlers were early risers. They had gone ahead with breakfast without her, and jelly and toast crumbs splattered the counter and table. Someone had tried to toast the bread after jelly had already been applied, and the mess had left a black, sticky goo in the bottom of the toaster. The haze of burnt jelly wafted through the house. Two of the boys were arguing over whose fault it was.

"We didn't want to wake you up, so we helped ourselves," one little boy told her, wiping his fingers nonchalantly on the curtains.

Melinda sighed and then started back upstairs to get dressed. Then she paused and went back. Quickly she counted heads. "Six. Where's the other one? Who's missing?"

"Annie. She's locked in the basement," one of them told her, licking the butter knife and slipping it back into the jelly jar.

"Locked? What do you mean, locked? That door doesn't have a lock."

All six children turned and pointed toward the door to the basement stairs. Melinda saw that someone had pounded three long nails crookedly into the doorframe, preventing the door from swinging open.

"Who did this?"

Every child shrugged. Muttering again, Melinda rummaged through drawers and finally found the hammer in the breadbox. She pried out the nails and flung open the door. The little girl stood on the top step, her crumpled face streaked with tears. Melinda reached for her, and the child caught Melinda in a stranglehold around the neck and began to cry noisily.

"You and me both, honey," Melinda sighed. She turned to glare at the six culprits.

"Wasn't me," said one of the boys with his mouth full.

"That wasn't very nice to do to your sister," Melinda told them all.

Ryan came downstairs, looking a little haggard with face unshaven and feet bare. Melinda felt a little tremor at the sight of him. What would it be like to see him like that every morning?

"Well now," he said, tucking his flannel shirt into his jeans as he crossed the living room. "What have we here?"

Melinda told him. Ryan reached out for the little girl, who went to him willingly. Ryan held her gently against his shoulder and made comforting sounds. After a while, her tears stopped, and she rubbed her running nose vigorously against Ryan's shoulder. He didn't even blink.

"What do you say we clear all this up and make some real breakfast?" he said briskly and started doling out assignments. "You guys carry the toaster out to the back porch, and you open the window to let the smell out. You see if you can find any eggs out in the henhouse. But go quietly and don't scare them, and don't drop any on the way back in."

Relieved, Melinda felt her tension begin to seep away as Ryan took charge. She lifted Annie from his arms and took her to the sink to wash her up.

After a decent breakfast had been made, consumed, and cleared away again, Melinda stole out to the henhouse to make sure the Ostler child had bolted the coop door behind her. The air was cold but fresh, and Melinda took the opportunity to hike down to the orchard to check on the pigs in their shed. All seemed to be well. The snow was clinging wetly to the tree branches and was beginning to drip. The temperature must be rising. Melinda felt a rise in her spirits and decided, charitably, to phone the hospital to see how Carmella was doing.

When she came into the house, bedlam had taken over again. It was amazing how quickly the peace had shattered. The Ostlers had decided they enjoyed cooking and were still in the kitchen. This time they were making an unrecognizable mess with powdered sugar, milk, and butter. The electric beaters had scattered powdered sugar all over the counter and floor and had covered the children as well. They beamed up at her as she entered, their faces dusted like floured scones, their blue eyes bright with joy.

"We're frosting the cookies," one said with a proud, gap-toothed grin. "Do you have any green food coloring?"

"Sorry, I don't." Melinda sighed.

"That's okay. We'll use strawberry jam to make it pink instead."

Melinda put a hand to her head. "How very resourceful. Where's Mr. Delaney?"

Benji, a lanky, baby-faced ten-year-old with too-short jeans, answered her.

"He went to his house. He took his little boy with him."

Melinda sagged against the counter and eyed the group gloomily. So Ryan had gone back to his place after all. She felt a keen sense of desertion. Well, she couldn't blame him. If she could've hightailed it out, she would have. Maybe she'd go over to the Delaneys' herself and leave the Ostlers to themselves to finish their destruction of her peaceful home.

"Don't you have *anything* green we could use?" another child called from inside the fridge.

Melinda heaved a sigh and pulled herself together. She couldn't desert them now. Her poor house needed her to protect it as best she could. "No green," she said firmly. "And no strawberry jam, either. Please put that back and clean everything up, and then we're all going downstairs."

"To do what?" another child—Hector? Henry?—asked.

Melinda closed her eyes briefly. "I don't know yet, but I want you all in the basement where I can keep an eye on you."

She found a recipe for playdough in the back of a cookbook and whipped up a batch to keep the children entertained. Benji complained that he was too old for playdough. The baby tried to eat a chunk and, finding it too salty, promptly spit it out again—all over the throw rug. Melinda then retired the playdough and gave all the children paintbrushes and the last of her watercolors and set them to painting on big squares of butcher paper. For lunch she fixed peanut butter sandwiches again, feeling a sudden, distinct distaste for cooking. She sent them all to the basement again to eat on blankets like a picnic. It wasn't the best solution, but it kept them out of her kitchen for a while, at least.

She took the opportunity to quickly mop up and do some dishes, and then she ran upstairs to pull her hair into a braid. She could think of a million and one things she had to do, and the prospect of doing them all by herself seemed a bit formidable. When on earth was the children's father coming back? Melinda knew that if they were all going to be stuck there again that night, she had better come up with improved sleeping arrangements. And she was at a loss for any more entertainment for the children. It was the first time she'd ever regretted not having a TV.

She peeked into her living room on the way downstairs and found that Winston Churchill had wet the couch and fallen asleep with his head at an awkward angle. Melinda carefully propped him up with a pillow and went to tackle the next installment of Ostlers.

The next wave wasn't long in coming. By one o'clock Melinda had scrubbed the couch, cleaned toothpaste off the mirror upstairs where someone had done finger painting, repotted the uprooted Easter lily, and reshelved the books the toddler had pulled out. Two books would need Scotch tape. She had rescued Abigail from the clutches of two little boys who were playing tug-of-war with her, and put a stop to one of the boys who was throwing lighted matches over the basement stair banister at his screaming sister. She had wiped noses fourteen times and vacuumed up a pile of sugar one child had spilled. In a fit of creative insanity, she thought up the bright idea of mixing up a big bowl of soapy water for them to blow bubbles with. It was too cold to do this outside, so they went into the basement. The game lasted about three minutes and ended with a sobbing baby with soap in his eyes, a wailing five-year-old who hadn't wanted his bubbles to pop, and a large puddle on the floor.

Melinda ran her hands through her hair, shredding her French braid. Outside, the temperature had dropped again, and the wind was spattering icy crystals against the windows. The snug cement room was starting to feel like a prison cell. Taking the situation in hand before the Ostlers could, she set them all to cutting out paper chains from the painted butcher paper and making Christmas cards for their family and friends, not that she expected them to be here for Christmas—heaven forbid!—but because the idea of Christmas kept them happily occupied. She was fishing in the cupboard above the fridge for more Elmer's glue when the front door opened. Ryan stamped his feet on the steps and came in.

She tried not to run to greet him. "I thought you'd flown the coop."

He laughed, took off his gloves, and blew on his hands. His newly-shaven face was pink with cold.

"I just had to supervise some things. I can't let the guys do all the work. I meant to be back sooner, but someone from the insurance company showed up again. I grabbed some supplies while I was there. I brought back everything I could think of."

"You're a saint! Where's Tanner?"

"I left him with Jenny. You don't need another body in the house."

"Thanks."

Ryan unloaded his pack onto the table. He'd brought diapers, blankets, clean clothing in the toddler's size, a couple of Tanner's toys, a box of Popsicles, a bag of hard candies, and a portable heater.

"Is Santa here?" one of the Ostler girls asked, caught up in the Christmas preparations in the basement.

Melinda pushed the bag of candy into her hands. "Take that downstairs and fight over it," she ordered. The girl happily obliged. From the sounds that issued from the basement, it appeared the Ostlers were diligently following orders.

"You survived while I was gone?" Ryan teased, producing a stack of *Hardy Boys* books from his bag. "I found these."

"Lovely. The older boy insists he's too old to do any of the activities I suggest." Melinda gave Ryan a brief recap of the morning's events. "At least we haven't broken any bones yet. But Abigail ran away and is holed up somewhere hiding from everyone," she finished. "I've never felt so sorry for myself. It's noble of you to come back at all. Would you like some hot chocolate?"

"I would, actually. I'm frozen stiff." Ryan moved closer to open the cupboard, and Melinda got a better look at him.

"You're a funny color," she said. "Did you strain something hauling all that stuff?"

"I'm just tired and cold, that's all. I've had a sore throat since the fire."

Ryan kept the children busy building miniature corrals and barns from craft sticks to hold the cardboard horses they'd made earlier. For a blissful couple of hours, the house fell relatively quiet. With everyone occupied, Melinda collapsed into a chair and closed her eyes. There was laundry to dry and supper to think about. She needed to take bread out of the freezer, and she really ought to clean the bathroom. But for a while she just sat, guiltily enjoying the peace. Her head was throbbing.

When Melinda went out to the kitchen to start supper, Ryan's appearance alarmed her. He was sitting at the table with the children, his head propped on one arm. His skin was flushed, and his face looked thin and aged. She saw that his eyes were a dull green when he straightened and looked at her.

"To bed," she ordered firmly.

"I'm all right."

"No, you're not. You have a temperature. I can tell without even touching you."

She marched him upstairs and settled him in the spare room on the air mattress. Ryan slid into bed completely clothed and rolled over to press his face into the pillow.

"I'm sorry. You didn't need this," he moaned.

"No problem." It was becoming her battle cry. All she had to do was believe it.

Ryan closed his eyes and lay still. Melinda sat on the edge of the bed and touched her fingers to his forehead. His skin was hot and dry. She slid her hand down to his cheek, feeling the roughness of his whiskers. He turned his head and kissed her palm. It was a simple gesture, but it sent warmth flooding up her arm to her face.

He fell asleep almost immediately, and she let herself linger a moment, just watching him. She knew his sickness probably wasn't serious and would pass in time. Most likely he was just run down. But she couldn't help feeling concerned—just on the edge of hysterical, actually, the truth be known. She brushed the hair from his forehead and thought back to the night Tanner had disappeared. In that brief, desperate time, prayer had come easily to her, really for the first time in a long while, longer than she liked to admit. Did she have to wait for a true crisis to access that relief and sense of guidance again? The throbbing of her heart confirmed what she already knew—that she could turn to prayer whenever she wanted to. That was another thing she had let slide for too long. It was time, she knew, to correct some things.

How long she sat there, mulling over her life, taking stock of herself, she didn't know. After a while she realized that she was praying again, a quiet murmur in the back of her mind. *Let him recover. Let him be all right. I need him.* She stopped and thought about the words flowing through her mind. *I need him.* It sounded pathetic to her. Weak. But then, was it really weakness to connect with another person? Wasn't that, after all, what people were meant to do? And wasn't that, essentially, what prayer was—recognizing another kind of connection, accessing a source of strength outside oneself?

Ryan's eyes were closed, his face slack in sleep. There was no one to see or hear her. After only a slight hesitation, she folded her hands together, closed her eyes, and gave her soul over to the prayer. The uncertainty fled. Once she started, the words seemed never to stop but just rolled out of her as if her spirit had been waiting for such an opportunity. She imagined God not as a fierce, critical parent, the way her mother had always portrayed Him, but as a friend, someone gentle and intelligent and open. And so she spoke to him as she would to Ryan, to her grandfather, and she found herself welcomed instead of judged.

Some time later, she wiped the tears from her cheeks and went downstairs to check on the children. The house seemed empty somehow with Ryan confined upstairs, though how it could seem empty with so many children crammed into it, she didn't know. Someone was crying—Horace? Hubert?—and she shuffled resignedly into the living room to see what needed to be done.

At eight o'clock, Ryan padded downstairs looking somewhat better for the sleep.

"Do you think you could eat anything?" She looked doubtfully at the leftover chicken soup on the stove. It had congealed into an unappetizing yellow mess. "I can warm something up."

"Not yet, thanks. I'll just have some juice."

She poured a glass for him, and he sat at the table. "I'm sorry I'm being a burden, especially right now."

"You're not a burden," Melinda assured him. "Just having you here is a support." She went to throw a batch of laundry in. While she was downstairs, the phone rang, and Ryan answered it for her. She heard his deep voice murmuring in the kitchen, and the soothing sound melted the tension from her tired limbs. When she came back upstairs, he nodded at the phone, now on its cradle.

"That was John Ostler. Carmella is recovering nicely, and he's home now. He's on his way to pick up the kids."

"Hallelujah!" she answered fervently. She set about gathering up blankets and discarded clothing while Ryan returned to bed. She was in the kitchen trying to find a clean dishrag when she heard a shriek from the basement. She froze an instant, envisioning another disaster—fallen bookshelves, maybe someone playing with the pilot light on the old furnace—before she rushed down the stairs.

Judy Ostler was crouched over something in the corner of the basement, where Melinda had placed some boxes of old clothes and other things she'd intended to haul to Goodwill. The girl was shrieking and hopping in excitement, forgetting all pretense of teenage dignity.

"Come see! Somebody come look what I found!"

Melinda hurried forward to peer over the girl's skinny shoulder. A pair of ugly brown curtains, which had once hung in the living room, had been dragged from one of the cardboard boxes. And now, lying curled upon them, was a pile of orange fur. Abigail gave Melinda a reproachful look, as if asking her to stop all the noise.

"What's the matter? It's just the cat," Melinda began, and then she stopped short, staring. Judy shot her a wide grin. "See?"

There were kittens curled up beside Abigail on the faded curtains. Her mouth open in astonishment, Melinda reached a cautious hand to move Abigail's long fur aside to get a better view.

"There are four of them," Judy gleefully informed Melinda. "Three orange ones and a black one. See? Aren't they cute?"

Melinda eyed the tight-eyed little bodies, estimating the kittens to be no more than an hour old. She put her hand on Abigail's head. The cat began to purr deep in her throat, revving her engines.

"You little sneak, you," she said when at last she found her voice. "I thought you were packing on a lot of weight this winter. You little trickster."

"Who's the daddy cat?" Judy asked her, jigging up and down as her brothers crowded down the stairs to see what the excitement was about.

"I have no idea. I think the Purdys have a black tom, but I'm not sure," Melinda said, still dumbfounded. "What am I going to do with four kittens?"

"I'll take one," Judy said promptly. "I'm sure Mom won't mind. Can I have the black one? Please? Is it a boy or a girl?"

"I don't know, and I'm not about to find out," Melinda said firmly. "Come away now, and let Abigail feed them in peace. Don't make any loud noises or try to pick them up, okay? Give them time to adjust. Now run and get yourselves ready, because your dad is coming in a minute."

The children cheered and scampered upstairs. Melinda sighed and rubbed Abigail's soft ears.

"You had to do this today, didn't you?" she said, chuckling. "You just couldn't stand not being the center of attention."

She spread a towel over a spare cushion and moved the little family so that they would be more comfortable. Then she gathered up the ruined curtains and threw them away.

"I'm sure Mom will say yes," Judy told her when Melinda re-entered the living room. "I'm going to name him Rat."

"Rat?" Melinda blinked, trying not to laugh as the girl was obviously sincere.

"Yeah, I saw a rat at the fruit stand once, and that's what it looked like, except it had a tail. A longer one, I mean," Judy explained.

"Rat won't be ready to leave its mother for a few weeks yet," Melinda said, wondering just how long it took to wean a kitten. "But when it's ready, it's yours. Now, everybody, get your things on, and Benji, you watch out the window, and tell us when your dad comes."

John Ostler appeared in due time, full of thanks and apologies. He whisked the children away in a flurry of farewells, toting a paper bag filled with sugar cookies. As Judy climbed into the car, Melinda could see that she was already launching into the can-I-have-a-kitten campaign. When Melinda had waved them away and closed the door, she sank gratefully onto the couch, stretched out luxuriously, and closed her eyes.

"Never," she said aloud to the suddenly silent house. "Never, never again."

As Melinda mused on the events of the past two days, she realized that it hadn't been all that bad while she and Ryan had divided and conquered the kids between them. His confident and cheerful efficiency had kept her sane. She didn't want to think what would have happened if she'd been on her own. She remembered the relief she'd felt when Ryan had come back with the supplies.

She slept like the dead and only awoke when the front door closed. Ryan stamped the snow from his boots on the mat. He carried Tanner on his shoulders.

"Are they gone, or are they still lurking about?" he inquired, poking his head cautiously into the living room and looking around.

Melinda laughed and sat up. "Yes, they're gone." She squinted at her watch. "It's eight o'clock. In the morning?"

"When I woke up this morning, I felt better, so I went to get Tanner," Ryan said, setting him down and unbundling him. "Jenny was an angel to stay with him all night. I couldn't impose on her any longer."

Tanner scampered off to reclaim his territory now that the Ostlers had vacated the premises. Melinda pushed her hair into some semblance of order and took a closer look at Ryan.

"You do look better."

"Whatever it was, it didn't last long." He tossed his coat over the newel post. "Maybe it was just my body's way of reacting to stress."

"You and Carma both." Melinda scrubbed her face with her hands. "I must have been out pretty deep. I didn't even hear you leave. By the way, you didn't hear the news. Guess what happened while you were in bed?"

"What more *could* have happened?"

"Abigail decided to have kittens."

"What?"

"Four of them, in fact. Three orange and a black." Melinda laughed. "They were a total surprise, but they came right in the nick of time. I was about ready to lock the kids in the garage with the chickens set loose to keep them amused."

"What are you going to do with the kittens?"

"One might end up at the Ostlers'. I don't suppose you could use a mouser at your place?"

"Nice try."

Melinda shrugged. "It was worth a shot."

She started to get up, but he waved her back and dropped onto the couch beside her. "Just sit with me awhile. You've been flying all over this house like Wonder Woman for two days. I haven't had a chance to have you all to myself."

"Mmm." Melinda sat back and leaned her head on his hard shoulder. "Thanks, Ryan."

"For what?"

"For helping out with the kids. I couldn't have held it together without you."

He picked up her hand and held it between both his own. His thumb stroked the tender spot between her fingers. "I didn't do anything. I brought candy and the *Hardy Boys*."

"You brought more than that," she tried to explain. "You were patient and calm. I felt like if you were there, everything would be fine and I could stand anything. When you were gone or lying there sick and the Ostlers were in hysterics all over the house . . . I didn't just miss your help. I missed *you*."

"Ah," he said. "That's encouraging. And?"

She punched him lightly. "You're going to make me break down and say it, aren't you?"

"Yes, I am." His eyes glittered.

"All right, then. Remember how I said it was nice to be needed? Well, I think I'm finding out that sometimes it's also nice to *need*."

Ryan's smile crinkled the corners of his eyes. "You've really been giving this some thought," he said.

"Yes. And I discovered that I don't just need you—I need God, too. I don't know if I can explain it right. I just . . . I don't feel such a need to prove myself now," she finished. "I don't have to do it all alone anymore."

"Ta da!" he cheered. "Pardon me if I share my virus with you." He gathered her into a thorough, breathtaking kiss.

Melinda gave herself up completely to the moment, letting her mind turn off and her thoughts grow still. She was filled with a great sense of relief, as if she had set down something incredibly heavy. She felt like she could float.

When their kiss ended, she kept her eyes closed and let herself be still, leaning against the cushions. She felt like she'd run a marathon over the last few days. Vaguely, she heard bells ringing. When the world came back into focus, she found that she was alone on the couch and that Ryan was on the phone. She lay in a comfortable haze and let his mellow voice flow over her. He returned a minute later, grinning like a little boy with a secret.

"That was your mom."

Melinda came back to reality with a jolt. She sat up and began running her fingers through her hair as if he'd announced her mother was sitting in the kitchen. "You answered it? What did she say?"

"She asked who I was, logically."

"And you said?" she asked apprehensively.

"I told her the truth. I'm the handsome man next door who has designs on her daughter."

"You didn't!" Melinda put her head in her hands in mock despair.

"Of course I didn't." He chuckled. "Give me some credit. I told her I was a neighbor and I was here to check on you because the roads have been blocked."

"Oh. That's all right, then. What did she say?"

"She asked my name and if I was married."

"She did?" Melinda gulped. "That's Mom. I'll bet she pounced on that."

"When I said I was single, she invited me to come up with you for the Christmas holiday."

Melinda covered her face. "The jig's up," she moaned. "She'll have us engaged by New Year's."

"Would that be such a bad thing?" Ryan gripped Melinda's wrists and pulled her to her feet. He held her tightly to him. She rested her head on his chest, feeling his pulse against her jaw and breathing in rhythm with his breaths. She was completely comfortable in his arms.

"No," she said, leaning back and tracing his jaw with her finger. "No, it wouldn't be a bad thing at all."

"Then I'm complete again," Ryan breathed.

Melinda didn't move or speak, but inside she was leaping and dancing. By some miracle, she had been given another chance at happiness. Her heart wasn't closed and unapproachable after all. It was a good thing to realize after two years of winter.

At that moment, Tanner wandered in from the kitchen and stood contemplating them indecisively. Ryan held an arm out to him, keeping the other around Melinda. Tanner's angel face broke into a wide smile and he scampered to join them, squealing and giggling as Ryan scooped him up. Melinda pulled them both into her arms in a fervent embrace. They were hers; they were staying. They needed her, and she needed them. She would cling to them fiercely, not out of weakness, but out of love. And that made all the difference.

ABOUT THE AUTHOR

Kristen McKendry began writing in her teens, and her work has been published in magazines in Canada and the United States. She received a bachelor's degree in linguistics from Brigham Young University and has always been a voracious reader. Kristen is deeply interested in environmental issues and agriculture, especially as applied to urban areas—interests that likely arose from sun-filled childhood summers spent on her grandfather's Idaho mint farm. A native of Utah, Kristen now lives in Canada with her husband and children.